Plié
Wicked Moves

A. H. Cunningham

Copyright © 2022 by A. H. Cunningham

All rights reserved.

No part of this book may be reproduced in any form or by any electronic or mechanical means, including information storage and retrieval systems, without written permission from the author, except for the use of brief quotations in a book review.

Cover Art: Nizzy arts
Cover Design: Brynn Harbon
Copy Editor: A.K Edits

Content Warnings

Please scan the QR code for the most updated content warnings. I'm always updating them based on reader feedback so if you have anything you recommend to add please email me at:

ah@ahcunninghamauthor.com. I want the reader experience to be safe and consensual!

One

Aisha

Time was a scarce commodity in my life. Like right now, as I guided my grandmother into our house with little success.

"Aisha, if you don't stop rushing me!" Momma pushed my arm away from behind her as she navigated the three steps that led to the redwood front door of our townhome. I stole a glance at my watch—I had less than fifteen minutes to get to the dance studio for my ballet class.

I lived exactly fifteen minutes away from the studio.

"Stop it, woman, she's just trying to help you. You old, you gotta deal with it," said Pops, zooming past us up the ramp that led to the door. The ramp had made its debut after Pops' second surgery for a broken hip from a nasty fall a few years ago.

Dutiful granddaughter that I was, I flew in from New York for the surgery. At the post-op appointment, the doctor had explained Pops needed more help than Momma could handle if I wanted to keep them both healthy. After that news, I bought a scooter for Pops, flew back to New York, quit my dance spot in the off-Broadway musical I'd been part of for two years, packed up my rental, and returned to South Florida in less than a week.

Two and a half years had passed.

It had been the wisest, most tough decision in my life. I owed so much of who I was to the two of them. They had raised me, the child without a mother and an absent father. So, when they needed me, there was no hesitation that I'd be their support.

"Pops, don't rush up the ramp! It's not a race," I admonished. My frown morphed into a smile when he winked at me from the front door as Momma finally made it inside.

"Ok, Momma, you take it easy until I'm back home, alright? I'll cook."

She waved me away, and everything squeezed in worry. Momma's temper had flared up at her appointment, where we discussed some changes she needed to make because of her osteoporosis.

An eighty-five-year-old who could pass for sixty, Momma still thought she was thirty. With her tall, big-boned frame, just-sprouted white hair, and agility, I understood her frustration. At least the new recommendations were nothing that a daily walk, calcium, and medication couldn't manage. She just needed to slow down, and I needed to add this to my mental list of things to manage.

"You gon' head, Aisha. Aren't you late for your class?" Pops asked, and I immediately checked my watch again.

"Oh, lordy. Alright, Pops, I'll see you later!"

I hopped into my small SUV and sped out of the driveway. The modest neighborhood with its mismatched houses and their crowded small lawns flew by as I tried to make up time. My fingers tapped to the rhythm of my '90s hip-hop playlist until my ringtone blasted, interrupting my flow.

"I'm almost there, I'm almost there!"

Mila was holding down the fort at my dance studio.

"You better be, the parents are asking questions," she said through what I imagined were clenched teeth.

Two years ago, when I let go of my solo dancing career, I pivoted to entrepreneurship. It took a lot of hand-wringing and hesitation. I didn't want to leave my dance career, but in the end, I did it. That studio was my baby, and I only trusted my baby with my best friends.

Mila and our other best friend, Sal, had all met in Ms. Brown's School of Dance, one of the few dance schools for Black girls when we were kids. None of the difficulties of life had drawn us apart, and I knew I would be lost without the two of them.

Case in point, Mila's help today.

"Ok, so sorry. Thank you for manning the desk. I really need a new receptionist."

"Yeah, girl, you do because my pretty ass and I hate confrontation, and some of these parents can be...testy."

Ugh.

I knew exactly who she was referring to, but I didn't want to ask.

"Ok, girl, I'm driving in!" I said, feeding off the tension she transmitted. The parking lot of the studio overflowed with cars. Two of our most popular classes were about to start in—fudge, should have already started.

No matter how rushed, my chest filled with pride at the sight of the building. Ms. Brown's Dance Studio, it said in slick black letters; named after our old teacher's studio as an homage to her. The previous studio was unfortunately now gone, taken over by a new rental development. The new building was a simple one-story structure with large windows facing the main road that reminded me of the original.

Taking a deep breath to calm my adrenaline, I glided into the studio, ready for the class. Inside, the décor was more overstated than the exterior, all the details hand-picked, and the sight of them centered me even more.

Calmness surrounded me as I focused on the pictures of iconic Black dancers: Katherine Dunham, Pearl Primus, Carmen de Lavallade, Harold and Fayard Nicholas, Janet Collins, Arthur Mitchell, and Alvin Ailey. I aspired to have half the influence they had on the Black dancer community. I would have fulfilled my life's purpose if this little dance studio was the start of any renowned artists.

One of the doors of the two dance rooms closed as Mila returned to her Jazz 1 session, which had started on time. Unlike my Ballet 1 class…

My eyes turned toward the door of my lesson, where most of my dancers waited patiently in line. Only a few jitters and giggles escaped. More pride washed over me to see their discipline. These were seven to nine-year-old dancers, and already, they were exhibiting the type of control needed for professional dancing.

"Alright, dancers. File in," I said in my "Ms. Mac" voice as my older dancers called me, a nickname I secretly loved.

They all went in with smiles, in their soft pink, black, and brown leotards and tights in the accepted school colors. I let out a sigh of contentment and turned to the guardians who sat in the waiting area.

No distractions for my dancers, and that included their parents. They could watch the practice from screens outside each of the rooms.

"Thank you very much for your patience. I had an appointment that unfortunately ran longer than expected. I will ensure to—"

A loud scoff resounded in the quiet waiting area.

Someone had carefully employed the sound to unsettle me, but it fanned the embers always present when he was around. I rallied, ignoring the way my frown wanted to pop out at the rude interruption.

"I will ensure," I continued, "to add additional time to next week's—"

"Ms. McKinney, that cannot be the way you continue to excuse your tardiness. I think, at this point, we should get a discount instead."

A discount? In this economy?

I schooled my expression and forced myself to make eye contact with him.

There he stood, all smooth mahogany skin and piercing eyes behind fancy glasses, bald head contrasted by the thickest beard I had ever seen, dressed in his usual black tailored suit and white shirt that hinted at the powerful body beneath. The stoic gaze he trained on me incited all kinds of thoughts. None of them were appropriate for mixed company.

The Nightmare Dad, Mr. Davenport.

Every school has one. Teachers know who I'm talking about. The parent that has more to say than everyone else. The one that wants to hold the teacher accountable for every little misstep. The one that is vocal and annoying and rude and just a pain in your...

Ever since his daughter joined my class, we've been sniping at each other.

Correction—I didn't snipe. He was a client, and I never stooped low like he did. He did all the complaining, and I smiled my way through every single encounter, which I secretly suspected irked him. Which gave me all the pleasure.

I shouldn't let him bother me, but...he hated my school. This wasn't a supposition; I'd heard him on the phone telling someone that my school was a "raggedy ass excuse for a dance studio" right after I opened. He hadn't cared I was finding my footing as a small business owner.

Every other parent had been supportive, but this "I think I'm better than everybody" father couldn't see past his own behind.

The only reason we marginally tolerated each other was his daughter, Trinity. She was one of my best students. Trinity had fallen in love with the school and me as her teacher and demanded her father let her stay with the studio.

Two years later and we rarely addressed each other unless absolutely necessary. If only he knew how he played right into my private desires...

"Mr. Davenport, if you have any additional concerns, please address them with me in my office after class," I said with a serenity that really should be lauded as a Tony award-worthy performance.

His mouth pursed in annoyance. I stared at those lips and lost myself in inappropriate thoughts... He noticed my shift, and his nostrils flared in recognition before he shook his head. He was angry but curious. I ignored the way my stomach contracted at the knowledge that, yet again, he was disappointed in the school—the school which was an extension of me.

I'd stopped trying to gain his approval long ago.

Right...

"Everyone, if you have concerns like Mr. Davenport, don't hesitate to share them with me. You know I have your children's best interest at heart."

"Don't you worry, honey, we know you have a lot on your plate! Go on, go on to your class," Ms. Bonita, one of the grandmas, said, shooing me away. I reluctantly gave another smile, then shot a last glance at Mr. Davenport, wondering what those pursed lips could do to me... I took my time closing the door as conversation from the reception area filtered through.

"Listen, she won't tell you because she is a *professional*, but her grandma had a fainting spell and hurt herself, and Ms. Mac had to take her to the doctor. Her grandma and I are friends, so that's how I know. Which is why I told y'all she had a good reason when Mr. Trouble here started riling y'all up earlier. It's not even five minutes past the start time," Ms. Bonita said from her perch by the window. Her twin grandkids were in Mila's Jazz 1 class.

I really hadn't wanted to go into my personal life, but it couldn't be helped when half of my clients and their families were from around the way. Most of them were understanding, unlike Mr. Know-It-All...

Shaking away the discomfort from a second ago, I got my mind straight and started class. I didn't need Mr. Davenport's distraction; I had plenty on my plate already.

"Ok, dancers! Let's start our circle time with flex and pointe, you know what to do."

———

"Before I head out to the club, you need help?" Mila asked me with a concerned frown.

I sat in the studio's office, staring at the computer. A throbbing headache threatened to take over my concentration. These numbers looked like shit.

"What's going on, bebita?" Mila asked, calling my attention. *Bebita*. My heart warmed at the endearment.

I tried to shake off my concern, but it was too late, and she knew me too well. Still, I attempted to distract her.

"Baby, where do you think you're going with those booty shorts?"

"Here you go. I'm going to the club. I'm going to try out my new routine and costume early, see if it rips well and reveals anything I shouldn't. You know it's boudoir, darlin', not striptease..."

"You forget I've been to your shows, you might as well show them everything. You walk away almost naked."

"But not really. It's all an illusion." Mila grinned an innocent grin that didn't fool me. I let my eyes travel from the top of her long straight blonde weave, lingering on the dark smooth skin of her abundant cleavage and curvaceous body down to her black slides. Mila was one of the most gorgeous women I'd ever known, and our history was...complicated.

It had become normal for us to straddle the line between friendship and benefits. We had made it work for so long. We'd promised never to hurt each other and kept that promise. We weren't in love with each other, but the lust... That was another thing.

"Girl, if you don't stop looking at me like that, I'm gonna be late to my show and wet. Stop it. Also, why are you trying to distract me? What's going on? I can tell something's wrong since you didn't replace Ms. Jojo two weeks ago once she told you she wasn't working the door no more."

"Before we get into that, you never told me who was giving you a hard time earlier."

Mila rolled her eyes. "That piece of thick, delicious chocolate with his bald sexy-ass head and that beard..."

"Mila, focus!"

"Sorry, girl, you know I think that man is fine as hell. And I also know *you* think that man is fine as hell, no matter what you say and how much you fight him."

"I don't fight him!" I said, indignant.

"*Right*. Well, he told the other parents they should call for a meeting with you and state some things they'd like to see change. Something about not having someone on the desk isn't safe. Also, something about timeliness and transparency and... I tried to settle them down, but you know me."

Ugh, this man. Why was he so annoying yet appealing at the same time?

"Yup, you avoid confrontation like you're allergic to it."

"You know it, which is why I know when you do it too," she said, plopping her behind on my desk with an earnest look on her face that had me wanting to cave.

I sighed. Might as well come clean.

"Yeah, well, a few students have pulled out of the school. Enough that the numbers don't add up like before. I had finally gotten to a place where I was running black each month, and now I'm backsliding. I have to pay the starter loan I took out, and the rent, and some meds for Momma aren't really covered by Medicare and..."

I'd been trying to avoid thoughts of my problems, but they all came rushing back as I explained everything to Mila. I hated worrying. I wanted to just go with the flow. I needed a break.

"Damn, shit is tight again?"

"Yeah, girl, I breathed easy for six months, and here we are again."

"So, what are you going to do?"

"What I always do—figure things out. You know me."

"Are you going to go back to..." Mila trailed off.

"I might. I don't know. I have to sit down and study everything with fresh eyes, and honestly, I'm exhausted. I mean, it's a good idea, but... Ugh, I've been running it through my head the whole day and haven't reached a decision yet."

"If I'm conflict-avoidant, you're a magnet for overanalyzing. Decide; whatever it is, you know I can help with anything you need. Until you get a replacement, I can help. I have fewer hours with Migue at my other job now the drag pageant is done, and I'm sure Sal can help too."

"I know, I know. But this whole thing with Mr. Davenport riling up the parents, and I want to make sure my grandparents don't worry and..." I sighed. I didn't want to talk numbers, though; I wanted to create and dance and just not have to care. Why couldn't I just dedicate myself to my art without money worries?

"Aisha... You need to let go a bit, girl, relax, disconnect. You can't be fretting about every little thing you can't control. Trust that the right solution will find you. And remember, like my dad says in Spanish, 'you're not a gold pebble to be liked by everyone.' 'Cause I know you're worried about that man's words." Mila enveloped me in a hug that threatened to make me lose my composure.

"Who are you, and what have you done with my Mila?" I mumbled into her hug, and she poked me in the side.

"Ouch! Go on, you try out your new fit. Don't you worry about me, I'll be ok!" I promised her.

As Mila left for the night, I sat there looking at the computer, trying to figure out exactly what I would come up with next to stay afloat. Because if there was something I knew how to do, it was tread water.

Two

Knox

Steamed broccoli, grilled chicken nuggets, and apple slices for Trinity; grilled chicken breast with wheat pasta and a spinach salad for me. Every Thursday, this was our spread. It made things easy for me—Trinity loved the menu, and I was all about practicality and making sure my number one girl was always good.

I plated Trinity's food and placed it in front of her, making sure I kept my temper in check. She wasn't to blame for my bad mood right now, and, knowing her, she would call me out on my irritation if I let it out.

"Thanks, Daddy!" she piped up and dug in.

My chest filled as usual when I admired my baby girl, and I hoped I wasn't fucking up as the sole custodial parent. She sat there, the perfect mix of her mother and me, with wavy hair I had yet to figure out how to best style and warm mahogany-toned skin a lighter shade to my darker complexion. And her smile.

Trinity's smile had gotten me through some hard

moments in my life. Through kicking my father out of my life for good. Through a divorce I never thought would happen. Through the recovery from that divorce and the work I had to do to put myself back together. I knew I owed her so much just for keeping me focused on making myself a better man so I could be a good dad for her.

Her smile was all hers, which currently sported something green in between her two front teeth.

"You got broccoli between your teeth, Princess."

"Gosh, do I? Oh no, let me fix that," she said and ran her tongue over them. She sounded like an old lady; she'd been hanging out with my mother too much.

After her successful attempt, she flashed her teeth at me.

"You got it."

"Whew! That's good." And she went back to her food.

After I ate a few bites of my dinner, I got up from the table and made the last business call of the day as Trinity continued enjoying her dinner with little excited hums as she bit into her nuggets.

"Stephen, what's up, man?" I greeted my stepbrother and partner.

"About to sit down for dinner, which you should do too, instead of calling me to talk about business."

"Business doesn't stop, though."

"It does when we say so. Because we're the owners of the company."

"Commercial real estate never sleeps," I reminded him, strolling into the kitchen, so I didn't interrupt Trinity.

"It's real estate, not brain surgery. We were in several meetings together today and coincided for a couple of hours in the office, and still, you couldn't tell me what's on your mind?" Stephen grumbled, annoyed at my habit of calling him around this time to discuss any last-minute details we couldn't complete during the day.

"The meetings were with other people, and you know I tried talking to you several times, but both of our agendas conflicted. Listen..." I breezed right through his complaints. My temper was simmering enough for me not to want to engage in more back and forth. "We need to schedule a meeting to discuss our steps before we meet Kwon. This merger could be our next level up, and we need to come correct with our proposal."

"You couldn't send me an email, though?" he asked, and I could hear my nephew and niece in the background talking. The pressure in my head increased. Stephen knew this was important. There was no need for him to be an asshole about it.

"I'll drop an appointment in your calendar."

"Bruh, what has you pissed off?" Stephen asked. I could also tell he had moved away from the dining room.

"Nothin'... Well, not nothin'. It's just this woman."

"Oh, the ballet teacher again? If you just wanna call to shoot the shit, there's no reason to use work as an excuse."

He was right; I needed to vent, and I didn't always know how to reach out and just say so. Stephen was more than my stepbrother. He was my dude, my confidant. He'd been with me through some of the hardest trials of my life. Even so, I couldn't always open up to him.

I was assertive about my daughter's needs, but mine? Not so much. But Stephen understood that, so he encouraged me to talk even when I deflected.

"Yeah, man, she was late again. It's a bad look, bruh, like why can't she keep her shit together? I really wish I could move Trinity to another school, but..."

"I heard that, Daddy! No changing schools! I love Ms.

Mac!" Trinity yelled from the dining room. I pinched my nose, dislodging my glasses.

"Trin was loud and clear, so there's your answer. Why do you let her get under your skin if this is what Trinity wants? And what Trinity wants, she gets, we all know that." Stephen laughed.

"She's not spoilt."

"Are you gonna move her to another dance school?" Stephen taunted.

"No," I admitted.

"So yeah, what happened now? Did the sexy teacher smile too much at you?"

"Fuck off."

"Daddy! No cussing! I'll tell Gam Gam!" Trinity's singsong voice came from the dining room. Damn, my girl had bat ears, just like her grandma.

Thick lips and a perfect line of teeth flashed in my mind. She'd been wearing the same thing she wore every Thursday, and every time I saw that sliver of skin between her crop top and her high-waisted leggings with those thick thighs and hips and that pleasant smile that I just wanted to make disappear with my mouth... She pushed all my buttons.

Her calmness bothered the shit out of me. It was such a reminder of how I used to be before...well, before I realized people would trample all over me if I didn't assert myself.

I'd wanted to pull Trinity from Ms. Brown's Dance Studio since the second class. I couldn't, though, because somehow Ms. Mac had put a hex on Trinity and my parents. My parents helped with Trinity a lot, so I didn't dare piss them off, and I dared not make Trinity upset. So, I had to deal with Ms. I Don't Give A Fuck and her way of flowing into a room like the rest of us were some damn simps.

"I'll holler at you later. I need to get Trin to bed," I said as Stephen still laughed.

"If you call, I won't answer."

"Fucker," I said without heat, glad I could get some things off my chest, even if it was to Stephen.

"I love you too, bruh!"

Trinity strolled into the kitchen with her plate.

"Are you all done, Trin Trin?"

"Yes, I am, Daddy. Why did you leave me at the table by myself?" she asked, and I felt a pang of guilt.

This was a habit I needed to break. Trying to work through every minute of my day wasn't healthy... But I wanted to expand my business so that I could eventually decrease the hours I had to work and dedicate more time to Trinity. I needed to be to her what my father never was to me; a provider, a caregiver, her friend. It was overwhelming sometimes, but I pushed through.

"Sorry, Trin. I have to work on that, not working so much."

"Yes, you do. Work is boring anyway. It's more fun to watch some cartoons with me, or we can go out and play on my scooter." I took the plate from her and rinsed it, then put it in the dish rack.

While we bantered, we made our way to Trinity's room. She'd already showered when we got home after dance, so now it was just time to tuck her into bed.

"Did you pull your uniform already?"

"Yeah, I did."

"Did you put your backpack in the front?"

"Oh... I think so." Trinity chuckled.

"You think so? No, Miss Smart, either you did or you did not!" I said and showed her my tickle fingers.

"You can tickle me, Daddy," she giggled, giving me permission for a tickle fest.

I attacked with a gentle pressure that made my Trin Trin laugh until tears ran down her eyes.

"Ok, Miss Smart, you gotta go to bed now."

"Alright, Daddy. You make sure you go straight to bed too, ok? This morning you had some bags under your eyes," she said, wrapping me in her little arms. My heart mellowed under the hug while my ego bruised from the tired comment. But she wasn't wrong; I had been feeling ragged lately. Between trying to expand the business and be the best father to Trin, things were fraying around the seams. I needed a release valve.

"Love you, Trin."

"Love you, Daddy." My heart squeezed at her little voice telling me she loved me, and I wondered if her mom and I could have made it work for Trin's sake...but I knew I had made the right decision seeking a divorce. Trin needed a stable environment, and what her mom and I had created those last months wasn't stable at all.

I returned to the kitchen to straighten things out before turning in for the night. Everything in order, I made my way to my bathroom.

I turned on the shower and let the steam build up around me. Hot water hit my skin, and I let myself think of Ms. McKinney again.

She got on my fucking nerves.

Images of that serene smile she plastered on her face appeared. I wanted to fluster her, rustle her until she lost that airy composure. I envied her; I envied the way she made it seem all easy and seamless even when she was fucking up. She'd made some poor business decisions through the time Trin had been a member, and every single time, she dusted herself off and moved forward. And she made it look effortless.

Ms. McKinney intrigued me, but I'd never admit that. Not even to Stephen, even though he'd accused me of being weirdly obsessed with her. There was something about her that just called to me from the day I met her two years ago.

That first class had been a disaster. She hadn't had the names of all the registered kids, so she ended up giving free classes to three students that hadn't actually registered yet. Then she'd had technical problems with the music and got so excited about the class she ran past time until a parent asked her if it was a forty-five-minute class or longer.

Nerves I could understand, but Ms. McKinney had acted as if everything was ok, leaving me with a mixture of awe and annoyance in the pit of my stomach. I never could brush things off and move on. Since then, she'd become a puzzle, and I fixated on puzzles.

Ms. McKinney unearthed all my dark needs. Somehow my puzzlement and annoyance toward her progressed to a pent-up arousal that would have me in its grip from the moment I saw her in class until I went to bed. Every Thursday, and every Saturday, if Trin wasn't with my parents, this sphere of pressure formed in the base of my spine and the root of my balls.

The steam loosened my muscles, and the soap soothed my temper. The water hit my hard dick while I indulged in thoughts of Ms. McKinney and how I'd make her pay for every smile with my dick, my fingers, and my tongue.

My balls tightened, and the pressure on my spine amplified. My temper made my heart race twice as hard, goosebumps traveled across my arms, and still, I didn't touch myself.

It wasn't ever necessary.

I imagined the tight black leggings she wore today. I imagined the fold, that sweet spot where thigh met hip, the perfect handles for my hands. I imagined her as if I had already been with her, as if she was mine, and I...

"Fuck!"

I nutted so hard I impressed myself with how much cum painted the shower walls.

After rinsing the walls with my detachable showerhead, I finished cleaning up and dressing, finally laying down after a long-ass day. After the way I orgasmed, the tension I had carried most of the day dissipated. I felt much better even though my annoyance with that woman hadn't decreased a bit. At least this weekend, Trin wasn't going to class, a respite from this ill-advised, one-sided annoyance I carried for this woman.

My phone vibrated on the nightstand as I relaxed into sleep.

> Stephen: remember you agreed to take care of the kids on Saturday.
>
> Me: Of course. I already have the whole day planned for them and Trinity, and that way you can have some sexy time with your wife.

I smiled typing that.

> Stephen: Who said I was trying to...
>
> Me: Bruh, get yours. Y'all need it.

> Stephen: Alright you got me, we probably are gonna stay home and hopefully fuck the day away.
>
> Me: Good for you. At least one of us is getting it in.
>
> Stephen: you could as well! If you got laid, you probably would relax a bit.
>
> Me: Nah, I'm focused on Trin. That's my priority.
>
> Stephen: You can lay pipe and still have time to be Dad of the Year.
>
> Me: Fucker
>
> Stephen: I love you too!

Stephen wasn't wrong, though; I was considering finding a solution to my problem. And this weekend, I would finally take the last step toward ensuring I had some relief.

Three

Aisha

There were a few options in front of me to generate money, and this route was a familiar one. My grandparents had remortgaged their home to put up the seed capital for the studio, so I was the proud owner of two mortgages, medical bills for two octogenarians, and still paying off student loans for the things not covered by my dance scholarship. The studio was my only means of income, and when I lost some students, I was only making enough money to cover the bare bones for the business and home. My grandparents' pensions helped a little, but they'd both been blue-collar workers all their lives. There was no magical 401(k) funding their lifestyle. *I* was the 401(k).

So, after days of tossing and turning, wondering what I would do, I made a phone call.

A few days later, here I was.

Master Q's office was always a safe space for me. I sat on an oversized comfy chair, waiting for him. The office was a dark royal blue with sleek modern furniture, every piece in the room with a clear purpose. The walls were adorned with erotic art, which he'd told me he collected from Black artists, and my favorite feature—shelves with the most creative toys I had ever seen. I remembered the first time I had walked into this room, wanting to speak with him about opportunities to be a submissive for hire. He owned the entire building, which served as a membership club for kinksters of color, as well as a safe space for people to explore their sexuality.

I was very familiar with kink and professional submissiveness from doing it in New York during my years as a dancer—great for subsidizing my income—which had allowed me to explore my sexuality. After meeting a fellow dancer that was a dominatrix, my brain fired up with ideas. Why not be a sub for hire? With some investigating, I found some other dancers in the kink community in NY that did it as well, and they showed me the ropes. But then I fell in love...and there wasn't space for that while I was in love.

When I moved back and started looking for capital for my business, restarting the work seemed natural, and once I met Master Q, I presented the idea of collaborating with him during one of his quarterly educational kink workshops. He was happy to let me offer my services and for the money to go directly to me.

I'd put a stop to that six months ago, wanting to take a break and clear myself of some extra feelings I didn't want to feel. Now, I needed to put that aside and make money to cover my expenses so I could invest the profit right back into the studio.

"How are you?" That deep lovely voice resonated with warmth. Master Q's presence was larger than life. He was the type of man that had a magnetic field around him, with an aura that soothed and charged me at the same time.

I moved to stand, and he shook his head, taking my hand and giving it a kiss instead. I crossed my legs, attempting to ignore my natural reaction anytime Master Q was around. He was one of the most sensual people I knew. I didn't see him as anything but a mentor... Alright, I saw him as a fine-ass man I would love to fuck but keep as a mentor after.

"Oh, you know me, Master Q, staying busy. And you?" I smiled, hoping he wouldn't get into it tonight.

"I'm worried you're back so soon."

"Master Q..." I sighed. I had confided in him, telling him how getting into subspace was getting harder and harder when I didn't feel a connection to the dom.

He had explained it was something that sometimes happened to those that did kink for a price; your needs no longer were met in that transactional way. It resonated with me because I'd caught feelings I didn't need with the doms I was working with, projecting some of that want for things not to be casual.

"I want to make certain you're sure before I brief you. When we last spoke, you told me some club experiences had brought up memories of your ex-fiancé and your D/s dynamic."

I uncrossed my legs and planted my heels on the floor. "I'm going into this with zero expectations or concerns. Well, I'm expecting to get paid, but outside of that, zero concerns." I smiled, holding my posture, my back arched in the same line as when standing in first position.

Master Q had been the right person to present this idea to because his name was synonymous with trust in our kink community. That trust meant I could bring him this proposal where I knew I was getting the payoff I deserved for my time and service. Two sessions were enough to cover my grandparents' house mortgage payments.

Master Q's intense stare attempted to make me squirm in my seat, but I refused to back down. Showing any hesitation would have him packing me up and sending me home to pout.

"Master Q, I promise I'm good. Tell me about the baby Dom you mentioned this morning?" I relaxed my back, unfurling slowly against the chair. I crossed my legs again and rested my hands on my top thigh.

Then I waited.

"Aisha, you think your silence is intimidating...but we're not playing right now, so I'll allow it," he murmured, and I shivered at his words.

I grinned again, eager to break the trance of Master Q's scrutiny. I didn't really need all his silent, brooding censure. He knew it was my catnip.

"X is close to finishing private Dominant classes. One of the most natural Doms I've taught in a while. He wants to get some practical experience before he goes out into our kinky world on his own, be prepared if he meets a new submissive. X has had some play experience with subs during his time here at the club but wants to ensure he can be a good Dom in any environment. He's looking for a sub open to doing several scenes that can give him some range, teach him how to be the experienced one."

I nodded along, intrigued by this person. I liked that they were looking to work out the ideal scene for the sub instead of playing out their Dom fantasies on a submissive. It would be a fresh experience for me.

"As always, whatever the two of you decide to do once you get to know each other is your business. What he will pay for is didactic sessions on how to properly be a dominant," Master Q reminded me. He didn't have to tell me twice, but I knew it was important for him to say it. The money exchange was not and should not be for sex, and I rarely had sex in these sessions. But occasionally...

"One last thing—he values his privacy, so he'll be wearing a mask, same as you. Are you ready to meet him?"

The thrill that coursed through me at the question was reassurance enough for me. I was ready.

Four

Jasmine

The décor in Q's Space dripped Afro-exceptionalism. The sex club had rooms all around the top level of a courtyard looking down on a space set up for the best sex parties and reunions. We'd been assigned the Gold Room.

The room boasted black matte walls with gold accents elegantly spread throughout. Golden fixtures adorned the furniture. Gold and brown toys and tools were spread around the room, all familiar sights.

What wasn't familiar was the man standing in the middle of the room wearing gray sweats, a black long-sleeve t-shirt molded to his muscles, and a balaclava, exposing only his eyes.

Solid came to mind as we eyed each other.

Thick, smooth dark skin and *scrumptious* also came to mind.

A thrill of danger overtook me to see him waiting for me. I couldn't see his face, but what I could admire of his body had me speechless.

"Good evening, Jasmine," he said, using my alter ego for my sessions with him. His voice was a low rumble slightly muffled by the balaclava, and it traveled deep into my stomach as I shifted on my heels. This man had my curiosity—and other parts—piqued.

"Good evening, X. You asked for a professional submissive?" I said in my silkiest voice.

"I did. I've heard only the best about you. You honor me with your presence, and I look forward to learning from you."

Oh, I wasn't expecting that. Some of the baby Doms and Dommes were in it for the wrong reasons, narcissists looking for someone to be at their beck and call, and it wasn't always apparent until they interacted with a sub.

Master Q was an expert at it, but sometimes one or two slipped by. It took a sub's good eye to realize when a Dom's head wasn't in it for the right reasons. That was a personal red flag, and to have this man say it honored him to meet me...well. He was striking the right chord so far. The problem was I wanted him to strike other things too...

He waited for me to say something, but I was stunned and a bit intimidated. I needed to buck up. No matter what, I was the experienced one here.

"Today, you and I get to know each other and set our boundaries," he said, straight to the point, interpreting my silence for immediate submission. He wasn't exactly wrong. He was pressing all my subby buttons right now, and that mask on him just made it even more delectable. The intensity of his gaze made my skin pull, all of me taut, connected to his every move.

He gestured to the black and gold throne chairs, releasing some of the tension, and I sighed in relief as he sat on the other one across me, legs spread to accommodate their thickness, elbows resting on his knees. Sir X crossed his brawny arms in the middle, a clearly comfortable position for him, but it screamed danger to me. The fun type of danger.

My heart skipped a beat as I settled on the comfortable seat.

I'd done this so many times, both for my enjoyment and for money, but somehow, this was different. Never had my heart beat so hard inside my chest that I worried it would be audible. Other Doms had tried to dominate me based on their needs; very few had tried to get to know me well. Taking a deep breath, I regrouped, then exhaled slowly.

"Have you done this before?" I asked curiously.

"Negotiate?" he asked.

"Yes," I replied, crossing my legs. His eyes remained on my masked face, further impressing me.

"For scenes, I have."

"But not for long-term D/s relationships?" I tilted my head to the side, knowing the answer but wanting to see what he had to say. The beauty of this was that we got to incorporate some role-playing as well—me the inexperienced sub, him the seasoned Dom.

"That is why we are here tonight. I know Master Q enough to know he's not sloppy about preparing his classes, so I guess you're testing me. Gon' head, Jasmine, drill me." X relaxed, stretching those thick thighs, making my mouth water. His eyes assessed me with an intensity that I didn't quite understand, almost as if he was trying to puzzle something out.

His relaxed pose kept me more on edge, and I loved being on the ledge, teetering between safety and recklessness. He reminded me of a giant tiger switching its tail, waiting to pounce when I least expected it.

"No drilling." A giggle escaped me, surprising me. I shifted in my seat, trying to gather my bearings. This was honestly unprofessional of me.

Get it together, Aisha! Less flirting, more keeping open lines of communication. This conversation was key to our sessions.

I couldn't tell for sure because the lights were dimmed, but his eyelashes flickered at my giggle. His head snapped back, those penetrating eyes focused solely on me. I shivered, wondering if he'd seen me before. Had he recognized me from somewhere? This wouldn't be the first time I scened with someone that knew me in my vanilla life, but one of my requirements was no acknowledgment of our vanilla roles if we recognized each other. I trailed my eyes over him—the balaclava was doing its job.

My palms itched, and I wanted to run them up and down my legs, but I abstained. Was he as affected as I was?

"Ok, I'm willing to answer anything."

"Oh, ok then. Good to know. Let's proceed with the negotiations." I hoped my breathiness wasn't obvious.

"What does it for you? What are your kinks?" he asked, making me believe I imagined his previous reaction.

"Actually, I don't know," I answered, and he did a double take.

"What do you mean, you don't know?" Concern was laced in his tone. He knew I was experienced, so...

"Or let's say Jasmine doesn't know." Jasmine was a newbie in the scene, just like he asked for.

"Oh, gotcha." He nodded, impressed. "Alright, Jasmine, you and I are going to explore a little and figure out what you like...together." He stood up and sauntered to the wall where some toys hung in order. My eyes trailed his every move as he collected a whip, his strong knuckles surrounding the pommel.

He walked back and bent one knee in front of me, making me uncross my legs.

"Do I have permission to touch you?" he asked.

"Yes," I breathed, the scent of his cologne delicious. It was woodsy and citrusy and snuck up on me just as he did.

"Blu?"

"What?"

"Your cologne, Blu by Chanel?" I clarified.

"Yeah, how did you know? My d—someone I love dearly gave it to me for my birthday. I found it's more suited for night use."

"It works perfect for nights," I mumbled and heard his breath catch.

Oh, I almost moaned that into his ear, didn't I? I hadn't intended it to be that sensual, but it just escaped me. That happened to me sometimes; my friends would tell me I had been flirting with someone, and I wouldn't know.

I sat back to make space between us.

"Do you like pain?" he asked after a second.

"Mmm...I don't know. I mean, I've been spanked, and that's fun. Not sure I would want to be bruised black and purple after, but I don't know..." Jasmine didn't know what the heck she liked, but I had a limited pain threshold. Clamps, floggers, spanking, and light whips were all good... but canes and heavy pain were not my jam.

X wielded the whip in a leisurely motion and cleared his throat, and I felt that rumble in the apex of my thighs and wondered if he'd make me enjoy the whip more.

"Are there certain areas that are off-limits for me to touch?" he asked, and the fabric on top of his mouth muffled things a bit, but I could have sworn he sounded choked.

I considered his question while the sway of the whip mesmerized me, my pulse skittering in my throat as we watched each other.

Unless I was in a personal relationship, depending on how comfortable a Dom would make me feel in the first sessions, I usually made my genitals and sometimes my breasts off-limits.

After all, there's a plethora of nonsexual scenes to explore in BDSM.

My mouth had always been out of bounds, no matter what. But this person had me second-guessing my professional boundaries.

"Ahhh...no kissing," I whispered. Then something made me say, "Well, that's a soft limit."

Crap, why didn't I make that a hard limit?

X nodded solemnly, and I watched him take on the weight of the responsibility I'd just placed on him. That made me feel safe. Sheeze, I was losing my marbles. How was this man making me feel so safe when I didn't even know him outside of Master Q's vetting?

He loosened his grip on the whip's handle, the instrument almost falling from his hand.

"Thank you, Jasmine. I don't have any hard limits. You can touch wherever you please if I command it." In a flash, he whirled the whip, my breath catching before the swat heated my skin, the pleasure-pain delicious.

It was a medium swipe; he had correctly gauged my limit. If he'd hit me a little harder, I might have made the intensity a soft limit.

"Green."

With impressive speed, he swiped again. The sting radiated through my leg, making my muscle seize.

"Yellow."

"Alright, that tells me a lot," he said and stood up. I remained sitting on the throne chair, waiting for his next question, breath still caught in my throat. The surrounding air was as thin as the top of a mountain, and my heart raced, unprepared for the altitude.

"Stand up, Jasmine."

The room temperature had increased. I parted my legs a little, needing the balance. This was the first time I had ever negotiated boundaries like this. His presence awakened my senses to full awareness.

"During our sessions, what is the overwhelming way you want to feel?" he asked, standing behind me where I couldn't see him. I could feel his muffled breath tickling the top of my curls. He swiped my hair away from my left shoulder and gave it a tender kiss. He must have moved the mask away from his mouth because bare lips met my exposed skin, and I shivered with a moan of delight at the gentle touch. I was so keyed up by this exchange that a little kiss had me moaning. Wow.

"Do you want to feel loved? Do you want to feel excited, scared, on edge?"

I gasped at "on edge."

"Mhm, on edge and loved. How about excited?" he asked as he ghosted a lone finger down the middle of my exposed neck, bringing goosebumps in its path. That touch felt a little too good.

"Yes, that too, and... I...sometimes like to be...used," I said, thinking Jasmine would have already had a couple of exceptional dicks in her life to know what cranked her jam in that department.

And in this regard, Jasmine is me, and I am Jasmine.

I never made up my likes and dislikes for these sessions; I didn't have the range for that, hence why I used to be a dancer on Broadway, not an actor, and it was important for me to protect myself. I could do impact play with the best of them, but I wouldn't go in subspace during it if you hit me too hard. But the beauty of my time with X was that he was looking to truly curate the entire experience as if I was his long-term sub, and I wanted him to discover everything I liked.

"So, you want to be my dirty little doll?" he asked, and again, I moaned.

"Mmmm, loved, excited, on edge, used, and a little name-calling?"

"Mhm," was all I could say.

"Well, Jasmine, I look forward to making you my filthy Baby Doll."

"Ohhh," I sighed in contentment, "...what do you want me to call you?"

"You can call me Sir or Sir X. One last thing before we go," he said, and I was desperate for the session to be over so I could go home to my new vibrator that got me from zero to ten in less than two minutes. And I was already at nine point nine-five, so the job would not take long.

"Yes?"

"Do you like high protocol?"

I frowned, not having much experience with it before except with Master Q. I'd had some rituals with my ex-boyfriend, but I wasn't trying to think of my ex right now.

"I haven't much practiced it."

"This is beyond Jasmine answering," he said, stating a fact.

"Yes."

"Ok. Starting next week, I want you to wait for me in a certain position. Kneel, please."

I obeyed and felt a little cream gush out of me. This man was onto something here.

"Do you like being gagged?" he pondered, dragging the hard whip handle against my bottom lip as he prowled around me. I fought the urge to taste the leather with my tongue. He was all elegant strength, broad shoulders, and smooth dark skin.

All I knew of his looks was the relaxed way he carried himself with the slight steel in his back that hinted at danger and coiled restraint. I loved how relaxed he felt around me already, and I, in turn, felt oddly at ease with him.

In one session.

"I might enjoy it sometimes. Not sure, Sir," I said, and he froze next to me. He slowly turned, his eyelashes fluttered at me, and again, that odd feeling that he was trying to figure something out, figure *me* out, ran through me, making me shiver.

"When I ask you to assume the first position, this is what I'll be referring to: back arched and elegant, knees in front of you, hands on your knees. I thought I wanted your eyes down, but I lowkey enjoy how your big brown princess eyes have been following me around as I walk. So, we'll keep that. The mask is perfect, by the way. Do you have more like this?"

I nodded. I wore a crystal-encrusted mask that revealed just my eyes and had a crisscrossed pattern around my face, then chandelier-style strings dropping in front of my mouth. It gave the illusion you could see my face, but behind that open pattern, I had a flesh-colored breathable mesh that concealed my features.

"I don't mind not seeing your nose and mouth, but I want access to your eyes. Though I do want admission to your mouth...in case that soft limit changes to a yes," he said.

"Yes, Sir." I shivered, thinking that soft limit might go away if I didn't woman up real fast.

"I'd love to see you wear a skirt or dress next time if you so please..." he suggested. Sheesh, he knew what he was doing. He knew I'd be in here next week wearing a thong with my butt cheeks peeking out of a cute short dress just to please his behind.

"Yes, Sir, I would please."

Oh, I was in danger with this one.

"A'ight. Send me the rest of the things you've liked in bed and your play by tomorrow. You can send it to Master Q, and he'll give it to me. I want to see what does it for you, Baby Doll, so I can keep you on your toes starting next week. Ok?"

"Yes, Sir."

"Every session after we're through, we'll do aftercare, and during it, you'll put Jasmine away and give me your professional sub feedback. We cool?"

"Absolutely. You're missing an important thing, Sir."

"What is it?"

"We need a safe word," I reminded him, knowing many Doms got so excited they forgot to put the railings on the game.

"Shit, you right. What do you want it to be, Baby Doll?"

"I'm thinking keep it simple. Green, yellow, and red work," I said.

"Does not-Jasmine have a special word?" he asked.

"Yes, but you don't get to always ask about not-Jasmine." I chuckled at his urge to crack the code. But I was a professional only in this room. Outside of it, we weren't even acquaintances; at least, I hadn't recognized him. There was always the chance... I hoped he remembered that.

"Mmm, I would love to get to the point with you where you let me meet not-Jasmine...in depth. So, what can I ask about?"

"You can ask Jasmine what she likes in her play and in the bedroom, and you can rest easy. Everything she likes is what I love; the difference is Jasmine is discovering herself. I know myself real well. Can I get out of position, Sir?" I asked, breaking the enchantment we had created together this past hour.

"Yeah." He offered me his hand and helped me back up.

"Thank you for tonight. This negotiation was very enjoyable for me. I'll remind you of this, though: outside of these doors, there is no Jasmine, no X. So, asking things beyond what happens here can only lead to confusion. Does that make sense?" I asked him.

Because I had a prominent job in the community, being the ballet teacher for many people's kids here, I always maintained my anonymity in the club, even when I played in scenes for fun. I always wore a mask. Master Q and a select few that I trusted knew who I was, but to avoid messiness, I kept it tight in here. I didn't want X getting confused about what it was between us.

"A'ight, Jasmine, I hear you. But you know that beyond this professional arrangement, you felt something more today, and as long as I have your consent, I won't hesitate to explore that something..." he whispered in my ear, a promise and a threat all in one.

And why was my inner ho rooting for him? Gah.

"I'd like to see you try," I countered and sashayed my way out of the Gold Room, leaving him behind.

Five

Knox

My brain explored the conundrum of my night at Q's Space. The sense of familiarity I felt the moment Jasmine walked into that room had stayed with me for days after.

My mind percolated all I had learned in our session and all the questions raised. Who was she? Could my suspicions be correct?

I hadn't been able to stay still at home, so I headed over to my parents' house with Trin. I knew there would be some manual labor waiting for me there.

Every time I came to this house, I was tasked with work. No matter how short the visit or the reason I stopped by, my Momma always found something new for me to do.

"Oh, honey, so good to see you!" she said, going on her tippy toes to give me a big hug before she turned to Trinity with a kiss.

"And my baby, how are you, Trin? Come, I bought you some new dance outfits I want you to try." She held out her hand, and Trinity happily followed her.

"Momma, she has enough outfits." I shook my head, following the two of them. My mom had a way of spoiling her grandkids. Sometimes I felt she was overcompensating for the things she couldn't give me because of the instability of our house when I was a little kid.

"Oh, shush you. I get to do what I want to now that I'm old," she said.

"Old? Yeah, right. Just last week, that lady in the restaurant asked if you were my sister," I reminded her.

"Hi, Gam Gam! Daddy said in the car he hoped you wouldn't treat him like cheap labor today."

Yo! It always be your own.

"Oh, really? Huh. Knox darling, your father is in the kitchen installing one of those overhead hanging pot things for me. Go help him," she said, beaming as she breezed by me and up the stairs with Trin.

"Of course, Momma. I got it." I chuckled and walked into the kitchen.

"Son! How are you?" My stepdad was perched on a ladder, drilling holes into the ceiling.

"Why didn't you hire someone to do that? You sure you good, old man? You're doing a lot by yourself."

"Last I heard," he nodded toward the stairs, "I got help."

"That you got." I laughed, happy to assist him.

William had earned my undying support and respect through the years of marriage with my mom, a divorcee with a turbulent past and a moody twelve-year-old. That past was composed of an ex-husband that emotionally abused her and neglected both of us at the same time.

The dysfunction of our house in the first years of my life had marked me, a tattoo that no laser could remove. Of course, at that age, I didn't recognize William for the outstanding man he was. I'd still been attached to the idea of my biological dad coming through for us. Through the years, William proved he was the actual father I needed and brought so much peace to our household. And he'd gifted me two step-siblings who I loved.

We worked together while we exchanged opinions on the latest results in sports, October being a great month for old sports fans like William, who loved anything involving a ball.

I came down from the ladder to check on my phone. Saturdays were usually a day off, but I still stayed in touch with the comings and goings in the office and my emails.

I checked the work mailbox, and all was well. Then I switched to my personal inbox and read an email that ruined my otherwise chill Saturday.

"Pops, you good with me stepping out for a minute? I need to take care of something," I asked, already walking toward the door.

"Are you alright?"

"Yeah, I'm a'ight."

"Honey, if you're going out, get some ice cream for dinner!" Momma shouted from the second floor.

"And sprinkles, please!" Trini chimed in.

"I will!" Those two had ears like bats. I'd get them their ice cream—after I took care of this problem.

I PARKED in the familiar lot and power walked toward the building.

The door was unlocked. The chime went off, and no one was at the front desk.

Fuck. This woman, she was asking for trouble.

The neighborhood was quiet; most people that lived

here were old heads that refused to move to their kids' houses further west. It was an area most people didn't mess with. Even so, there were always some new young dudes wanting to prove something that needed no proof.

I heard music and looked up at the screen outside the first room to see Ms. Mac with her dance troupe, practicing some type of jazz routine. My anger rumbled, but I wasn't angry enough to storm into her session, so I sat in the waiting room and waited...for thirty fucking minutes.

Anger. If there was one thing I carried from my formative years into adulthood dealing with a narcissistic father, it was anger. Managing it, always keeping it at bay. Knowing the volcanic eruptions in the pit of my stomach were a consequence of bottled-up emotions. I had gone to therapy; I had done the support groups. I knew it was a problem. When I cared more—when I was invested in something or someone—was when it got challenging for me to control it.

I knew she had cameras in the waiting room on a feed on her laptop, and even though she was aloof, she was no fool, so she probably had seen me come in when she heard the chime.

My breathing exercises kept me occupied during my wait. I clenched and unclenched my hands, wishing I wouldn't allow this woman to get to me like this, but it was a fight I lost every damned time.

Finally, she came out with her teenage students right behind her and her friend, the other dance teacher.

"Oh, Mr. Davenport, what are you doing here on a Saturday afternoon? Trin's class was this morning," she said as if she hadn't seen me come in.

"You're doing another recital," I accused.

"Yes...yes, I am." She nodded slowly, perplexed at my accusation. Now that I said it that way, I realized how asinine it was, coming all the way here to argue about it, but I was in it now. Might as well stick to it.

I didn't—couldn't stay quiet when I had any concerns about things that pertained to Trin. If it was her school, her dance studio, or things with her mom, I always strived to be vocal and made sure I advocated for her.

"Alrighty, so...you're mad about it?" she asked and snuck a glance at her friend...what was her name? Ms. Torres, that was it; Trin's hip-hop and jazz teacher. Her friend smirked and shrugged her shoulder. A thread of amusement tickled my chest, but I refused to show it.

"The timing is horrible. Right before Christmas? We just had a major recital in May. A recital that required the help of a lot of us parents, so that you've added a major one during the holidays without doing some type of survey or something is fu—very inconsiderate."

She nodded along as if my word was gospel and the sun shone out of my ass.

For fuck's sake, she was always poised and professional in our interactions, but I knew deep down she wanted to tell me to go fuck myself.

Her not cussing, something Trin mentioned one day, made me want to be the one to make her break. Through anger or other means... A black and gold room flashed in the back of my brain, but I was determined to respect the boundaries established.

"Dancers, your parents are waiting outside, Ms. Torres will walk out with you. Remember, if you're going to leave without your guardian, you need a note from them." She gave one dancer a look, and the teen shuffled her feet. I nodded, my muscles loosening as I watched her in action with her students. One thing I always gave Ms. McKinney credit for was she was good to her students; she cared above and beyond what they expected of a dance teacher. It never ceased to impress me.

"My mom is picking me up," the teen shared, and Ms. Mac clapped once.

"Great! Ok, y'all, see you during the week. Remember, stay hydrated!"

The teens all filed out toward the cars of their respective parents.

"So, you were saying, Mr. Davenport, that you drove here to tell me how you were upset that I didn't do a survey to gather interest in the recital. Even though the email says it's optional and the May show remains our main recital. You also could have emailed me your thoughts, but again, you drove here...am I right?" she said with a pleasant smile that curdled my stomach. At least, that was how I interpreted the flutters and swoops that just went on. And that voice... I was almost sure I was right about her.

"Yeah, well, I was around the way."

"You were around the way?" Incredulity dripped off her every syllable, and my ears heated to the point it was threatening to singe the frame of my glasses. "My understanding is you live about twenty minutes away, same as Mr. and Mrs. Jameson," she said, referring to my mom and stepfather.

"Oh, so you keep track of where every student lives? Or is that special interest only for me?" She messed up, saying that, and I would hang onto this small thread. Before this, she'd had me on the fucking ropes, about to tap out.

"Oh, ahem...every student. I make sure I know that information in case of emergency and such," she said, bouncing back admirably. That was a very plausible explanation. I searched her eyes for any sign of acknowledgment that things had changed between us, my whole body heating as I studied her.

"I think you might have an idea for other families, but I bet with me, you know exactly how far away I live, down to the second," I taunted her, tired of being flat-footed with her and having this weird attraction to someone I didn't see eye-to-eye with at all.

The way she managed her business was haphazard, always flitting to the next thing. One day I arrived with Trin to find one room converted into a pop-up shop full of dance clothes. She'd announced to everyone that she was opening a mini clothing store, completely rearranging the summer schedule.

It lasted three months.

Another time she started adult dance aerobic classes at night, sending emails to all the parents. My momma came to support a class, and it was a shit show. The teacher that was supposed to be directing the class never showed up, so Ms. Mac had to step in and improvise. She had been mortified and emailed a couple of days later, canceling the classes.

I might overreact, but this damn recital felt just like one of her half-ass thought-out projects. And this time, it involved getting our kids' hopes up, and I didn't like that one bit. I protected Trin at all costs. Determination to ensure Trin had a better childhood than I had drove me, and that included being the exact opposite of my father. I needed to be involved, protective, and in the know about all her activities.

Trin would never have to endure her soccer teacher hitting her with a ruler while her parent was so oblivious, he didn't realize during pick-up... I shook the memory away. I didn't want to go down that road.

The straightforward thing to do was not sign up for the

recital, but that would devastate Trin. So the next best thing was making sure the thought process around the event was 100% sound.

"Look." I collected my thoughts. Maybe antagonizing her wasn't the move. Right now, I needed to convince her to pull out. Cut the cord before she got in too deep. I ran my fingers over my beard, then approached her.

Her eyes flashed, and I wondered if she would say more, but then the serene grin was back in place. Was she thinking what I was thinking?

"I want to make sure you're in this. I know you have a lot going on with the studio right now." I gestured to the empty desk. "Maybe this isn't the time to jump on another venture. You have less than three months to pull this off. For the May recital, you prepare from January. This feels rushed." I needed to appeal to her sense of rationale if she had any.

She hesitated, and I knew she was truly taking stock, but then the chime startled us, and Ms. Torres walked back in.

"They all left safe and...oh, you still here? Boy, you really like to ride my girl's dick, don't you?"

"Mila!"

"Ms. Torres, always the gentle one," I said, nodding at her.

"Oh, never mind me." Ms. Torres smiled, giving us both the deuces and strolling peacefully to the back office.

"Does your friend talk like that in front of the—"

"No, she doesn't; she's a professional. But you must admit, you do like to complain a lot, and it was only adults in here when she said that." Damn, I was proud of her for giving me a bit of sass and pushback. I respected that.

I had been seeing red earlier, and though I'd simmered down in her calming presence, I wasn't done with her.

"Think about what I said. Maybe next Christmas is the right time to start a holiday show."

She paused, still thinking, then shook her head adamantly.

"No. You don't get to tell me how to run my business. If you'd like Trinity not to participate, though it will be heartbreaking, I'll respect it. Same as you should respect that this establishment," she gestured around, "isn't yours to dictate the goings on. Now, if you'll excuse me, I need to work on our new show."

She sashayed away back into the dance room and turned on the music real loud as if to drown my presence.

Fuck. I guess if I couldn't convince her to cancel it, then I needed to make sure this show went on flawlessly.

Damn it.

Six

Aisha

"Come on, y'all, dinner is ready," I called over to the living room, where Momma and Pops sat glued to the TV. The aroma of salmon with Brussels sprouts and brown rice made my stomach grumble. I didn't have time to eat myself as I had somewhere to be in less than—I checked my watch—thirty minutes.

"Earth to grandparents!" I singsonged loudly.

"We can hear you, child!" Momma exclaimed from her favorite corner of the sectional, paying me no mind as I tapped my feet on the tile floor. I needed to settle them and get them to eat dinner, so they could both take their meds before I headed out for this networker. I knew if I left, they'd eat whatever they pleased and would forget a pill or fall asleep in front of the TV, Momma curled up on the sectional, Pops reclined on his favorite chair.

I didn't plan to be home late. Their schedules were predictable, and today, they'd had their weekly long walk in the park with their friends, who I affectionately called The 80th Floor Gang, and that meant an early bedtime.

"Fine. I'll just bring you the food," I mumbled to myself as I picked up the plates from the dining room table and walked them over to their spot. Momma granted me a sweet smile that said, "I knew you'd figured it out eventually," as if I hadn't tried to break their habit of eating in front of the TV.

I set up their foldable tray stands in front of each of them and placed their plates.

"The usual?" I asked, knowing their drinks of choice for dinner. Always lemonade for Momma and the solitary glass of beer for Pops; it was the only time he drank.

"Thanks, honey," Pops said when I gave them each their drink.

"You look real nice, Aisha. Is that outfit new?" Momma asked, prying her eyes away from the TV now that she had everything she needed in front of her.

"No, I had it in my closet and hadn't been able to use it." I shrugged. I rarely wore business cocktail attire; it wasn't something I needed in my career, but if I wanted to elevate the studio to one of the prominent small Black-owned businesses in the area, I needed to put myself out there.

"Well, good for you. You enjoy yourself, ok, and don't you be worrying about coming back early. We ain't no babies to be put to sleep. Remember!" Momma started hitting her stride now, and I knew exactly what was coming next. "I wiped your behind!" Momma and I said at the same time.

"Oh, you think you're smart, don't you?" Momma said with a cackle.

I laughed, walking toward the door.

"I learned from the best. Be good, you two!"

I rolled up to Mila's apartment and waited in the car for my friends to come down. When we'd heard of this Young Black Business networker planned by The Center for Athletes of Broward, we all concluded it would be a good place to promote our business.

For me, it was all about meeting like-minded people in the arts as well as supporting The Center's work, which gave opportunities to the kids in our neighborhood with additional mentorships and resources for their life after high school.

Mila's reasons were more nebulous. She'd wanted to start her own business for a while but was always tight-lipped about what that business entailed. She was a collector of information; people usually spilled their guts to her because of her deceptively sweet, affable demeanor. Whatever her venture was, she needed to gather intel before she moved on with her project.

Last but not least was my other best friend, Sal, the smartest of the three of us, hands down. She hated when we said that, but there was no shame in admitting you had a brilliant friend and giving them their flowers. She was a freelance software developer and had mad skills with anything web-related, and on the side, she did other work, but I tried to pretend I didn't know because it made me nervous for her and her Robin Hood tendencies.

These two girls and my grandparents were the reason I was well-adjusted in adulthood. Trauma bred from parents that cared less about my well-being, but all the security and safety they deprived me was gifted in abundance by these girls and my Momma and Pops. I often wondered where I would be without them. My mom had left me behind in the hospital when I was born but had the decency to call my grandparents. A few years later, they found out she'd passed away from an overdose. Sadness swirled inside me at thoughts of my mom, of the tormented life she led and the opportunities we lost. So yeah, thank god for my tribe.

As I bopped to the music, they both emerged from Mila's apartment building. Mila wore one of her little black dresses that molded her thick frame to perfection. She had a way of wearing clothes that, on anyone else, would seem risky or revealing, but Mila wore them with an innate elegance.

Sal had grumbled the whole day today in our group chat because she hated dressing up. She'd finally settled on a burgundy jumpsuit that draped beautifully over her plus-size body, flowing as she walked.

"Ugh, she didn't let me put makeup on her," Mila complained as soon as they got in.

"First, I know how to apply makeup, y'all know this. Second, you also know I don't like to wear it," Sal said in her husky voice from the back seat, unbothered by Mila's annoyed tone.

"Hello to you, too," I said with a smile.

"Oh, I'm sorry!" Mila reached over and gave me a peck on my cheek, then reclaimed her seat and strapped on her seat belt. "It's just that she gets on my nerves. If I had flawless skin like she does, it would be a wrap," she continued.

"Your skin is beautiful," I said, and Sal just hummed in agreement from the back. We had already lost her to her cell phone. It didn't bother me; I knew online was where Sal lived most of the time.

"Aww, thank you, baby girl. I try to keep everything supple," Mila said, touching her cheek.

While Mila and I kept up our conversation with Sal interjecting at odd times, my phone rang.

"Oh, are you gonna answer him?" Mila asked with a tone I didn't appreciate.

"Of course, I will," I said and answered through my Bluetooth connection.

"Hola, Papa, como esta?" I asked in my accented Spanish. I didn't handle my second language well, and the reason was the man on the phone right now. My father, always flitting in and out at odd times.

"Aisha, how are you, Bella? You don't call your old man no more!" my dad said, and a twinge of guilt assaulted me. Mila shook her head and mumbled something, and behind me, Sal's judgment lurked as the fourth passenger.

My father was a deeply troubled individual with the best of intentions. He loved me, and I was glad I had him in my life. I'd never met my mother, so having even a piece of him... That's why I didn't mind him being inconsistent—better inconsistent than not present at all. And if he sometimes tried to hit me up for things he needed, well, wasn't that what family was for?

"I'm sorry, Papa, it's been busy at the studio. I have a lot going on, but you're right. I should check in with you more."

"I went by your house, but those grandparents of yours, always trying to block me from seeing you like you're not a grown woman. Wouldn't tell me where you were. But that's alright, I'm gonna stop by the studio in the next couple of days. Just to see you, you know. I don't see my Bella enough."

Sal harrumphed.

I tensed at Sal's censure, worried he'd heard her, but he continued. "You gotta keep practicing your Cuban, ok? That Spanish you garbled when you picked up needs work.

I know your American grandparents' family didn't care about you learning your heritage from my side, but it's just as important, you hear?"

"Alright, Papa, see you soon."

"Alright, Bella, adios."

Guilt and annoyance battled inside me, a common occurrence every time I spoke with my father. I would have learned all the Spanish, all the Cuban cooking, all about my culture if only my dad had been more present, and every time he came around after months of being MIA, he would press me about my dedication to my Cuban heritage over my American side, which is what I knew the most.

No matter what I did, I couldn't win with him, but I also knew this was part of his problems, of the demons he fought every day.

"Aye girl, I don't know why on earth you let that man fluster you. That ain't a father. That's a fucking scrub," Mila said.

"Mila, that's unkind!" I chastised her, knowing she meant well, but she was adding to my annoyance.

"Mhm," Sal said from the back, and I already knew she disapproved. The boundaries she set with her own family were made of steel, and she didn't understand why I didn't do the same with my father.

One day, she had made a point of saying my dad hadn't even fought for me to have his last name Solis, a comment that hurt to this day, so I shouldn't go out of my way to appease him on anything. She wasn't wrong, but I couldn't help myself. He was family, and I believe you help family, no matter what.

With those conflicted thoughts, we drove the rest of the way in silence, the girls letting me stew in my worries.

The rooftop bar for the networker was full of good-looking young Black professionals mingling and laughing in the darkening afternoon. I took in the beautiful scene, the purples and golds in the sky accentuating the deck bar's burnt orange and wood décor. There was a small pool on the opposite side of the bar, still full at this late hour with hotel guests.

Servers wandered about with platters of mini appetizers and white and red wine on trays. I plucked a glass of white wine while Mila grabbed the red, and Sal made a beeline to the bar.

"Ok, so here we are. Now we need to do the adult thing and mingle. But I honestly just want to find a table and chill," Mila said. I was tempted to do the same when I noticed two men approaching us. I smiled at the sight of them, one taller with medium brown skin and the other with a mahogany complexion and a wide, gorgeous smile.

"There's my bro-in-law," Mila mumbled, but I knew she loved Mason Brathwaite, the host of the night.

"Ladies! You made it! I bet Mariana twenty-five bucks you'd show up, and she said you'd flake, so I thank you for coming through!" Mason said with his charming smile that had ruined panties once upon a time. Now, he was in a committed relationship with Mila's sister and their boyfriend, Daniel, who Mila adored.

Beside Mason was his best friend, Gabo. The two of them were The Center for Athletes of Broward's founders and had started a monthly networker a few months ago. The idea of the event was to foster collaboration in the community so that we could further our own causes and support The Center's mission.

"So good to hear my sister didn't trust I would attend," Mila said in a deceptively sweet voice.

"I said you would come, so don't get mad at me; I want zero problems."

"Lies, he wants all the problems, all the time. How are you, Aisha? Good to see you here," Gabo said, enveloping my hands in his larger ones, then turning to embrace Mila, who he treated like a little sister.

"Oh, hi, Gabo! How are you? Mason, thanks for having us. I'm looking forward to the connections we'll hopefully make." As I blabbered, Sal approached us with a glass of whiskey neat, her drink of choice.

"Little Sal! Sal—" Mason started, freezing when Sal held one finger up. And it wasn't her index finger.

"No need to use my complete name, not today, Mason." Sal shook her middle finger at him, and he guffawed.

"Dude, I don't know why you don't like your name. It's beautiful!" Mason shook his head but relented.

"So, each of you has your reasons to be here today. I know Mila won't tell us what she's cooking up, but what about you, Aisha and Sal?"

"I need a couple of new accounts, so I'll do the rounds, get a couple of rich assholes to give me money to do the bare minimum to make them the latest app," Sal said in a dry tone that made us all stare at her, wondering how her dry wit would translate to networking. Before any of us could say more, she turned around and left us there to wonder.

"I guess she has a plan," Gabo said.

"Guess so." Mila chuckled.

"How about you, Aisha, what's the goal? We can always point you in the right direction. Today's group of people are all connected to me, Daniel, or Gabo, so we know they are trustworthy," Mason said.

"I'm looking to get a few sponsors for a Christmas show for the studio, and hopefully a few people that want to give scholarships to some kids in the neighborhood that have asked about doing classes, but their families can't afford the tuition." I shrugged, uncomfortable with the ask, but knowing this was the name of the game, and with some openings from the kids that had left the school... Well, now was the perfect time to help new students.

"That's what's up. I know someone that would probably be glad to help. We were just speaking earlier about opportunities for sponsoring community work. You want me to hook you up?" Gabo asked me, and I nodded emphatically, glad to have this potential opportunity. What were the odds Gabo had someone already lined up?

"I'll be back in a minute," he said, walking away in search of this person.

Meanwhile, Mason kept us entertained, making us laugh. Gabo's tall frame materialized once more, wading through the crowd, and right behind him... Broad shoulders and a penetrating stare behind glasses, always assessing. Those judgmental, beautiful brown eyes made me stand at attention, my belly dissolving in a shower of confetti.

Mr. Knox Davenport.

"Knox, this is the woman I mentioned who is looking to — I'm gonna take a wild guess that y'all know each other..." Gabo trailed off as he saw Mila's smirk, Knox's scowl, and my serene smile. I'd be damned if this man would see me surprised, but inside, I was gobsmacked.

What were the odds? Ugh.

Seven

Aisha

"Imagine my surprise when Gabo, one of my old homeboys from school, told me he knew this dance studio owner looking for sponsors for her Christmas show...and scholarships for more students. Imagine my surprise when he said the name of the studio," Mr. Davenport said in a low voice as we stood by one of the tall tables at the perimeter of the rooftop bar. He'd placed a hand on my elbow, taking advantage of my surprise to maneuver me away from the group with the excuse we were gonna talk business.

I extracted myself from his grasp, but I couldn't help the shiver that traveled through me at the masterful way he'd moved me from point A to point B. In another time and place, a particular black and gold room... I would love to be manhandled like that, but not by him. Not here.

It didn't help that he spoke those angry words right in my ear with his warm whiskey and woodsy scent surrounding me, making me lightheaded in the best of ways.

"What I do in my private time, such as attending this

cocktail event, is none of your business, Mr. Davenport." I beamed, giving him that grin I knew he hated.

"But you're searching for sponsors for a show you feel strongly about putting together. If you don't have the money, you shouldn't be doing it."

I stared at him, refusing to break eye contact, with the same unbothered expression, but inside... Inside, a tornado emerged. How dare this man get into my business! And what if he was slightly right about hosting the show without having the bread to put it together? People used sponsors for things like this all the time. I didn't need his approval.

Outside of the tuition he paid, I didn't need a dime from him.

I needed that.

Fudge.

"For fuck's sake, woman, why don't you let me help you? I have connections; I can help. I don't want to see you fail. Trin loves you and the school—if I come on too strong, it's because I care!" he said in an odd moment of sincerity that made me blink twice. Why would he care, and what was this wave of familiarity I felt, this sense of been there, done that? I hated déjà vu. Momma always said it was our ancestors calling our attention. What message was I currently missing?

"Oh. Well, you sure have a weird way of showing it," I said, breaking my smile and crossing my arms over my chest.

"Don't get me wrong, I won't let you pull any shit that might hurt Trinity, so if I think you're wrong, I'll call you out," he added.

"Ah...right. Ok, then." I shook my head, wondering what had made me think, even for a second, that this man had my best interests at heart.

"Look, we're always arguing." He sighed and placed his

hand palm up on the table between us. I stared at that hand and wondered why I felt so compelled to fold and touch him. I felt nothing but animosity for this man. Every time I had to deal with him, my stomach burned in a pool of acid, but here he was, showing me another side of him, and I wanted to cave. That sense of déjà vu, of wanting to trust him, hit me hard, making me lightheaded.

"Yes, we are." I cautiously placed my hand next to his and hoped he understood the gesture. *I don't trust you yet, negro, but I'll show good faith.*

He nodded, staring at our hands next to each other, his palm up, mine curled up palm down, before his gaze shifted to watch me from above his glasses, an air of anticipation emanating from him. I didn't know what he wanted.

"Trin told me one of her friends changed dance schools. Her last day was on Saturday," he said, and I wondered if this was a question or a statement. The thought of losing another student made me tense up. I still hadn't figured out where my dancers were going, and they were all super cagey about the reason they were leaving.

"I thought I was doing good, that I was a wonderful teacher. According to the students, they enjoy the program..." Words escaped me, the air of defeat trying to circle me, but I wouldn't let it get me down.

"You're an excellent teacher. You annoy the shit out of me with your bad business moves, but I've never doubted your teaching skills. Something is off. Trin said Keisha's mom told her not to say where she was going, but she's going to another school."

I started at his words. Why would they go to another school? And were we having a decent conversation? Us? Oil and water?

"Are you being nice to me right now?" I stared at him,

surprised at his concern, and he chuckled. The sound was a deep rumble, like hot cocoa on a chilly night, and I wanted to cuddle up and let the sound soothe all my worries away. Where the heck did that thought come from?

"I guess I am. Don't get used to it, though."

"I wouldn't dare." I shook my head, trying to dispel the sense of camaraderie, which was sure to be a trap to convince me to cancel the show or something equally senseless.

"If you need a sponsor for the holiday show, my company can do it. Count on us," he said. I was about to decline the offer; I didn't want to be indebted to him. He'd think he could tell me what to do. Next, he would want his darn name on the building.

"There he is! Knox, Liam was able to make it." A tall, lanky Black man wearing glasses and a pleasant smile approached our table, accompanied by an elegant, equally tall but stronger-built East Asian man with a serious face.

"Sorry to interrupt! Hello, I'm Knox's brother, Stephen, and this is Liam Kwon, a potential partner for our business. Kwon, this is Ms. McKinney, right? She owns a ballet studio." Knox's brother was his physical opposite, apart from their height. Where Knox was frowns and scowls, Stephen was smiles and kindness. The potential partner seemed to be more in line with Knox. Liam Kwon offered his hand to Knox, then me, and didn't crack one smile.

Well.

"Nice to meet you both. It seems you gentlemen have business to discuss. I'll go around the room and meet some prospective sponsors." I pushed away from the table, collecting my wine glass at the same time.

"But we just agreed we were going to sponsor you," Knox said with a frown.

"Did we? Oh great, what are we sponsoring?" Stephen asked, and I watched Knox subtly step on his foot. Stephen's face scrunched up in pain, then went completely smooth. "Yeah, where is my mind? Of course, we agreed."

"Really? Because less than a few minutes ago, your brother didn't know I was looking for sponsors," I asked, curious to see what Stephen would say next.

"Ms. McKinney, I assure you my brother and I are proficient in that device we all carry now...ahem, a cell phone. Yeah, we're good with texting and shiiii—"

Yeah, right, and I was born yesterday. But I had to commend Stephen here for the cover-up story. Lord knew what Davenport had told his brother about me. You know what? I didn't want to know.

Another stomp. I wanted to laugh, both at Stephen's dig as well as the sibling dynamic, but I really was wasting time here. I needed to move on.

"Nice to meet you, Mr. Kwon. Hopefully, I'll see you around other networkers?"

"It would be my honor, Ms. McKinney. Godspeed with your endeavor," Mr. Kwon said.

"See y'all later," I said with a wave, twirling to head to my destination.

"Ms. Mac! Ms. Mac... Aisha." Mr. Davenport followed me all the way to the bar. His voice and my name, a combination I didn't know if I wanted to repeat.

I didn't know if I could take it.

"Yes, Knox. I guess we're on a first-name basis now?" I whirled around, and warm hardness met my hands. Oh, my badness, the man was ripped underneath all those frowns and scowls.

"You're going to take our help, and no, I won't take advantage of our sponsorship. I won't tell you what to do because of my donation," he said in a low tone, his whiskey-scented breath making me close my eyes. I didn't want him to see how affected I was by his nearness.

"But you *are* telling me what to do," I pointed out, my pulse skittering.

"I'm telling you what to do, yes, but because it's good for Trin. And I suspect it's good for you too. And maybe you'll also find a damn receptionist. Gabo said some of their students are looking for part-time work."

Darn, I hadn't even thought of that, and here this man was, thinking of my business more than I was. I didn't think it was a good idea to accept, but beggars and all. I thought of Momma's meds and how Pops needed a new scooter and...

"Alright, Mr. Davenport, your company is the sponsor of our Winter Extravaganza," I said, knowing I would regret those words.

Eight

Knox

Q's Space became a haven for me during the hard days of my divorce. I'd always known I had Dom tendencies, but my ex-wife didn't like to be bossed around, in bed or outside of it. And I loved her, so I adapted to what she loved.

When I finally realized there was no fixing us, that I didn't have the tools to be the best husband for her, when she allowed her love for pills to be greater than us, when our daughter noticed Mommy was always sick... That was my rock bottom.

How could love not *be* all we needed?

I had nurtured our relationship, or so I'd thought. I'd been a good father; I worked my ass off and provided for my ladies. Sure, I fucked up—I was abrasive, possessive, stubborn, my temper could use work, and I could be an asshole—but I'd loved her.

I'd fucking loved her.

So, when I recognized my marriage was over, I turned to

the one thing I had denied myself for years: the kink I'd left buried deep inside.

I didn't do shit without the knowledge to do it well, so even though I had dabbled in scenes here and there and met some like-minded women, I knew I wanted to do it better. Do it well. And that was how I met Master Q.

"So, how did your first session go?" Master Q sat on the chair opposite mine. He handed me a glass of whiskey, but I declined.

"Nah, I want to be 100% for this next session. Thanks for sharing what Jasmine sent. The session went well. I... I'm drawn to her."

"You haven't really seen her, though." Master Q lit up a blunt and inhaled. The sweet smell of indica hit my nose, making me consider getting one of my own after my session with the lovely Jasmine.

"I guess you aren't doing a scene at the public party today."

"No, I'm taking a bit of a break. Gotta get some shit off my mind before I find a new sub," Master Q said.

"Mhm. All good?" I asked. Q was just a couple of years older than me, but in life experience, he was light years ahead. He had that type of know-it-all, street-smart wisdom that told you he'd seen some shit in his life. Master Q took a minute to answer, seemingly in his own world.

"Oh, yeah, I'm good, bruh. Just found out some shit... nothing that can't be resolved."

"A'ight. Well, if you need to talk..."

"Thanks, I appreciate it. Don't think I didn't miss you not answering my question about you seeing her. When she tells you it's all fantasy, believe her." The warning clanged through my brain, a warning bong to a situation I was trying to navigate as best as possible. Based on my encounter with her during the cocktail hour, either I was wrong about Jasmine, or I was right, and she was in the dark.

I didn't know which one I wanted to be true.

All I knew was that Jasmine was making me see Ms. McKinney in a different light, making me wish this wasn't all fantasy. For all I was abrasive with her, Ms. McKinney had captured my attention since day one. I'd kept that instinct at bay, but now, things were meshing. I could put a stop to all of this, but something told me I would end up losing. So, I'd keep at it, still wondering if the elusive Jasmine was closer than I realized.

THE GOLD ROOM. When I first walked into this chamber, I thought it was flashy with its black walls and gold accents everywhere. But today... Today, the room didn't hold a candle to the woman waiting for me on her knees.

For fuck's sake, how was I supposed to keep my shit together?

A gorgeous expanse of smooth umber skin, covered by a little gold dress that barely concealed anything. Tonight, she wore a mask of gold jewels that obscured everything but those big brown eyes and long lashes. Eyes that widened in appreciation at the sight of me.

My dick hardened at her appreciative glance. This was why I'd told her I didn't want her looking down—her eyes... they spoke to me. I knew the connection I felt with her the first time wasn't just in my mind. That same pull that told me somewhere deep down we were kindred spirits, had walked a similar path. There were people you met in life, and in just a few conversations, you realized they had something that called to you. Jasmine called to me.

She felt the call, too.

"Good evening, my Baby Doll," I greeted her.

"Good evening, Sir," she said in that silky voice, barely audible.

"I'm honored that you're granting me your time once more."

She gasped, and I bricked all the fucking way up. I needed to get my head in the game. She had me flustered with just a good evening and a gasp. I searched her face, the hope in my gut that this was Ms. McKinney as disconcerting as it was walking into this room last time and realizing it could be her.

"Today, we're gonna continue exploring your kinks. You're gonna do everything I ask you to do. No deviation," I told her, getting into the right headspace.

"Yes, Sir."

I stepped toward her and ran a finger along her ear, feeling the shudder that went through her body. I needed to focus, regardless of who she was. We were here for a reason, and we both had established some ground rules. Concentrating, I got my head back in the game, even though curiosity vibrated in the back of my mind.

I kept her there, still kneeling, and stood behind her. I wanted to keep her off balance. Excited.

"You remember I told you this was first position, right?"

"Yes, yes, Sir."

"Alright, second position is this," and I gently pushed her down until her face was on the floor and her ass was up in the air. The softness of her skin zapped through me, making me ache for a longer touch.

The movement had her gold dress sliding up her ass. Her ass cheeks were perfectly plump and dimpled, and I wanted a bite of them.

"Rest your head on the floor, shoulders all the way down, and curve up that pretty back of yours so your ass and pussy are all I can see."

She obeyed, curving the small of her back until her booty was high and proud, her dress completely off her behind now, giving me a full view of her gold thong.

I knelt behind her and ran the back of my hand over one of her ass cheeks.

"Ohhh..." Jasmine whispered into the otherwise quiet room. One thing she'd mentioned she liked was listening to music during her scenes. I figured it was because it brought her comfort. I'd do that for her another day, but tonight, I wanted her off-kilter. She said she liked to be on edge, and I wanted to deliver.

I wanted to build that excitement. The silence in the room was an added element to the uncertainty she must be feeling now.

"You please me, Jasmine, wearing this gold dress, short as fuck, showing me all your ass. You're such a good doll," I said, then bent over and licked her other butt cheek.

I could smell her earthy, scrumptious pussy, and my mouth watered at the thought of more nights with her. *Of more days.* But that wasn't part of the scene today, no matter how much I wanted to dive nose-first between her thighs.

I stood up again and watched her legs shake, but she kept the position just as I commanded her.

"This is second position. And whenever I say, you will immediately drop into it, ok?"

"Yes, Sir X."

"That's my good little slut." I slapped her ass. "Your pussy is trying to eat that thong of yours."

"Oh yes, Sir, I love this new position. I can't wait to see what else you show me."

I finally sat behind her and stayed quiet for a second. I could see her squirming; her pussy was wet, and the shit was thumping. I wasn't lying when I told her it wanted to eat her thong. Just watching her hole throb like that told me her grip must be glorious.

I slid my hand into my sweatpants and stroked myself a few long thrusts, then adjusted my dick and yanked on my balls. I knew I could come without touching myself, and I needed to keep my shit together. It was heady to be responsible for her high, for Jasmine to trust me like this and not even know me...

"Sir?"

"Yes, Baby Doll?"

"I want to see you."

"Oh, do you? I don't think so, not yet, at least."

"Oh, please, Sir, I can hear you touching yourself and—"

I was so glad I'd thought of it before—I was ready for this. I grabbed the flogger next to me and let it swing against her ass. The strips connected with her skin, the leather making her ass welt red.

"Aaahhh," she moaned.

"I'll tell you when you can watch me touch myself, ok?"

"Ok, Sir," she purred. Oh, she was into this. She was enjoying herself, and I craved her buy-in.

"First position," I commanded.

She took her time, knowing the view she was giving me. She lowered her ass slowly to her feet and sat back up gracefully.

"Stand up," I asked her.

She did so again with her distinctive grace, the gold dress draping back over her ass. Damn, that dress was going to give me a heart attack.

"Turn around." I waited for her to do so. "You see the table behind me?"

"Yes, Sir."

"Good. What do you see?"

"I see a bunch of toys." She stood tall and sure in her heels, those big brown eyes not missing a thing.

"Ok, grab your toy of choice and come back to me." I wanted her to choose what she loved the most, which would tell me more about how she liked to be stimulated.

She came back with a G-spot and clit massager. I tucked that knowledge in my mental cabinet, and the hope that this was Ms. McKinney flared again.

"Sit on the throne and spread your legs like the queen you are. I'll tell you what to do with the toy."

Fuck. Fuck. Fuck. I loved watching her follow each instruction. I was getting obsessed with the cute breathy hitches she let out whenever she particularly liked a command.

She really liked this one.

Her pussy was tormenting me, with cream leaking between her legs as she sat spread eagle in front of me. She was turned the fucked on, and I wanted to make her wild before the night was done.

"Wet it all up for me," I commanded.

She smiled and guided the toy into her mouth, tongue snaking out to wet the toy all over. She then spit on it for good measure, the nasty ass. How did she know I'd love that?

"Ok, turn it on and push it right into that pussy of yours.

She's hungry and needs to be fed. Make sure I can see it all."

She moaned as she followed the command step by step. Pulling the thong to the side, she thrust the toy inside her with a smoothness that spoke to how wet she was. The silence had been a tactic to unsettle Jasmine, but now I was the one suffering for it as the squelching noises of the toy massaging her walls resounded around the room.

The smell of her earthiness mixed with her perfume made my mouth water as she followed my every command. Her eyes never left mine as she pleasured herself, a spotlight above pointed right at the chair, exactly as I had planned it all before she arrived. The light shone on her pretty pink pussy with the landing strip of dark brown hair. My fingers vibrated with the need to touch her.

When I told her to push it in, she did so. When I asked her to grind her clit against the toy, she lifted her hips and whined on that shit. To have so much power...hers over me. Dominating her was going to become my favorite pastime.

My dick was leaking now at the sight of her pussy swallowing the toy. She was on the brink of coming, her pussy throbbing around the vibrations. But just when I was feeling myself for how well she followed my instructions, she defied me by pulling the toy out.

What the fuck was she doing?

Oh...

"Jasmine." I let my bass rumble through the room.

"Siiiir," she whined, trying to edge herself without my permission. So she liked to delay her pleasure. But that's not what we were doing tonight, and for that, I would punish her.

I got up from my chair and stalked toward her. She

closed her eyes, her chest falling and rising to the beat of her breathing.

"You don't get to decide how and when you nut. That's my job. Open your eyes," I murmured.

"Yes, Sir." She did, her eyes glassy with lust. I didn't think she was in subspace, and I felt a pang of disappointment for not being able to take her there, but I knew we were only starting out, and I was just getting to know what worked for her. I would get her to the brink of it soon enough. But tonight, time was running out, and I wanted to give her all she deserved.

I smacked the flogger against her leg, soft enough to know it would stimulate her even more.

"Aarghhh!" She moaned, dropping the toy to the floor and holding on for dear life to the arms of the chair. Denying me her orgasm.

"Oh no, Baby Doll, your pussy is mine right now. Every time you cross that door, that pussy has a first, middle, and last name. Sir X's Pussy, you hear me?" I asked, and before she could even catch my intentions, I glided two fingers inside her and used my thumb on her swollen clit. That did it. The unexpected touch made her buck and thrash on the chair, her pussy gripping my fingers so tight I thought I would never get them back. Her wetness gushed down my hand.

"Yes, give me the nut. Don't you ever deny me like that again. Your orgasms are mine, Baby Doll. Look at you, soaking my hand and my chair, you nasty little doll." I rubbed her clit once more, and she gasped and cried out in pleasure.

Her voice rang clear in the room, and the whole thing was too damn much. I came as well, no stimulation, my nut busting out of me and ruining my sweatpants.

"Look at this mess you made." I gently pulled my hand out of her pussy and showed her how wet it still was, then pointed at my crotch. Then, unable to help myself, I slid my wet hand into my sweatpants and jacked the last two pumps of cum with my pussy-soaked fist.

"Oh, my word, you're nasty... Ohhhh!" She wailed and came again.

I was still spent from my orgasm, but I knew my work wasn't done yet. The hidden panel in the wall held a pantry and mini fridge. I strolled back to Jasmine, who still lay spread eagle on the throne chair.

"Here you are. Chocolate milk and donuts." I presented the glass and plate with a flourish and felt my heart beat faster when she stared at me adoringly with her big, beautiful eyes.

"Oh, Sir, you're on point today."

"Am I?" I asked, sitting on one of the many rugs on the floor. Jasmine hesitated, then got up and settled herself next to me. Her lusty scent still lingered, making my dick want to valiantly try for round two.

"Ok, so aftercare and debrief," she said, turning her head to take a bite of the donut. She hummed in pleasure, and it made me grin. I loved me a woman who loved her food. In two nights, the little details I captured of her made me want to dig deeper, and that scared the shit out of me. I wasn't ready for more—or so I had thought—but here I was, hoping for this woman to be Ms. McKinney.

"What do you think?"

"I think that for a first scene with an inexperienced sub, this was a great introduction. The entire time, I was engaged. You used the silence of the room as an added tool and kept me on edge. I selfishly did not like that you didn't let me edge my orgasm, but it means you were paying attention. And I hadn't fully shared that, so that was ok. I did feel the scene was basic..."

Damn, basic? I mean, all her feedback so far had been complimentary, but basic? Damn.

"Not in a bad way, but like an inexperienced kinkster can digest this."

"Ok, and did I take you to subspace?" I asked, already knowing the answer.

"You know you didn't, but that doesn't happen to me all the time. And I'm a long scene type of girl, so it's hard to get me there in a short period."

Bet. She didn't know she'd just thrown down a gauntlet.

"Ok, I'll have to be more creative next time."

"Uh...don't forget this is for Jasmine, not for me."

"You're Jasmine, didn't you say that?" I watched her as if my eyes could convince her to speak as she turned her head again to take a sip of her milk.

"You know what I mean," she protested.

"Look, I felt I was into the scene and had planned it well, but as we went through it, I wasn't sure I gave you what you needed today. So then, I didn't get what I needed."

"What do you mean?" She shifted and faced me fully, putting down the plate of half-eaten donut and the glass of milk.

"You were aroused, but I don't know if your mind was as stimulated as other parts...and it feels like you need to disconnect. I don't know... I might be wrong, but it feels like you're carrying some stuff."

She sighed, shaking her head. "Remember what I said —don't."

Shit, I needed to tread lightly. I wasn't looking to spook her, but in this environment, I felt I could open up to her, talk to her in a way I never allowed myself to before.

"I got some shit on my chest too, so I get it. I was looking forward to fully letting go, but I didn't get you there, did I? So I couldn't get myself there either."

"What's on your chest? Never mind, what am I even asking?" Jasmine shook her head, but I was glad to hear she was curious. I was glad she cared.

"Some work stuff. I'm working with a potential new colleague. It's a bit of a trial period, and they're a little conservative, which I respect, but I don't know how well I'm connecting with them." I hoped she connected the dots.

"Oh. Have you tried inviting them to dinner or a fun activity? I always find some common ground with people when you try outside of the four walls of an office," she said, and she pulled closer to me, eager to give me some ideas. Her wanting to help set me at ease. I wasn't being too explicit about my merger, but still, being able to talk about it with Jasmine was fucking nice. Having someone act as a soundboard outside of my brother or my parents felt good.

"Hmm, you could be right. I might need to take them out on some type of non-work-related activity, see how we jive outside of the…office."

"Ok, so about stimulating my mind. This is our first scene. If you don't hit a home run in the first inning, it's alright." She shrugged.

"Who likes baseball in this day and age?" I joked.

"Excuse me, Sir X, baseball is America's pastime, a'ight? And I love it. I watch it all the time with my— Oh, I gotta go. I have stuff to do at home. This was good. Don't overthink it too much; a tense Dom is a preoccupied Dom, and that's contagious. I enjoyed myself so much, I promise!"

Jasmine spoke quickly, gathering her things as she approached the door. She paused by the door, turned around, blew me a kiss, then waltzed out of the room. She had been about to open up even more, and I was eager for any crumbs she had to give me. But she put up her walls, and I could only respect that. But I wanted more of this.

Talking to her... I could get used to that.

NINE

AISHA

THE ROOM BUZZED with chatter as parents waited for me to call the meeting to a start. I hadn't lost any more students in the past week since announcing the recital, but I was worried.

The sense of unease that something larger was happening and the fact my dancers were keeping me in the dark about where they were going wasn't sitting well with me. Besides that, I was alright; public speaking was easy for me. After a few years on stage as a dancer in a few ballets and on and off Broadway, having to stand to talk to a few parents was nothing.

There he was, Mr. Davenport, chatting in a low voice with another of the fathers. I enjoyed seeing those glasses of his perched on his broad nose. The ghostly feeling of recognition whispered behind my ear, and I shivered. The ancestors hollering again.

I'd been surprised to see him tonight, but it seemed he'd dislodged the stick up his behind, or Trinity really had him wrapped around her little finger because here he was, behaving for a turn.

I had emailed all the parents, suggesting a Daddy ensemble to surprise the dancers. The response was enthusiastic, and I was happy to see it. I had a good mix of parents from my different age brackets here, including a grandpa who said he had moves for days.

I avoided letting my eyes linger toward Mr. Davenport's corner because, honestly, just his presence confused me.

That last interlude we had at the networker wasn't enough for me to forget all the times he had been difficult and confrontational. I'd mentally hit the reset button regarding him and was back to keeping him at arm's length with my smiles. His being a sponsor of the show did not mean I needed to pay him any pointed attention. Right?

"Good evening, parents!" I raised my voice just enough for it to carry around the chamber. Sal, Mila, and I had set up some folding chairs around the perimeter for all. The room quieted as I waited for everyone's attention.

"I called this meeting to present an idea for our next recital. I want to produce a father routine, where we have our fathers take to the stage and surprise their dancers with some choreography."

The fathers nodded along, some smiling, some exchanging words and jokes. Mr. Davenport watched me intently, fully focused on what I had to say. He needed to stop staring at me like that. I didn't need his brand of attention.

"I think the choreography should be collaborative. I could, in theory, put up something intricate, but it wouldn't be fun, and the idea is for this to be fun for everybody. So, I want to ask if you're interested in the choreography being hip-hop, African-American dance, or jazz. Let's put it to a vote! Jazz?"

Only the grandpa raised his hand, and I stifled a laugh while the other parents murmured and avoided eye contact with me and each other.

"Ok, African-American dance?" This was a little more popular with some parents, but not even half of the room raised their hands.

"And last but not least, hip-hop." Most of the hands went up at last, just as I had suspected.

"Great!" I clapped my hands. "We've found the genre of our choreography. I would love to have one father be a spokesperson for the group, and from there on, we can plan on a practice day. The father in charge can create the obligatory group chat and assist with coordinating the wardrobe and music selections. I will, of course, do the mix and create choreography based on your choices. Do we have any volunteers?"

My gaze lingered on each face around the room as fathers shook their heads until my eyes collided with his. Mr. Davenport raised his hand, and that sensation of familiarity made my stomach contract.

"I can volunteer," his voice rang clear.

Oh, my goodness, why was that sexy to me? I really didn't want to find this man any type of attractive.

"Ok, it looks like Trinity's Dad is the Boss Daddy Executive, or BDE for short," I said, hitting them all with my calm smile as some fathers caught onto the acronym and guffawed.

Across the room, I saw him give me the same energy back, smirking.

"I look forward to our collaboration, Ms. Mac."

Why did 'collaboration' sound like a dirty word on his lips?

Oh, pickles I miscalculated on this one.

MOST OF THE parents had filed out of the studio, eager to get back home to their families and dinner. I needed to head out soon too, and make sure Momma and Pops were settled for the evening. The mortgage payment for the studio was due soon, so I also needed to sit down and study the numbers. The income from my sessions was helping, but I still felt the emptiness in my stomach every time I opened my accounting books.

I turned off the lights and marched toward the reception area to find Mr. Davenport seated.

"Oh, don't you have to get back to Trinity?" I asked, startled to find him there.

"Nah, she's with my parents tonight. Whenever I have evening engagements, I make sure she stays with them," he said agreeably.

"Why are you being so nice?" I asked, attempting not to appear too flustered.

"Listen, I think you and I should start over," he said.

"Start over?" I repeated.

"Yeah. Look, I know I can be bullheaded..."

I snorted. It just escaped me before I could stop it. I felt exposed. I crossed my arms over my chest and tilted my head, inviting him to continue.

"Damn. Ok, yeah, I'm stubborn and can be an asshole..."

"Hmh."

"And impatient."

"Mmmhmm."

"And difficult. But it's because I care." He spread his legs wider as he leaned forward. Dang, were his thighs always this thick? Those jeans were really working hard right now.

Silence.

"Oh, so no noise now, huh? I hope you believe me, though. I care about your success."

What in the fresh living inferno was happening right now? Did someone snatch this man's soul and replace it with a normal human being's?

"Look, Mr. Davenport—" I started.

"Knox."

"Excuse me?" I dropped my arms, the way the *x* sounded off his lips making me stand at attention.

"Knox. Please call me Knox."

"Oh, ok... Knox."

"Yeah, that's better..." he trailed off, waiting for me to reciprocate.

"Ms. Mac works well," I said with my smile. I desperately needed to get this conversation back on track.

He smirked, and then...the man laughed. His laugh was a warm breeze after a wintry day, and I closed my eyes to enjoy it.

"When I offered to sponsor, it was because I want you to succeed. It's obvious you must be going through something; first the receptionist, then the dancers—"

The door chime went off, and in walked my father in a cloud of acrid-smelling weed, booze, and his signature cologne.

This night was going from weird to bizarre.

My dad stood by the entrance, tall and lean with his dark complexion and the looks he still held onto after all these years. The looks that I had inherited, and the ones

Momma blamed for getting her daughter suckered into a toxic relationship.

"Papa, what are you doing here?" I asked, tightening my arms over my chest.

"I told you I'd stop by to visit you." He stared as Mr. Davenport stood up and offered him his hand. I felt a frisson of unease run through me at my dad's presence. I always wanted to be around him until he was around—then I wondered why I was so eager for his attention.

"Hello, Mr. McKinney, I'm Knox Davenport, father to one of Ms. Mac's dancers."

"Boy, I'm no McKinney. That's her momma's last name, may she rest in peace. Her grandparents wouldn't let my baby girl carry her name just cause I wasn't around for her birth. Mi nombre is Juancho Solis, at your service." Papa dapped Mr. Davenport, then turned to me again. I instinctively shifted closer to Mr. Davenport.

"So, Ms. Mac...do you want to continue our conversation later?" he asked, giving me the choice. I appreciated that so much. I knew why Papa was here, and it was for no good reason.

"Actually, I think we need to finish today, make sure we're on the same page." I stared up at him, and his eyes flashed with something. That something singed me. He nodded at me, then lifted his eyes to my papa.

"I'll wait for you then. I'm going to the bathroom for a moment and will be right back," he said in a tone that let us both know he was just a shout away. I appreciated his gesture and giving me a little privacy at the same time. Papa wasn't an evil man...he was just selfish, and sometimes that selfishness had a dangerous edge to it. His addiction made him do unpredictable things at unpredictable times.

"I thought he wouldn't leave. Why don't you tell him to

go, hija? I need to talk to you," Papa said, settling himself in one of the folding chairs. "Sit, sit, you're making me dizzy with all your standing and walking around." He chastised me until I sat on the chair opposite him.

"Papa, I'm at work."

"So what? You don't have time for your old man? Listen, I know those grandparents of yours are always trying to poison you with stories about me and how bad I was to your mom. But I loved her, and I love you. I have some issues, but I'm working on them."

Right, that's why he reeked of alcohol and herb. He was trying real hard. Last time he was here, I made him promise to work on cleaning up. For a few months, he had complied, gotten a new job, and been doing much better, but here we were again.

"What do you need, Papa?" I sighed.

"Listen, I'm short on my rent, and my landlord gave me till the end of next month to pay him. If not, he's gonna kick me out."

"What happened to your job at the car shop?" I asked. He was a whiz with cars, and when he was sober for more than a day, he could do magic with vehicles.

"That hijo e' puta fired me, talking about I wasn't in my five senses."

"Papa, no cussin', and I thought you were gonna stop drinking." I hated that my voice broke as I asked.

"Mija, you know I'm doing better. If I drink a little during the weekends—"

"It's Tuesday."

He waved my words away. "Are you gonna help me or not?"

"Papa, I don't have it."

"You don't gotta lie to me." He bristled and stood up

abruptly. I expected this unpredictability. He'd done nothing to me, but years ago, when Pops was in his prime, they had gotten into a fistfight.

I stood up as well, and at the same time, Mr. Davenport came back into the reception area.

"Oh, Mr. Davenport, I... Yeah, we need to finish."

"Ok, alright, alright... I don't want to interrupt you in your place of work, mija. I'll be back in a few days, ok? Think about what I said. You don't want your old man to have any difficulties, right?" Papa smiled. "Davenport, make sure you don't stay here too long with my daughter, ok? She needs to go home to get some rest. See you, mi amor." And with that, Papa walked out just as he came in.

All the air I'd been holding sifted out of me in a long exhale. I was exhausted, my head pounded, and I just wanted to go home and lock myself in my room.

"You good?" Mr. Davenport asked me.

I couldn't muster my serenity right now, so on top of dealing with my father, Mr. Davenport got to see me down. Crap.

"I'm alright."

"No, you're not." He approached me, stepping into my personal bubble. He examined me, the heat of his body surrounding me. I felt his breath on the top of my head, and the feeling of him so close to me was akin to sliding into my cold bed and pulling my warm weighted blanket on top of my body.

I kept my eyes down and waited for his chastisement. I was sure he would find something to berate me for, and I couldn't deny that I looked forward to his words. To the banter that would ensue.

I needed to feel something other than this dread and

despair suffocating me, and I knew he could distract me with a few well-placed words.

"I know what it is to love an addict, and if you ever need to talk... I'm here." I shook at the sensation he created in me, afraid of what would happen if I let him just a fraction in. And his voice. Why did it invoke feelings in me that weren't there a few weeks before?

"You do?"

"Yeah, my father... I could keep you here for hours with stories. I'm so glad I was here. I don't know much about your father, but if he's like mine?" He shook his head, the resigned sadness behind his glasses calling to me.

Someone who understood. Mila complained about my dad because she didn't get it. She had two loving parents that doted on her. Were they imperfect? Yeah, but they were good, kind, and present. Here was someone who had been through the trenches just as I had. But did I really want to let him in this deep—did I want to address the sense of familiarity this all brought tonight?

"Yeah, it's not easy to love an addict," I agreed, acknowledging his willingness to connect. But that was all I had to give tonight. "Thanks for staying, but I have to close now." I took a step back, creating some needed space between us.

I wasn't ready.

The magnetic pull he was generating was so hard to combat, but I stood still, staring down at my jazz shoes till I felt him shift.

"Good night, Ms. Mac."

"Good night, Mr. Davenport."

Ten

Knox

Words were coming out of my brother's and Liam Kwon's mouths, but they weren't registering with me. Two days since I'd seen Ms. Mac and our last interaction lingered, intruding on my thoughts.

I had no time to dwell on other's people's problems, especially hers, but I couldn't help but be drawn to everything in her orbit. My sense of sureness increased every time I dealt with Ms. McKinney. Every time I was with Jasmine. I wanted her to let me in.

It had pissed me off when her father finessed her for money, and she had been conflicted when she declined him. I knew addiction was a disease, but I also knew some people never wanted to get better. And her father was one of those.

It took a child of one to know one. The difference between Ms. Mac and me was that I'd understood during my young adulthood that my dad wasn't willing to change, and I stopped expecting anything from him. It helped that I had a true example of a dad in Will, who supported me and showed me true parenting.

I wondered if Ms. Mac had that.

"So ideally, we would maintain our operations in each city and collaborate in major cross-state projects." Stephen finished, and I had no fucking clue what he was talking about.

"That makes sense. I want to have a presence here in the Florida office, though. I'm thinking of relocating eventually once we've fully established the New Jersey branch. But I'm not convinced there is enough overlap for a need for a merger..." Kwon answered, and I fazed out again. I wanted this merger; I wanted to expand the reach of our realty company, slowly partner with other people of color, and create a conglomerate, but Kwon was more cautious than I expected.

There was something about Liam Kwon that reminded me of Ms. Mac. I didn't know why, as they couldn't be more different. But there was this air of wait-and-see they both exuded that made my thoughts circle back to Ms. Mac and the way she kept entangling me in her complicated life.

Alright, that was BS, and I knew it. The woman had tried her best to keep away from me. She didn't want me to sponsor the show, she sure as hell didn't want me to be the "BDE" as she fucking called me in that meeting, and she'd been hesitant about me staying behind while her asshole of her father tried to get money from her. But I wanted to be in her presence more.

Something had shifted for me since she decided to do that show, and I'd adjusted my strategy with her. Somehow knowing more about her, about why she was late sometimes and how she was struggling with dancers leaving the studio, made her more...accessible, more human. Clearly, I was on some bullshit because it made me want to help her even though she'd never asked for it.

"So, more time will help us solidify more of these differences in opinion," Stephen finished, glaring at me while Kwon nodded agreeably.

"Alright, gentleman, this was a good meeting. I'm going to head out to my Airbnb now and run some numbers," Kwon added.

"I know you didn't rent a car; why don't you let Knox take you?" Stephen offered, and now it was my turn to glare at him. I knew it was payback for zoning out on this meeting. This project was all mine, and Stephen was just going along because he felt ambivalent about our growth. I was the one that wanted to expand, and now I was the one fucking things up.

"Uh, sure. Kwon, do you need a ride?" I offered, cornered. I was going to be late.

"Thanks, Davenport, I appreciate the offer."

I let him walk out, then turned to Stephen.

"You're a—"

"A great brother and partner who just carried this two-hour-long meeting while you daydreamed. Talk to you later." Stephen smirked and walked out of our boardroom.

"Daddy, I don't like being late for class," Trin complained as I took my time parking. No matter how fast I wanted to get to the studio, I'd never speed with the most precious person in my world in the car. So here we were, fifteen minutes late.

Trin had never been late for class.

"I know you don't, and I've never brought you late. This

is a fluke," I said while I put the car in park and stepped out to open the car door for her.

"What's a fluke, Daddy?"

"Something that doesn't happen often. Look, Miss Smart, I'm sorry, a'ight? I had to take my colleague home, and that hadn't been in my plans."

I spoke straight up to Trin. She might be seven years old, but she was smart as fuck, and I didn't underestimate her intelligence by talking down to her.

Trin sighed, deeply disappointed in me, and walked in front of me toward the studio entrance. I felt like shit for getting her in late, but that dramatic ass sigh made me want to laugh.

"It's ok, Daddy, you can't be perfect," she said as she opened the door and waltzed in, reminding me of another woman who had a tendency for dramatic entrances and exits.

I followed behind her, stifling my laugh, glad Trin could make me smile like this. Usually, I'd be mad as fuck that I got here late, but I would take this feeling instead. Matter of fact, I'd been feeling more relaxed since...

"Oh, Trin, this is highly unusual. You missed circle time, was your ride here alright?" Ms. Mac's voice floated out of the dance room and into the reception area. I flushed hot at the insinuation that I was the reason Trin was late. I mean, I was, but Ms. Mac didn't get to insinuate that.

"Sorry, my daddy had a very important meeting that ran late."

Fuck, Ms. Mac would probably hold onto this till the end of days. I stood in the middle of the waiting area, making sure Trinity got into Room A.

"Oh, it's alright, sweetie. It's not your fault." Trin walked into the room, and then I faced Ms. Mac as she stood in the doorframe of the dance room, her beautiful brown eyes and long eyelashes languorously moving up and down.

Those fucking princess eyes.

It had to be her.

I felt that shit everywhere; her voice made the heat transform into electricity and her stare made me want to yank her against the door next to her and...

"Mr. Davenport, tsk, tsk, tsk." And with that, she closed the door in my face.

———

"Pops, can you come and get Trin? I have to do something before dinner."

"Ok, son, I'm on my way."

Thank god for my retired parents and their help with Trin.

My ex-wife had needed time to get her life back together, so having sole custody of Trin with visitation rights made the most sense for us. I'd never thought I'd push for something like that until I realized my ex needed way more than I could provide, so having my parents' support was essential.

I needed to have a word with Ms. Mac and her pleased ass self, grinning at me as if she'd won a contest. I needed to remind her that...fuck, who was I kidding? I just wanted to hang out with her for a minute, but having Trin around wouldn't be conducive to the ideas I had in my head, so I called my Pops.

When the class ended, Trin came out smiling and chatting it up with the other dancers, then did a double take when she saw Pops, running into his arms. She loved her grandparents, so for her, going to their house was an upgrade.

"Hi, Pops! Are you here to pick me up?" she asked after giving him a hug.

"That's right, bug. Gam Gam made some delicious meatloaf."

"Yeah! You have more work, Daddy?" she asked.

"I have a couple of things to iron out with Ms. Mac after her last class, so I'm gonna hang around for a little longer."

"Alright! See you later, Daddy!" Trin threw her little arms around me and smacked a kiss on my forehead, her love radiating into me. My forehead still tingled as she strolled out hand-in-hand with Pops, leaving me face-to-face with Ms. Mac.

"What do we have to talk about?" she asked curiously.

"Show-related topics." I nodded, proud to have something I wanted to run by her.

"Really?"

"Yep," I said, lifting my left leg and placing it over my right one. Her eyes flickered as she watched me move, then went back to my face.

"Ok, then." She nodded and went back into the room.

Usually, when I was here, I fired up my laptop and got some work done, but I wanted to focus on something else.

This fixation with the woman was untimely, but here I was, eyes glued to the screen outside the room. I needed to get my shit together fast because the excuses I kept making in my head that this was all for Trinity were running low. But I'd do that tomorrow. Today, I would admire her while she danced.

The older teens were now in her dance room for the last class of the day.

She seemed to be showing them a new routine, and I

was mesmerized by the graceful way her body moved. She did some type of curtsey before she vaulted through the air with minimal effort, her feet pointing perfectly down, then just as she had jumped, she landed on her feet in third position. I could only thank Trin for the knowledge.

It was as if springs lived in her legs as she performed the move again, then got on her tippy toes, practically walking on air as her legs moved in rapid motion.

Those legs... The strength of her calves and thighs was pronounced as she raised one limb and remained on her tiptoes on the other, extending her entire body.

Her arms seemed to seek something, and I felt that pull in the bottom of my stomach. With a graceful flourish, she dropped back into the same plié—again, thanks, Trin—and then finally turned to her dancers and grinned.

A force hit me at seeing her smile, strength, and grace. I wanted to harness the power of everything I felt and deploy it on her.

I wanted her.

I stayed in place as she continued showing her dancers the steps until, finally, they ended the class. At this point, I was bricked up after seeing her flexibility and imagining how much she could do with those long legs of hers and her strong thighs.

Shit.

The door swung open, and I adjusted myself, not wanting to alarm her or her students. Suddenly, another dance room opened, and three teens walked out with Ms. Torres and Ms. Mac's other friend. She was the quietest of the three and kept mostly to herself whenever visiting. I had completely forgotten about the jazz class concurrent with Ms. Mac's.

"Remember, dancers, please practice these first steps at home, alright?" she said with that permanent serene smile.

"Bye, Ms. Mac," the dancers said in a chorus as they departed the studio.

Then there was silence.

"Sooo, what are you still doing here, Davenport?" Ms. Torres said with a smirk while their friend stood next to her, face down in her phone.

"*Mr.* Davenport," Ms. Mac emphasized the mister, "was waiting for me to talk about the show and his sponsorship." She finished with a tilt of her head to one side.

"Oh, for real? He wants to talk about the *sponsorship*? Do you want us to wait?" Ms. Torres asked, and I felt the overwhelming urge to answer her no. I also didn't miss her emphasis on the word 'sponsorship.' She was on to me.

"Nah, I'll meet you at the bar, alright?" Ms. Mac said, and I pumped an imaginary fist in the air. Her other friend raised her head as if alerted to my excitement and squinted her eyes at me.

"You." The friend pointed at me. "Walk her to the bar. She shouldn't have to walk alone just because you have the hots for her and—"

"Sal!" Ms. Mac exclaimed.

Sal shrugged her shoulders. "Just sayin'. Let's go, Mila. I want my whiskey," she said, holding her hand out to Mila, who was still smirking. Mila twirled her fingers at me, then winked at Ms. Mac, who pretended not to see it.

"I'm sorry about Sal. She can be..."

"Honest? Yeah, I see that." I nodded and saw Ms. Mac's eyes squint just like her friend a few moments before.

"What do you want, Mr. Davenport? We've been exchanging emails about the sponsorship."

"That we have." I nodded, thrilled to have her standing

so close, so suspicious. I still loved sparring with her, at least, that hadn't changed.

"So?"

"So..." I trailed off, stretching the moment as I moved closer to her. I was still in awe of her dancing and still bricked up, all because of her company. She turned to look behind her but otherwise stood her ground. "So, I think you're understating your overall expenses for the show."

I'd asked her to send me a projected profit-and-loss statement, wanting to hopefully cover all the expenses she had so that the money made in tickets went straight to the studio coffers, but when she'd sent her estimate, several line items were missing.

She stared at my mouth, and I couldn't help but lick my bottom lip, then bite it for good measure.

She coughed and broke her stare. "You think I did what?"

"You downplayed your expenses. You know damn well that the T-shirts for the dancers won't cost $2 a pop." I took another step closer to her, inhaling the scent of earth and clean sweat.

"I didn't do that!" she protested, then went quiet when I moved even closer, leaving a sliver of space between us.

"You did because you're proud, but I told you I wanna help. So, send me that P&L again, alright, Ms. Mac?" At this point, I could stretch my neck down, and my lips would brush hers, but I wanted to respect her boundaries. We'd gone from barely tolerating each other to this charged—

Ms. Mac jumped away from me and widened the space that I'd been contemplating erasing. I'd let her off light this time.

"Ok, sure. Sure. Sure. Yes. I can do that all for the kids.

Yeah, for the kids. So, I have to head out to meet my friends..."

"Yes, let me walk you." Her eyes widened, and her chest rose and fell, and I felt thirsty as fuck suddenly.

"No need. It's just down the corner, it's just our spot. Our regular spot." Mark this as a first—Ms. Mac flustered. I'll be damned.

"Nah, I can't let you walk down there on your own, let's go." I offered her my arm, and she stared as if I'd just whipped out my dick and waved it at her.

"Uh...ok." She nodded and placed her soft hand on my biceps.

We walked out together into the darkening evening, and I wondered if all of this was really for Trinity or me.

Eleven

Aisha

I had to endure a lot of jokes and innuendo from my friends last night, and I hadn't been ready for it. I hadn't been able to explain Mr. Davenport's presence after class, and then he'd asked if he could walk me inside the bar and sit down and have a drink with us. The second he left to pick up his daughter, it began.

"So, did the two of you review his Peen and L?" Mila started.

I sipped on my margarita and ignored her.

"Nice, that was inspired. I think he had his entire presentation inside his pants. Did you see how tight those slacks were looking?" Sal asked Mila.

"Sal!" I chastised her, but really, I just wanted to nod and agree because those slacks were truly packing.

"What? Just because I'm inexperienced doesn't mean I can't admire some."

"Girl, you're not inexperienced." Mila shook her head.

"Trust me, I am. But that's a'ight, I just need me a man

that wants to play with my...numbers," Sal finished in a dry tone, then downed her whiskey in one shot.

"Y'all straight up evil. That man is out of bounds. When I opened my school, I promised myself I wouldn't tangle with any parents. Two years I've kept my vow. It's messy, y'all, or it could get messy, and I'm trying to build a legacy, not a reputation."

"Mr. Davenport is on that same page about building...he's trying to lay some pipe," Mila nodded sagely, and we all busted out laughing.

I WAS STILL SMILING a day later as I stopped by the pharmacy before my session tonight. I needed a few personal items, and I knew I'd be in no headspace after a session to stop.

I couldn't wait to see what my Dom For Now was planning to do; the last two sessions had me excited about his development in kink. But like I had told him, I had no plans on getting my cables crossed with him.

Someone called my name as I turned into the aisle with all the Black hair products.

The voice wasn't recognizable, but that wasn't out of the ordinary; I was horrible with voices.

"Aisha, girl! I thought that was you." A tall, thin, light-skinned woman approached me, and I instantly recognized her. She had been one of the mean girls in Ms. Brown's dance school, and she and I had exchanged a few words back in the day.

"Hi, Roxane. Last I saw you, you were telling me all about your contract with the big-time ballet in Cali. How did that go?" I asked curiously. I hadn't begrudged her the appointment. Roxane could be nasty, but she was an amazing dancer and had the right body for it compared to me. I'd been glad for her as we needed more Black dancers everywhere. Didn't mean I couldn't be a little petty.

"Yeah, well, I had some artistic differences with the dance director."

"Oh, for real? That sucks."

"Yeah, but that's alright. I'm in talks with the Miami City Ballet."

"That's what's up!"

"How about you? Last I knew, you were on Broadway," she said mockingly. See, this is why you can't be nice to ain't shit people.

"I was, but I returned a couple of years ago because of my grandparents' health and reopened Ms. Brown's school."

"Oh well, that's nice, I guess," Roxane said dismissively, and I wanted to get on with my night; she was really messing up my vibe.

"Oh yeah, well, it is nice to me. Ms. Brown meant the world to me, and continuing her legacy is an honor. Listen, I have to go. I have an appointment, but all the best with the Miami City Ballet."

"Thanks. You have a good night, and have fun with that little school!"

I turned the corner into the next aisle and let my eyes roll all they needed to.

CRAP, I was late. Usually, Sir X arrived earlier than I did, set up the room, then left it so I could wait for him with our protocol, but the pharmacy run had delayed me. I checked in with Master Q, who laughingly told me I was late and that Sir X had been avidly waiting for me.

Well, I guess I wouldn't be waiting in position for him.

I sauntered into the room and found him sitting on one of the thrones.

He looked menacing with his black balaclava, all-black t-shirt, and sweatpants. And were those Space Jam 11s? Damn, that made him even hotter.

A chameleon.

He stood up and strolled toward me, and something told me to assume first position, going onto my knees for him.

His eyes flashed, then he smiled.

"Thank you for wearing my gift, Baby Doll." He'd left the gift with Master Q, who'd brought it to my studio.

The gift comprised a strappy black bra, panties, and a short flared leather skirt that attempted to cover my bottom.

Category: leather vixen.

The bra consisted of strips of black fabric crossing my chest, holding my breasts up and plump. The panties covered my mound and buttcrack, with straps fanning out from each of those spots. He'd even gifted me a vinyl cat mask with silver metal chains covering the bottom part of my face.

"It's my pleasure, Sir. Thanks for the outfit. It's very sexy."

"Is it your pleasure, though?" he said, looming over me. I could feel the coiled strength radiating from him and I felt oh-so-powerful, harnessing his dominance through my submission.

"Is it, Sir?" I stared up and fluttered my eyelashes at him.

"Well, you got me twisted then. This is how you repay me...by being late for our appointment? I'm disappointed, Baby Doll." He walked around me, making my stomach clench at his words. His disappointment was mine. A calloused finger ghosted along my right shoulder across to the left, waking the hairs along its path. The sense of déjà vu enveloped me, making the air thick.

Low jazz played through the speakers, the brass melody meant to put me at ease. I felt anything but ease. His tone told me he had a punishment waiting for me, and I was on pins and needles. My nerve center flickered alight, oversensitive. Every move of his amplified my anticipation. I regulated my breath with deep exhalations as I heard rustling behind me.

"Baby Doll, stand up and go to the St. Andrew's cross."

"Yes, Sir." I rose and strolled toward the X contraption.

I started turning around when I was stopped by his warm hand, slightly squeezing my neck.

"No, I'm strapping you with your back toward me," he breathed against my ear, and I let all my anticipation escape with a sigh. The warmth of his body heated my back, and his woodsy scent lured my eyes close.

Two large hands held my hips in place, preventing me from budging. Silly man, I didn't want to budge. I wanted to stand here and relish his nearness and how masterfully he was using his silence and disappointment to rile me up.

One hand slid unhurriedly up my side, his fingers ghosting along the underside of my breast, extending my arm until it was aligned with the cross.

He harnessed my hand, then repeated the same devastatingly soft gesture on the other side.

I wanted to feel his hardness nestled on my leather-clad behind, so I pushed back against him, and all I met was air.

Oh, he's taunting me.

"You don't deserve to feel my dick, Baby Doll. You were a bad doll coming in here late, letting me worry about you.

Do you know how excited I was to find you in first position in the new fit?" he asked.

"No, Sir."

"Nah, of course not, 'cause I haven't made you wait for anything, Baby Doll, but that changes today. I'm gonna show you what happens when you're bad." He followed the statement with a tap of my butt cheek. I pushed back, moisture already coalescing between my legs, needing some relief. As far as my restraints allowed, I assumed my doggy-style position.

The trombone of the current jazz song ripped through the room, and I waited. I knew I must be a pretty sight with my behind up in the air, the leather skirt and panties adorning me for his view. I hoped against hope he'd touch me because I was keyed up and needed a little adjustment to stay in the game. The fact that I possibly knew who was behind the balaclava and the muffled, sexy voice was daunting.

A good Dom would see that.

"You need me, Baby Doll?" He grabbed a handful of my butt cheek and squeezed, then grunted, and his hand molded my ass with a reverence that made me even wetter.

"Yes, Sir," I sighed.

"But you weren't on time. Do you think you deserve what I had planned for you?"

"I do, I really do. I promise I'll do better next time." Lust roared inside of me, demanding release. My brain switched from that in-control place to the dreamy no-responsibility oasis I went to when in subspace.

"If you want some of what I had planned, you're gonna have to show me you're sorry. So, I'll have you count out loud the seconds you were late to our meeting."

Math, right now? This negro had me messed up. I

couldn't even think of what I ate this morning, let alone figure out—

SLAP!

"Stay with me, Baby Doll. How many minutes were you late?" His hands were now riding up my behind, over the line of my back, and he settled them on my shoulder blades. The warmth of his touch grounded me enough to follow his words.

"I was twelve minutes late," I grumbled, and he chuckled. I mean, I wasn't about to round up and get in more trouble.

"Alright then, how many seconds were you late, Baby Doll?"

This man had me over here carrying a one over and keeping the zero and...

"Seven hundred and twenty seconds."

"That's right. Count till seven hundred and twenty without messing up or slowing down too much, and I'll give you what you want."

"Sir, how do you know what I want?"

"Oh, I know you want to feel this dick. Figure out if it will satisfy you. Let me tell you right now that when we're ready to fuck, trust and believe my dick will deliver. You'll never want for anything ever again," he said close to my ear, and I gasped at the promise behind the words.

"Sir..."

"Only if you consent, Baby Doll, only if you consent." Oh, I wanted to consent alright, but I felt he and I were getting in too deep too quick, and this was just supposed to be sessions for him to practice, not to carve out a space in my brain named *Favorite Dom of the Year*.

"Yes, Sir." I sighed in acquiescence, both of us knowing it was just a matter of time.

I wiggled my ass back and forth, needing the air to relieve me.

"Don't play with me, Jasmine," he growled. "Start counting."

Alright, I can do this.

"1... 2... 3... 4... 5... 6... 7... 8... 9... 10..." I counted, mentally spacing out the numbers with a Mississippi to ensure I was going at the right pace. At first, nothing happened.

I was up to twenty when the torture began.

Again, he got real close behind me. I could hear his steady inhalations and felt his heat. Our hips were a breath away from each other, and I wanted to connect with him, so I pushed back. I met air again.

A vibrating noise started, and then I felt it, a wand gliding up between my legs against my covered pussy.

I was damp and so needy. The vibrations made me thrust my hips back, wanting the contact to be even more direct.

"Ahhh...oohh... Fudge... 21... 22..."

"Remember, Baby Doll, you mess up or stop, and I stop too. And you start all over again, ok?"

"Ahh, yes... 23... 24..."

The wand stimulated my pussy, the vibrations making my lips quiver and my clitoris yearn for more. He caged me against the cross and kept at it with the wand, shifting it with excruciating slowness up and down my mound.

"Do you want to feel it against your bare pussy?" he taunted.

"Ohh yes, please... 32... 33... 33."

The vibration suddenly stopped, and I cried out.

"Please, Sir!"

"Start over again, Baby Doll, you messed up."

Fudge!

I rubbed my legs together in desperation, hoping to ease some of the tension he had created with the wand. My heart pounded in my chest with the anticipation of what else he would do now that I needed to count again. I couldn't deny a thrill at having to begin once more.

"1... 2... 3..." I started over, trying to focus on just the count and not the way my brain matter morphed into fluffy cotton, my thoughts all centered on how amazing I felt all over. My skin tingled with the need to be touched, wetness pooled in my panties, my breath was loud as a megaphone, and still, I kept it together.

"60... 61..."

"Spread your legs, Baby Doll," he commanded, and I spread my thighs farther, still holding onto the cadence of the numbers. I adjusted my count to the beat of the jazz music, the rhythm keeping me in check.

Sir X's hands skimmed my waist, making my breath catch. Suspense kept the air thin around me.

"70... 71... 72..."

His thumbs hooked on my panties, and I exhaled, impatient for his next move.

"90... 91... 92..."

He leisurely slid the fabric down my legs, his breath kissing my thighs, making me erupt in goosebumps as he knelt behind me.

"100... uh... 101... 102..."

My pussy throbbed in expectation of what would come. Because something was coming.

Hopefully, it was me.

"125... 126... 127..."

Sir X kept me waiting, kneeling there, his eyes piercing

me the way I wish *he* would pierce me. I felt his stare even though I couldn't see him.

"187... 188... 189..."

He turned on the wand again, making me jump at the unexpected sound in the room as he gently placed it between my legs where I needed it the most.

"Mmmm, 200....201... 202!" My legs shook as the wand pressed against my clit. The restraints held me as sounds flowed out of me, at how good it felt to be pleasured like this.

"Baby Doll, I can't hear that count," Sir X admonished me.

"450! 451! 452! 453!" Oh, I needed more stimulation, I needed more. I couldn't—

Swoosh.

"Oh Gahd, 490!" He swatted my ass with a riding crop, the slight pain the perfect grounding I needed. Here I was, appreciating impact play because of Sir X.

"Keep counting, Baby," he said, his voice sounding strained to my ear. He'd turned off the wand, leaving me on the edge. Just the way I loved it.

At this point, I was floating; I felt as light as a feather. He swatted me to the beat of my count.

"500... 501... 502."

Swoosh.

"Keep that count, Baby Doll." He felt it, too, his voice tense as he kept up the taps on my bottom.

Warm, soft lips touched my shoulder, and I stopped, my heart thrumming at his gentle touch.

I couldn't stand the tenderness in the middle of so much stimulation. I couldn't...

Another kiss between my shoulder blades. Oh, those lips were so gentle on my skin.

"650, 651...ahhhh!"

Sir X brushed my curls off my neck and pressed another kiss, and I felt the touch of his tongue.

"690... 691..."

He turned on the wand, and I knew the end was coming; I just needed to keep myself together through the finish line.

The wand met my pussy again, and he turned up the vibrations to a stronger stimulation, liquifying my insides. It was all roiling underneath my skin, and I just needed to let go, but not before I finished this danged count.

"717... 718, ahhh, right there... 719... 720!" I finished, and I let go.

The buzz traveled through my needy clit, and Sir X's hand snaked across my waist as he pressed his whole delectable, firm body against mine. My heart and pussy synched up to the same desperate pulsing, the ache to be filled washing through my veins, and when I felt his hardness... I came apart, trembling all over.

"So, you liked it?" Sir X asked me while I sipped on my chocolate milk. We sat on the floor, leaning on each other's backs. Our aftercare always seemed to happen on the floor, requiring both of us to touch. I really wasn't treating these sessions as if they were professional ones, and I didn't even know how to reel it in. I enjoyed spending time with Sir X.

Not liked. I loved spending time with him.

"You don't need to sound so smug about it," I scoffed, but inside, I was impressed. This was one of the top sexual scenes I'd ever had in one of these sessions.

"Oh, I had yo' ass counting twice. I'm gonna feel smug," he reminded me.

"Alright, Sir X, you deserve that smugness. What did you originally plan to do before this punishment?"

"Never mind that. We still have a few sessions to go. Just know that they are all within the parameters of your boundaries and what you mentioned you enjoy or want to explore."

"I know that." My chest expanded at his care and excitement for these scenes just for me.

"Good, because I want you to walk away from each of these sessions absolutely relaxed and on a high if I can."

"I sure will today, and I sure needed it."

"Oh?" I felt him shift, and I turned around to meet his eyes. He straightened his legs and relaxed with his arms supporting him, and I sat cross-legged next to him. We still touched thigh to thigh.

"Yeah, work is... It's hard right now. I'm trying to build something bigger than me, something for the community, but roadblocks, they won't let me be great," I confessed.

"I'm sorry to hear that, Baby Doll. You seem to be someone that knows how to persevere, though."

"Yeah, I know how to bounce back and get on my feet again over and over. It's in my DNA, so it'll work itself out. I have a few things I'm planning to do." I sighed.

"You need a space where you don't have to worry about it, though," he hedged, and I realized that, again, we had ventured into the realm of the personal. Fudge, this man made me forget myself.

"Yeah, you're right, and I will. But now it's time to leave until next time."

His shoulders slumped, then he raised himself up, his

posture back to the strength I noticed the first day I met him.

"A'ight, Baby Doll, listen, I... Can we exchange numbers?" he asked.

I froze, every system in my body pausing at the possibility, mixed with the hesitation that snaked through me because I didn't want to mix things up in my head. If this was who I thought it was... He only had two ways of contacting me, through my studio or Master Q. I didn't know if I wanted to take this step yet.

"I... I don't think that's a good idea, honestly. I..."

"I just want to contact you, be able to text you. Just think about it. No pressure." He nodded, and I was glad for the reprieve.

"Alrighty, I'll think about it." But I knew deep inside I'd do no such thing.

Twelve

Knox

After an extraordinary Friday, this Sunday was an unusual one. I didn't have Trin with me—this was the weekend when my ex-wife had visitation rights. These weekends were difficult because even though my ex was a good mother, I had completely lost trust during the last months of our marriage when I felt nothing was going right.

After a couple of years of accompanied visitation with my parents, we transitioned to stayovers at her apartment a year ago. I felt uneasy every time I dropped Trin off at Chantal's, but I knew those were residual feelings from before her recovery. Chantal had her shit together with a nice apartment in a safe area in the city, was back at her agent job, and religiously attended her NA meetings.

I just couldn't get past the fact that her addiction became more important than Trin and me.

I couldn't just stay in the house, so I called the dance studio and let Ms. Mac know I'd be around to help with the scenery. She'd emailed asking for help from any of the parents that were handy, and I was determined to ensure this show was a success. And to spend more time with her after our last session.

The more I understood about Ms. Mac and her current situation, the more I wanted to help, for Trin's sake and lowkey for Ms. Mac's.

A couple more kids had left the school in the last few days. Trin had told me while we spoke on the phone Saturday night, so I knew things were getting tight. It also explained her work at Master Q's studio. Again, I was making the assumption it was her, and I didn't know how to broach the subject. After all, one of her asks was not to acknowledge if we knew each other outside the club. Master Q had explained this was a blanket rule for her, and I didn't know what to do with that.

Outkast's "Aquemini" blasted through the speakers as I walked into the studio. The chime alerted Ms. Mac to my presence, and she and her two friends strode out of the first dance room.

"Oh, Mr. Davenport!" she said with a huge grin. Her smile calmed some of the unease I'd been feeling since yesterday when I dropped Trin off at my ex's. My heartbeat regulated just being in her mere presence.

"Look, ladies, more help!" She gestured at me. Ms. Torres grumbled, and Sal walked right back into the room, saying nothing.

"Don't pay them any mind, they're a little annoyed with me right now. I got them working on a Sunday. But we need the free time!" she said animatedly, her hand sliding up my biceps and closing there, my stomach flipping lazily, making me yearn for more of her touch. She gently tugged me to the room, and I followed her gladly.

We entered the dance room, where several half-made

props were lying around on a large gray tarp protecting the floor. She let me go, and I felt bereft of her force tugging me into the room. Her hand had felt good as fuck on my arm.

I watched Ms. Torres sit in front of a prop on the floor and grab gold spray paint. Sal, on the other hand, was on her laptop lying on the floor belly-down, completely oblivious to the rest of us.

"These are some old props I've used in other shows that I'm trying to repurpose. I usually hire someone for this, but I reckoned I could figure something out with what I already had. What you think?"

"Why just not hire the same contractors as before? And this is just a question, I'm not trying to be a dick," I said, walking toward her in the opposite corner of the room with my hands up in a sign of peace. If we could keep from annoying each other, it would be a successful day.

"I could, but I'm trying to save as much as I can of the money to inject back into the studio."

I nodded, then looked around one more time. It seemed I was the only parent willing to give my Sunday away.

"You know we're gonna need reinforcements, right?"

She sighed. "Yeah, but we can start with spray painting what we have here today!"

"A'ight, Ms. Mac, show me what you want me to do."

———

Two hours later, I was deep into reconstructing a London phone booth into a dream capsule. I sawed away some of the top designs and was in the process of repainting the booth in black; then I was gonna add some silver stars with spray paint.

Ms. Mac sauntered over to my area and ran her hand

over my biceps again, making the hair on my arm stand in attention.

"Tell me, love, what do you need?" I asked, her hand feeling a little too good on my bare skin. The endearment escaped my lips, but it was too late to take it back. Served me right for wearing a sleeveless muscle shirt. She kept caressing for a little longer, then startled out of her trance.

"Oh, nothing, nothing. I was wondering if you were thirsty? You haven't stopped since you arrived."

"Am I thirsty? I could drink... What you got?" I asked, my eyes trained on her hand still touching my arm.

"I got lemonade, water, and beer."

"Yeah, ask her which beers she has," Ms. Torres piped up from her area with a mischievous smile.

I turned back to Ms. Mac with my eyebrow raised.

Ms. Mac squinted her eyes at her friend, and even Sal raised her face from her laptop.

"I have Budweiser, Corona, Blue Moon, Modelo..."

"I'll have a—" I started.

"Also Heineken, and Guinness, and um, Red Stripe. When you called, I figured beer would be nice, but I didn't know what you like, so..." she finished with an abashed smile.

Damn. She really got all of that for me? I hadn't even told her what I liked, but I guess that was the whole point—she enjoyed being extra-prepared. I snuck a look at Ms. Torres and saw her smirk with a slight nod, then glanced at Sal, covering her mouth with her hand, her eyes crinkling at the corner.

I didn't want to embarrass Ms. Mac, but I wanted to show her my appreciation.

"Thank you. You *honor* me with how many options you got for me. I'll take the Guinness; it's my favorite."

Her big, beautiful eyes widened, and I wondered if she'd noticed the word. Eyes flitted around, a hint of panic, then... A delighted grin blossomed on her lips before then she squeezed my arm one more time and went to the back.

Damn, did she get it?

She took care of everything, bringing us drinks and snacks. She fussed over Sal, who I learned was on deadline to complete a software update for one of her biggest clients. Then she turned to Mila, showering her with words of encouragement as they discussed a prop, then again to me, her hand warm on my arm as we agreed upon what to do with the next prop that needed major redesign.

The chime went off again, and a frown formed on Ms. Mac's face.

"Who could it be? No one else volunteered for design work..."

She got up from the floor where she'd been painting and walked toward the dance room door.

"Hold on, let me get it. This is why you need a receptionist." I scoffed, and her hand froze on the door handle.

"Oh ho, we're doing really well today. Let's keep the peace," Ms. Torres said from the floor, and I had to admit I really liked her friends; they weren't letting me slide at all.

I breathed in and out, trying not to let the fact that this woman kept taking chances with her security make me mad with worry. I breathed in and out because I felt like becoming a caveman, carrying her away from the door and taking care of it all by myself.

But I wasn't anyone to her but the father of one of her students.

I wanted to be more than that. *And again, where the hell are these feelings coming from?*

She stared at me for a second, and I nodded my head.

She opened the door and walked out, and I followed.

A teenager from the dance team stood just past the threshold, tear-stricken and wringing their hands.

"Jan, what happened, honey? Where's your mom?" Ms. Mac asked, worry written all over her face.

"Mama wants to pull me from the school. I heard her on the phone, she said the bills are piling up, and you're more expensive than the other school, but she didn't want to hurt your feelings, and you know how everyone is afraid of your grandma, ain't no one wanting to mess with her baby, and..."

"Oh, Jan, I can understand your frustration. And Momma is harmless. I don't know why she has that reputation for being a badass in the neighborhood. Does your mom know you left home?"

"Yeah, I told her I was gonna go to the corner store. I mean, it's a block away. For real, I was gonna go there," Jan said when she saw my face, "but then I started thinking of the show, then the competition you were telling us about... and I just don't wanna leave the school. Ms. Mac, it ain't fair! I know she don't got the money, but..." Jan crumbled into Ms. Mac's arms.

Ms. Mac's stricken face made my insides crumble. And what was that about another school?

I stood there, unable to do much, just providing silent support to Ms. Mac while she gently calmed Jan.

My cell phone vibrated in my pocket, and I pulled it out, annoyed at the interruption.

> Chantal: All is well but remind me again, what's Trinity's allergy again? It developed when... well, you know, and I wasn't sure.

What the fuck? Had Trinity eaten something that caused a reaction? She couldn't have strawberries. Right after the divorce, she broke out one afternoon after going to the fair with me and eating the fresh berries. I had a bad feeling this morning, and I should have trusted my gut.

> Me:... I wrote all of it in that document I gave you at the beginning of the year when she started staying with you.
>
> Chantal: The cleaning lady threw it away. I wouldn't be texting if I had that, would I?

And she was going to give me sass on top of everything. I needed to go. Trin needed me, and I couldn't do much for Jan or Ms. Mac right now.

I cleared my throat and saw Ms. Mac's hopeful gaze on me. Her eyes sucker-punched me in my gut. I wanted to be in this together for her, but I couldn't, not right now.

"I gotta go."

"Oh...ok. I...ok," Ms. Mac said. "Jan, honey, can you give me a second? I have to talk to Mr. Davenport, but I'll be right back with you. Why don't you go into Room A and hang out with Ms. Torres and my friend Sal?"

"Nah, no need. Take care of Jan. I'll hit you up later." I pushed my phone back into my pocket and headed toward the door, ready to check on Trin. My mind was on one track.

I wouldn't focus on how Ms. Mac's face fell as I dismissed her again.

Damn.

Thirteen

Aisha

About a week after the episode with Jan, I couldn't figure out which school was poaching my dancers. I had a talk with Jan's mom, who didn't want to share more, saying that Jan must have heard wrong. When I offered a partial scholarship, she thawed real quick, thanking me for the offer. It ensured Jan stayed, but it raised a heck of a lot more questions in my mind.

I'd been working with Sal, searching the dance schools in the area to see if there were any new ones, but nothing was popping up online. Mila was doing her through-the-grapevine investigative work, but no luck there either.

I tried not to dwell on the mystery too much. I had to focus on the good of the school and the students that were there. I'd made a couple of phone calls to some colleagues I worked with in the past and was excited to have found a potential additional teacher who agreed to start soon. That news had settled some of my worries, bringing my goals for the school back into perspective—expansion, elevation, and growth.

After a grueling week of classes, rehearsals, and getting ready for the show, I needed a break, so we got together at our spot. We were the only women in the sports bar, which was a corner away from the studio.

The bar was a community institution, and we loved coming here. No one messed with us. No men came to shoot their shot with wack-ass bars. It was paradise.

"This week was rough," Sal said, downing some whiskey.

"Yeah, is shit getting harder, or are we getting older and more tired?" Mila asked.

"Y'all getting old, that's what's happening," Ol' Man Joe said, bringing us more drinks from the bar.

Ol' Man Joe could be anywhere from sixty to a hundred and ten years old, but no one really knew. He'd owned this bar since he was a young adult and had kept up with the times with soft renovations here and there to keep the place up-to-date.

Mostly it was your straightforward wood and leather games bar, and Ol' Man Joe was your straightforward Black elder that knew everything but didn't bother with half the shit that happened around him.

"Joe, how you gonna call us old?" Mila protested, and I laughed.

"I call it as I see it. You three have been coming here since before you could drink... That was a long time ago," he said, shuffling his way back to the bar.

"Damn, we really were reckless coming in here with no ID." I remembered the old days when we would sneak into the bar on game nights and thought no one would notice.

Oh, but Ol' Man Joe would notice, alright. He'd let us stay but wouldn't serve us any alcohol. He always said better here than somewhere where no one would look after us.

"Mhm. Y'all were always trying to get me in trouble," Sal said, and we both stared at her in surprise.

"We? We tried to get *you* in trouble?" Mila asked.

"I don't know what you are talking about," Sal said.

"Girl, you were trouble when we were in school, always trying to sneak out of your house and drag us along on your adventures. For all you were introverted, you didn't just stay home."

"Lies. I've always been a homebody," Sal said nonchalantly and shrugged her shoulders.

I made eye contact with Mila, and she stared back. We were getting dangerously close to the one thing Sal hated talking about, so we left it alone.

Sal had changed after a long-term relationship that had been no good for her. She'd always been the quiet, no-nonsense one of our trio, but her joy in life had diminished after that situation.

"Sure, baby, you were, but you'd get rebellious sometimes," I smiled.

"Rebellious, please. I'm sure my Mama was unlocking the door for me to escape," Sal said, then took another swig of her drink.

Time to change the subject.

"I forgot to tell y'all that Mr. Grumpy called me trying to apologize after class on Thursday. But I didn't answer, so he left a voicemail."

"He still doesn't have your number?" Mila asked.

"No, why would he?"

Now Mila and Sal looked at each other.

"Hey!" I protested.

"Don't 'hey' us. You know that man is attracted to you, and lately, it looks like he's been trying to shoot his shot," Sal said.

"No, lady, I disagree." I shook my head, but darn if I didn't feel flutters in my belly.

"Pfff," Mila said. "You know that man has the hots for you."

"He doesn't, he can't stand me. Besides..." I trailed off, wondering if I should mention my new Dom client. If I should mention how my thoughts immediately went to Sir X when Knox's name was mentioned. My emotions were tangling up.

"Besides?" Sal's eyebrow quirked up.

"My new Dom client is kinda sexy."

"Ohhh, you've been mighty quiet about this one, girl. Spill the tea," Mila said.

"Listen, you know I have my rules about my Dom clients."

"Mhm. Yep, rules, so you don't think of that asshole—" Sal started.

"Nah, nah, I don't want to talk about James right now. He's in the past." No need to bring up my ex right now.

Mila made a disgusted face, which I ignored.

"As I was saying. This Dom... Sir X...the way he's going about his scenes. It really has me intrigued. Mostly, new Doms still haven't fully figured out the power dynamic."

"True, true." Mila nodded along.

"So, this man, well, he gets that already. And his scenes have all been about figuring out what works for me."

"So, have y'all rubbed privates together already?" Sal asked.

"No, and you know I don't always do that."

"You're right, you usually don't...unless you're attracted to your client." Sal finished her whiskey.

Darn it, why did my friends know me so well?

"So, what are you going to do about this double ill-timed attraction?" Mila asked.

"Well—"

Mila's eyes widened, and Sal did a double take.

"Speak of the devil," Sal whispered.

A shiver of awareness swarmed through my body as I spun to look behind me.

There, by the entrance, was Knox Davenport with three other men.

He'd already seen me and approached our table with a single-mindedness that made me cross my legs on the high stool I sat on, leaving his friends to trail after him.

Before I could catch my breath, he stood next to me.

I should be annoyed with him.

I should be mad. He was a prick the last time I saw him.

I couldn't, though, not when he was staring at me like that, as if he'd come just to see me and was intent on knowing all my desires and hopes.

I would spill all my guts to him if he asked.

Fudge.

"Ms. Mac," he said, and his deep voice rumbled inside me.

"Might as well call me Aisha. We aren't in the studio right now."

He smiled, perfect straight teeth and thick lips surrounded by an opulent beard.

Oh my goodness, I'm in trouble.

"Hey, Aisha, so we're finally using first names?" The

way he said my name was tantalizing. I had to cross and uncross my legs again. I stared at my friends in alarm. Mila covered her mouth in mirth, and Sal just widened her eyes.

"So, listen, first I wanna apologize for bouncing with no explanation last week. I know your dancer needed comfort, and I could tell you needed support, and I wasn't there for you. That was messed up, and there's no excuse." He extended his hand to me, and I reluctantly touched him.

"With that being said, do you mind if I explain what happened?" he asked, and I looked behind him, wondering if he was just gonna ignore the fact that he had three friends with him. I gave them a shy grin, remembering his brother Stephen, and the three of them just shook their heads and smiled back. They were all various types of attractive. I mean, birds of a feather and all.

"Ah, yeah, of course, you can explain, but don't you wanna make introductions first?" I asked.

"Hello, Aisha, nice to see you again. Ladies," Stephen said.

A thick-set, big boy handsome, dark-skinned man stepped forward after. "I'm Denzel. Pleasure to meet you, ladies."

Right after came the third friend, the shortest of the group, with a smile that probably dropped panties wherever he went. "I'm Toño."

After we made the introductions, the men asked if they could push another high-top table close to ours, effectively getting us all to hang out together.

I'd said yes, but I didn't know how to feel about it all. I didn't hang out with the families of my dancers outside of work. It was smart, and I did my best to keep a professional line drawn. The aunties that brought their grandkids had seen me grow up and couldn't care less about my boundaries, but besides that, I kept my distance.

But Knox Davenport... He made me want to bend all my rules, and that was very scary.

"So, can I explain now?" he asked once our friends hit it off and had their own conversation going. I don't know how he did it, but with his body, he'd created a cocoon around us, his frame blocking me away from the rest of the group and keeping me in our own private space. I was glad for the high stool because my legs had stopped properly working as I felt Knox's body heat and inhaled his yummy scent.

"You can explain." I nodded and sipped my drink.

"My daughter was with her mom. And her mom... Let's just say the last few years have been rocky for her. And she had her for her weekend and couldn't remember what Trin was allergic to. Trin got a rash. She texted me in a slight panic."

"Oh no, is Trinity ok? I mean, I saw her on Thursday when your folks brought her, and she was fine." I held onto his arm, my hand having a mind of its own, just like last Sunday when he came to help.

"Yes, yes, she's good. It wasn't an allergy; she had rug burn from playing on her knees with her dollhouse and then scratching it. Her skin is super sensitive, and..." He shook his head.

"And her mom didn't know this?" I asked, trying to keep any judgment from coloring my tone.

"These last few years...she's doing her best." He rubbed his beard, then peered over his glasses to inspect my drink.

"If you say so. I mean, I can see how good of a father you are to Trinity. And you're doing so well. It's just odd that if y'all share custody, I've never met her in two years," I said, wondering what the story behind it all was.

"Maybe one day I'll tell you all about it," he said with an odd intensity that made me squirm in my seat.

"You need a refill?" he asked.

"Mmm, I shouldn't..." I didn't want to say that we had plans to smoke weed at Mila's condo and didn't want to get too drunk.

"Alright. Just say the word, and I'll take care of you."

"Oh, will you now? What changed? Because less than a month ago, you hated my guts."

He reared back and shook his head, then let out a bark of laughter that made me think I might not need any weed to get high tonight.

"Trust me, I've never hated you."

"Well, sir, you have a funny way of showing it." The flutters were becoming a full-blown ruckus inside of me.

"What did you just call me?" He stepped closer. His thick thighs rubbed against my legs, and I couldn't breathe properly.

"I...what did I say?" I asked, wondering at the thrill I felt as he stared at me as if I was prey.

"Mhm, I'm gonna let that slide, but you call me that one more time, and I won't be able to answer for what comes next." The sexy smirk he gave me made me want to lean over and bite his bottom lip.

Man, when did this attraction sneak up on me?

"Don't overthink it, Aisha. I can see you overanalyzing what's happening, and it won't do you any good."

"I...excuse me? It seems you think you know me."

"Not as well as I wish I did." He stood so close I could smell his whiskey-sweet breath, could almost taste him. And underneath it all was a scent I recognized, tickling my nose, waking up my eye even though I'd refused to see.

Yep, the air just completely left the building because I could access none of it.

"Ah... Well, I gotta go. My girls and I...we were just leaving when you arrived, and..."

"Really? You were just leaving? It didn't seem like it." He raised an eyebrow, and I attempted to make eye contact with Mila with no success. She was into whatever conversation she was having with the sexy teddy bear. I turned to Sal, and she caught my SOS eyes.

"Aisha, you ready to leave?" Sal raised her voice over the music.

"See? I told you. I gotta go," I told him, a strange urgency to leave driving my every move. I jumped off the high stool, and that was a mistake because our bodies brushed together and...

I wasn't supposed to be this close to the father of one of my students—this was not professional. But I couldn't think straight as I let momentum carry me closer until I felt his solid body against mine, and for a second, I yielded to his strength as his hands slid over my waist.

"You a'ight there?" he asked, amused, his eyes half-mast and clouded with the same desire that had me running for cover.

"Yeah, I'm alright, just jumped with too much force." I laughed and attempted to detangle myself from him. He made it twice as hard, offering no help. Instead, he stood closer, his arms not moving as I created some space between us.

"Ok, so we're gonna go now, and I'll see you tomorrow for Trin's class, right?" I asked, compelled to open a door I wasn't certain should be opened.

He stayed quiet for a minute, searching my eyes, and I looked away, unable to handle the scrutiny.

After the seconds stretched into what felt like minutes, he nodded, stroking his beard.

"You'll see me tomorrow."

Now the door was open. And I walked away, my heart pounding as I imagined what would happen next between us.

Fourteen

Knox

Tonight, I wasn't holding back.

Jasmine activated all my protective tendencies. What first annoyed me about her—that smooth operator demeanor, that people-pleasing ability, her going with the flow? Now I understood it all for what it was, a deeply embedded kindness despite what life had thrown at her.

I wanted to negotiate a D/s relationship with her outside of these training sessions, but I knew she was skittish about it. Every session, we ended up opening up more and more to each other, but the walls she put up prevented us from delving even further.

I respected that. I'd gone into this protecting my identity, leery of what exposure I was bringing to myself, but Jasmine... She was worth the risk. Now my job was to show her she could trust me beyond these sessions.

To prepare for tonight, I asked Master Q if I could donate a new piece of equipment to the Gold Room, and he was all for it.

The plans for this scene enthralled me the whole week. Jasmine had shown me in glimpses during our time together how she thrived in the sweet limbo of anticipation. That gap right before finishing where I could entrance her and gain all her attention, that's when she blossomed into her true self.

With that in mind, I would usher her to that sweet spot...and there she would stay...until she couldn't take it anymore.

After a brief chat with Master Q, where he did all the heavy lifting because my mind was on what was about to come, I headed back to the Gold Room.

Any anxious energy dissipated at the sight of her. Jasmine was in first position in a shiny black leather bodysuit. The bodysuit covered her torso, leaving her arms and legs bare, and had two holes exposing each breast, presenting her like a snack. Shiny black star pasties barely covered her areolae with something sparkly dangling from each of them. I had asked her via Master Q to wear one of her favorite outfits, and this was what she wore.

Aisha smiled, plush lips painted in deep burgundy, and her grin touched me like a caress. Her mask sparkled in the light as it covered the upper part of her face and the sides, exposing only her mouth and eyes to me.

Tonight, I would turn her the fuck out.

"You're breathtaking tonight, Baby Doll. You're already pleasing me, and we haven't even started."

"Good evening, Sir X." Her eyes journeyed from the top of my head down to the soles of my feet, igniting my ever-present need for her in their wake. Then, as she left me to deal with the devastation her eyes wrought, she turned to the corner and studied the contraption in interest.

"Are you curious about what's beneath that?" I asked, getting myself back on track.

"Yes, Sir." She nodded and turned those huge, gorgeous eyes on me.

"I won't keep you in suspense." I approached the gold drape and unveiled it with a whoosh. A standing bondage seat emerged from within. She gasped behind me, and the sound made me want to bask in that second where I imagined her picturing all the different ways I could tease her on this device.

"Do you like it, Baby Doll?"

"I'm curious," she said hesitantly.

Smart girl.

"Come. You can stand up and look at it yourself."

The click of her heels was audible behind me as I held back on looking at her again. I'd been overwhelmed by all she presented to me so willingly, and I'd need a realignment before I took us both where we wanted to be.

"Sir?" she asked, recognizing I was taking a second to compose myself.

"Come, Baby Doll, you can look from up close." I extended my hand to her so she could study the bondage chair. The chair was a black metal frame that we'd secured to the floor and a suspended gold pad for lying down or sitting on, with chains and cuffs to secure the person to the seat.

"The possibilities are..."

"Plenty, and I want to explore them all with you." I knew that shit came out strong, but I wasn't holding back with her today. I knew with a deep certainty that I knew the woman behind the mask.

My hand itched to run down her long braided ponytail

all the way past her ass. I wanted to wrap the hair and yank her to me, but we were just starting.

Jasmine stayed quiet while she openly studied the chair and surreptitiously studied me. I allowed it, but I was stiffening up as she wet her lips with her pink tongue, imagining what I was going to do to her. Imagining where we could go now that she'd opened the door wider between us.

"You got your fill?" I faced her, letting her see her effect on me, and pulled on my dick, giving it room to grow. I felt all the tension as she licked her lips once more.

"Not yet... Sir." She smirked.

"Baby Doll, I might be relaxed with you, but don't mistake my relaxation in this room for complacency. I'll punish you if you play games with me. Let me speak clearly. I want us to take this to the next level."

"What's the next level for you, Sir?" She cocked her head, waiting for my answer.

"If you'd let me, I'd collar you..." She stiffened at my comment, and I backed off for the moment. "But I'll take these moments together...for now."

I was deadass serious, and I hoped she knew this was a promise. I would respect her boundaries, but I knew there was something more between us. I just needed to wait for her to see it too, and use these scenes as proof of how good we were together.

We stood facing each other, not breaking eye contact, the cold of the room making the hair of her arms stand to attention while we engaged in a battle of wills. She shifted her gaze first and blinked, breaking the growing tension between us. I was keyed up and ready to roll. The possibilities for tonight taunted me to begin.

"Too much talking. Get on the bench."

She fluttered her eyelashes at me, then complied with

my command. Knowing her power over me, she took her sweet time getting on the gold cushion, spreading her legs on each side of the seat, then scooting all the way to the edge. I almost choked on my tongue when I realized the bodysuit was crotchless, her bare pussy winking at me as she awaited her next command.

"Lay down."

Again, she complied with grace and fluidity oozing from every cell of her body. She clutched the chains on either side of her.

I got to work. With my phone, I switched the low instrumental music that had been playing and turned it to my freaky time playlist, turning up the volume to change things up a bit.

I itched to touch her so badly, so I let go of my inhibitions and held my lips shut, keeping the groan in when my hand met her silky thigh. I ghosted my hand up and down her smooth legs.

"Open for me."

She widened her legs and lifted them until they were aligned with the cuffs and chain on the frame.

The strap of leather caressed her ankles and held her in place. I continued my handiwork, letting my hands stray occasionally between the dewy skin of her upper thighs close to her progressively wet pussy. Jasmine's hard breaths were music to my ears, and if it were up to me, they would be the only thing playing, but I wanted to make this memorable for her too.

I ran a finger up her inner arm until I met the cuffs that had her tied to the frame, her arms extended next to her.

The last touch was a golden gag.

"Lick it," I whispered to Jasmine, and we both shivered when her tongue snaked out to meet the new gag.

I took the gag and licked it as well, and Jasmine's moan invaded my sense of purpose, and for a second, I was tempted to sink into her warm pussy and fuck her until she screamed my name. But that would be taking the easy route.

She opened her mouth and showed me her pretty tongue, then winked at me. She was just fucking with me now, but my dirty doll had no idea what was coming her way.

I strapped the gag on her, and she moaned again. Her perfect lipstick was smearing. I welcomed making a mess out of her.

"Ok, let's look at this pussy of yours."

I pulled a low stool and sat right in front of Jasmine's pussy. Her umber legs shimmered in the dark room, the spotlight pointing right at her as 112's "You Already Know" serenaded us. I could see her chest rise and fall, fast as if I had her running a race, and in some ways, I did.

Again, I ran a finger from her knee up to the soft skin between her thighs and let it linger right beside her pussy.

Damn, my mouth watered, hoping for a taste, but I had a plan.

She was just being herself, and I kept trying to ditch my plans and just fuck her raw.

Damn.

I groaned when she clenched her walls, pushing moisture out of her opening, and an image of my cum running down her legs assaulted me.

Fuck it.

I ran my tongue right there where she was clenching, accepting that, for the moment, she'd topped me into giving her head without saying one word.

The taste of her... I needed a minute because I was about to come in my pants, and we'd just started, but *damn*, the taste of her. She tasted tangy and smelled like wet earth on Sunday morning after a rainy night made for cuddles, and my tongue would never be the same after feeling her wet silkiness. And that pussy trick? That was something I vowed to experience with my dick. But for now, I let her squeeze my tongue as she pulsed around me and made other parts of me pulse with her.

She was already so close; I could hear it in the pattern of her breathing and the way her red nails clawed at the bench. But the dead giveaway was her grinding her ass against my face, and I was happy to oblige her. For now.

With an impressive show of strength, she wiggled her hips down closer to me and lifted her ass off the bench so she could rub her clit, then her hole, and lastly, her ass over my waiting mouth, and that's when I lost it.

I sank my fingers into her soft thighs and kept her in place.

"Don't you fucking move."

"Yes... Oh yes, Sir."

Then I gorged myself on her. I wanted to smell like Jasmine, taste like Jasmine; I wanted to percolate in her essence so not even a shower would take the scent of her away from my beard and face. I'd have to bottle this shit up and use it as my beard oil, her pussy was that addictive.

And her moans? It took all of me not to give her all this dick to see if she'd keep moaning or transition to screaming, another experience I promised to fulfill.

I could smell the scent of her lotion as she rubbed her thick thighs against my face, and I stopped what I was doing to her pussy to bite the velvety skin of her inner thigh. She squeezed her legs so hard around my face she was about to strangle me, and I couldn't think of a better way to go to my maker.

I used her thighs to dry some of the juices off my beard, then went back to my work.

Jasmine's panting grew ragged, so loud now I could only hear her and her wetness as I slurped on her clit, and just when I knew she was about to cum, I pulled back.

"FUU!"

Fuck that gag because I would never know if she was cursing or saying something else, but I could see her wide glassy eyes, pleading for her orgasm.

"No, Baby Doll. Slutty girls don't get to come when they want. You're so needy; look at how you've left my beard. All I can taste and smell is you."

"MMMM." She humped the air and again started clenching, trying to entice me to taste her. And fuck, she was succeeding, but the reward of having her desperate to come was a bigger one.

"Hoes like you just wanna come and not do the work. Have you pleased me today?"

She nodded enthusiastically, and she wasn't wrong. Every single command I'd given her, she had followed, including how fucking sexy she'd dressed for me.

"But what if I want more?" I asked as I slid my hand into my pants, pumping myself up as drool trickled down the sides of her gag.

Fuck!

"SSSHMM," she moaned, and again, her hips searched the air.

"What?" I shook my head, but I knew what she was trying to say. I kept stroking myself way slower than I wanted to, just to mess with her. This part I hadn't planned, but she had tempted me with her impressive Kegels, and now she needed a little funishment...

"Only eager little sluts like you clench their pussies to

get some head. And I love me some slut pussy." I squeezed the head of my dick, hoping I wouldn't be all talk and no walk.

I tapped her arm once, checking in with her, and she tapped her hand back, letting me know we were in the green zone. She and I had agreed on some nonverbal cues through exchanging notes. I was glad I'd thought of that because it made it easier to check in with her in times like these.

"If I pull my dick out, will I cross your boundaries?" I asked, knowing this was something she'd moved from a soft limit to a go last week in her paperwork after our scene. She'd given her new limits to Master Q, and he had communicated them with me. I purchased this chair the day after Master Q shared the recent development.

Jasmine shook her head vehemently, and I tapped her once again on her arm. Again, one tap back.

I pulled my length out of my boxers, and it smacked right back against my belly. I got closer to her hand, my dick inches away from her fingers.

Her eyes closed, then she opened them and fluttered her eyelashes at me again. I nodded, and she ran one finger from the base to the tip of my head, the soft touch increasing the pressure on the base of my spine until I was afraid I'd come without much more stimulation. She jiggled her hand, took me in her grasp, and tried to run her hand up and down my dick, and my knees buckled. I pulled away from her, and she moaned in protest.

"Nah, I know what my doll wants."

I unstrapped the gag from her mouth, and she exhaled, her lips stretched out, lipstick and drool smeared down her chin. I tugged on my balls because I wasn't ready for how beautiful she'd be, how reckless she'd make me want to be.

She didn't have time to think. I shoved my dick into her open mouth and begged to all I wouldn't nut in the first five seconds because Jasmine knew how to give head.

The muscles of her neck tensed as she took me on a wet and wild ride. Then she showed me she knew magic because she made my dick disappear down her throat and then swallowed.

"Fuck! Jasmine!" Fuck, I felt my eyes roll to the top of my head.

I didn't want to come, but she already had me leaking like a broken faucet.

"Slow down, Baby Doll," I commanded, but she kept on going, the nasty sounds of her slurps the most erotic thing I'd heard in my thirty-six years alive.

She moaned, ignoring me, too far gone in her high. The chains clanked against the metal frame as she attempted to bring herself to an orgasm, but I couldn't have that.

I inserted a finger into the side of her mouth and pulled my dick out.

"Noo!" she screamed.

"You don't get to come giving me head." There was clearly a god out there.

"Sir, please," she pleaded, a mess of lipstick and saliva.

Fuck my plan. She was begging for it.

I yanked off my mask, her eyes widened, and then before she knew it, I kissed her. Lust and want drove me as our tongues tangled. I'd never been kissed this way. I'd never kissed anyone this way. The caress of her tongue against mine was what I cared about. I didn't care about anything but this lightness in my legs and my arms and the hardness of my dick and the precum seeping down my head. I didn't care about anything but the next breath this woman would take, and I only cared to rob her of it and then return it through my kiss.

This was the kiss of all kisses.

She bit my bottom lip hard, and the tremors in her body shook me as she orgasmed. And just when I thought this couldn't feel more otherworldly, she sucked my tongue into her mouth, making me spurt all over her belly and side as we kissed through our high.

I reluctantly let go, our pants mingling loudly in the otherwise quiet room. The playlist had ended, and I stood here without a mask in front of her.

Walls down.

"Let me go," she whispered.

I searched her eyes, but she wasn't making eye contact with me. She was breathtaking, chained up, legs in the air spread open, with her lipstick now gone. I peeked down at my dick and saw the red smears left behind by her lips.

"Let. Me. Go."

Our gazes met, and I could see the panic and anger in her eyes.

"Hold on."

"Now, please!" She raised her voice, and I could tell the high had hit her bad and now she was tanking. I didn't want her to leave without us talking; she needed aftercare, and I needed to know she was ok.

I hesitated one second too long because she started yanking her arms, and my muscles tightened as I realized how mad she was. I pressed a hand on top of hers, and once she calmed, I let her out. My fingers felt twice as big as I tried to free her, and the entire process took me longer than it should have. By the time I had one of her hands free, she tried to help with the rest of the restraints with an urgency that had my mind racing, trying to figure out what was wrong.

"Thank you," she said as she hopped off the bench and went to her clothes. She threw on a maxi dress, then turned around, still masked, and stared at me.

"I'm going to ask Master Q to find you someone else." White noise surged around me until her mouth was moving, but I detected no sound.

With those last few words, she whirled and glided out of the room, shedding Jasmine as if she was a costume.

Fifteen

Aisha

There were so many reasons I should have known better. So many reasons, and I picked at each one like petals on a flower. When Knox yanked his mask off, he also yanked open the door I'd left briefly ajar, hoping we could ease into our knowledge. And now I was having second thoughts.

One, he was the father of one of my students, and I didn't mix work and pleasure. Not anymore.

Two, I thought I had been ready to go back and do scenes for work, but by the second scene, I'd realized he had a pull on me. Same pull as my ex...

Three, I'd learned with my ex that even though kink was my thing, there were certain Doms that could make me forget myself, get me so high in a scene that I lost all sense of reality. I chased that feeling—craved it, honestly—especially when I was going through hard times. But all highs have a low, and when my ex-boyfriend and Dom left me, breaking our engagement, I fell into a deep depression. I knew I couldn't afford to have such lows again. I had too much riding on my sanity—my grandparents, my students, the school, heck, my friend's livelihood.

Four, I didn't like this man! I didn't like his arrogance and nitpicky ways, his commands and bossiness. But fuck did I love his arrogance, his nitpicky ways, his commands, and his bossiness. I was making zero sense!

But the most important one, five: he and I were not compatible. We didn't gel well. We rubbed each other the wrong way unless we were trying to caress each other's genitals.

This couldn't work. There. I felt a little better.

Then came the other thoughts. How I'd loved our conversations after our scenes; how he was helping with the show, still in his own way but always there supporting; how he'd thawed with me in our day-to-day as the scenes progressed. I wanted to reset the clock and start over yet again with him. Knowing a little about his father explained some of who he was to me and made me want to know him on a deeper level. I wanted time, wanted to explore what could be more, but it just felt reckless. Reckless with my heart, knowing my tendency to give it too quickly.

As Sunday progressed and I took my grandparents to their bingo game, then to the grocery store for the week's shopping, my mind kept wandering back to the most amazing kiss of my life. I came from the touch of his lips on mine, the way he moved his tongue and controlled the kiss with his sensual swipes.

Arghh.

After my grandparent's bedtime, I sat down to do some finances, my stomach curdling as I tallied up all the bills due. I'd probably be able to pay it all, but there wouldn't be much left after. What was I to do? Between that and my love life, my expertise in treading water seemed like a distant skill. I couldn't take being in my head anymore, so I called the girls.

"Three-way video at 9:00 p.m. on a Sunday... This is an emergency, isn't it?" Sal drawled, dressed in a big tee, wearing her black-rimmed glasses. Mila, on the other hand, seemed to be at her parents' house.

"No, ya regreso, es una llamada importante. Papa, please, I'm no little girl. I can take calls after nine. Por favor." Mila spoke in rapid Spanish, the image bobbing up and down as she navigated her parents' house. "Girl, I'm here for Sunday dinner with the parents and Mari and her men. What's up?"

"I fucked up," I started.

"I'm sure whatever it is, you're overthinking it," Sal said, munching on an apple.

"No, I fucked up. I had sexual relations with one of my student's dads."

"So, you finally let that big hunk of chocolate goodness lay some pipe?" Mila said as I heard some shuffling behind her.

"Who's laying some pipe?" a voice asked in the background.

"Mari, get back out there! I'm on the phone."

"Aww, man, whatever it is, it sounds juicy!" Mari responded.

"Yeah, but it's nonya," Mila shot back, exasperated.

"Focus, Mila!" Sal called out.

I wondered why I'd thought this would be helpful. This required an in-person conversation.

"What happened, girly? Sorry, my sis was being nosy on her way to the bathroom."

"Never mind, we can chat tomorrow. Sal, are you good manning the door till I find someone? You can do all your work from the front," I asked. Sal had lost a couple of her key clients in the past week, and I was a little worried. I figured I'd prefer to pay her rather than anyone else. She needed the money, so I offered to pay more than I could afford. At least I lived in the house my grandparents had paid off with hard sweat and work. Sal didn't have that luck; her mom couldn't help her.

Sal stopped me. "No, no, no, you called us for a reason."

"My new Dom client...it's Davenport."

"Holy shit!" Mila shouted.

"Girl, do you have to scream so loud? I swear I lost some hearing," Sal grumbled. "But Mila is right. That's a plot twist I didn't see coming."

"Yeah, well...I kinda knew," I confessed, finally putting into words my thoughts and suspicions of the past weeks.

"Girl, this is more than a video call. Let's meet at Ol' Man Joe's."

"Nah, I'm ok, I promise. And I promise to tell you all everything on Tuesday." I thought I'd been ready to speak, but now that I had the floor, I couldn't articulate my feelings, and the list I had prepared for myself earlier seemed as distant as petals in the wind.

All I could think of was Knox Davenport and how he'd given me one of the best sexual scenes of my life. And I still hadn't had his dick inside me.

Trouble, thy name is Knox.

"So y'all kissed! Why am I more scandalized about that fact?" Mila asked on Tuesday as we sat at the reception desk, waiting for the first class of the day.

"I know, girl. I have my no-kissing rule, but the moment I saw him that first time, I amended it to a soft limit."

Mila stared at me open-mouthed.

"Even after all you went through with James, you took that risk?" Sal asked quietly.

"Yeah...I know."

"You know I think the depression had nothing to do with your kink and all to do with the fact you thought you were gonna marry that man. You have to stop mixing up the two," Mila interjected.

"I've had other partners I loved but never a Dom one. It was different with him," I reminded her.

"You've idolized that relationship in your mind to the point you've convinced yourself you cannot have a real—"

We all stopped when the chime sounded. We were an hour away from the first class, so the interruption took us by surprise. However, when I saw who it was, I remembered I had been expecting an arrival today.

"Devon!! You made it!" I exclaimed.

"Who's Devon, and when can I mount him? Hubba-hubba," Mila whispered behind me.

I shook my head and approached the waiting area where Devon stood, all lean muscles and smooth walnut skin under a white tee and whitewashed jeans with locs down to his shoulders. Devon had the gentlest eyes I've ever seen, a firm jaw, and heart-shaped lips that begged to be kissed—and had our entire dance crew in Harlem risking it all to have a night with him.

"Ladies, meet Devon, our new ballet teacher as well as our latest choreographer for our dance team!"

"Nice to meet you, Devon. I'm Mila, one of Aisha's friends." Mila walked out right behind me and thrust her hand toward him.

Easy, girl. Devon gave her one of those self-deprecating smiles that said, *I have no clue people masturbate to my ballet videos.*

"Nice to meet you, Mila. Any friend of Sha's is a friend of mine," he said in his faint Jamaican accent.

Sal had gone even quieter than usual.

"Sal?" I asked, worried she might not like Devon. She was very hot and cold with men and usually disliked new people.

"Hey," she mumbled and kept typing away on her computer.

I caught the end of Mila's eye roll and headshake.

"Don't mind our friend Sal. She's the quiet and deadly one of the crew," Mila said, ushering Devon to the reception area, where we had a few chairs.

"So, Devon, you gonna be my colleague?" Mila asked.

"Well, yeah, that's the plan." He nodded amiably and unfolded his tall frame on the chair.

"So, how is everything with you? Oh, I'm so glad to see you! I'm so honored that you took my call."

"Gyal, who are you trying to bamboozle? You know the honor is all mine; you called and saved *me*." He shrugged with an air that would deceive anyone into thinking he was just a run-of-a-mill dancer.

Out of the corner of my eye, I could see Mila vibrating to know the whole tea, but this wasn't one I planned to share.

Devon was one of the best male dancers I'd had the pleasure of working with. I met him during my short stint at the Dance Theater of Harlem and knew I was in the presence of greatness. He had continued his career with the ballet, and I moved on to Broadway, where I was better-suited and didn't have to eat two grapes and an egg white per day to keep up.

A year ago, he moved to South Florida and joined the ballet company in Miami, but a month into his tenure, he had a severe injury and underwent surgery.

He was now undergoing physical therapy and was back to dancing, albeit with some limitations, but with a visa attached to the theater he danced for, I wondered how he'd stay long-term. I still wondered how I could figure out a lasting solution for him, but for now, I knew he needed to focus on working and creating besides all the rehabilitation and conditioning he was working on.

"Oh, come on now, you know I gotchu, just as you did me when I was sad I was too fat to get any major roles." I shrugged.

"If you don't stop that nonsense. You were never fat, and if you were, fat dancers are equally talented as average-sized ones."

"Look at you with all the politically correct verbiage, ok!" I exclaimed, so glad for Devon's interruption. I needed a break from worrying about my love life. *Love life?*

"So, I figured you could observe tonight. We have a few classes. I do ballet in this room," I pointed to Room A, "and Ms. Torres here does Jazz and hip-hop in Room B."

"Alright, I look forward to that."

My cell phone vibrated in my leggings pocket, and I checked while Devon chopped it up with Mila and Sal kept acting like she had no home training.

Master Q: Do I need to kick Sir X out of the club?

What in the world? Why did Master Q have to go all medieval on my ass?

Aisha: What? No of course not! Look, I just can't

continue doing sessions with him, but he's solid. He'll do great with another sub.

Master Q: You're gonna have to do better than that.

I should have known when I freaked out and burst into Master Q's office asking him to cancel all my other sessions with Sir X that this would happen. Now it was going to become a bigger deal than it needed to be...

Aisha: I know him.

Master Q: And? This is not the first time you've scened with someone you know behind a mask.

Aisha: Yeah, but with him it's different, it's...complicated.

Master Q: I see... Well, I was asked to deliver the following message: We need to talk. And he's been checking in with me for messages for the past three days. Whatever this is, if you're alright and don't need me to intervene, then I'mma ask you to handle your business.

I let out all the air in my lungs, annoyed and excited at the message. He'd been trying to reach me, and I was glad he was. I wondered why Knox didn't just call the studio, but at the same time, I was grateful he didn't. It allowed me to keep things separate in my mind.

Aisha: I'll handle it Master Q

Master Q: Good girl.

Oh, Master Q, he can't turn that shit off.

The hour passed in companionable banter, and Sal even thawed out enough to join in the conversation with Devon. By the time class was about to start, I felt much better than the past couple of days.

Until the chime sounded, and in strolled Knox Davenport with his daughter. I'd forgotten he'd asked for her to do the Tuesday class instead of Thursday this week.

His eyes connected with mine right away, and it was as if there was no one else in the room with us. I felt his gaze from the top of my curls to the bottom of my pinky toes, and the warmth on my cheeks told me I was telegraphing my reaction to the whole room.

"Ms. Mac! How are you?" The little girl cannonballed into me, jolting me out of the trance. She gave me a tight squeeze that I returned with equal excitement.

"I'm good, Trin. How was your weekend?"

"Well..." She lowered her voice and peered at her dad, who was still grilling me with his attention, then back at me. She beckoned me to get to her level, to which I complied, curious as to what she didn't want to say out loud as she cupped her hand around my ear.

"My daddy was in a bad mood. He was nice to me, but I could tell he was *anchious,* and he told my uncle you were driving him up the wall," she whispered in my ear. Oh no, I hadn't meant to upset him. I didn't think he cared that much. My heart tripped at the thought of his weekend being ruined by what happened between us.

"Oh no, honey, I'm sorry to hear that," I said to Trin as my insides twisted in concern. I made eye contact with Knox again, and he raised an eyebrow, telling me everything Trin had said was right.

"It's alright. I made him popcorn because he loves popcorn, and we had movie night on Sunday, and that cheered him up." Trin puffed her chest proudly.

"Good job, you are such a wonderful daughter." I high-fived her and straightened up again, still feeling bruises inside from the news she'd imparted. My gaze connected with Knox's, and I felt his aura, his challenge, his need to talk. I shook my head and turned slightly away from his intensity. Right now, I couldn't handle it.

After clearing my throat, I addressed the parents in the waiting area.

"Before we begin our classes, I wanted to introduce everyone to Devon Reid, our newest addition to MBDS! He will teach Adult Ballet as well as all our advanced classes past the intermediate level. We are also opening a pre-professional level class that will be a collaboration between us both. Once your little dancers continue to mature, we will split the pointe classes between us. He'll be observing today's ballet class, so dancers, please give Mr. Reid a warm welcome!" I turned to Devon, who stood quietly as everyone clapped. My happiness at having him here stretched my heart the same way my smile stretched my cheeks. I watched him receive the warm welcome he so well deserved. When he flushed in embarrassment, I approached him and pulled him into my arms.

"You're good," I whispered in his ear, then detached myself from him, still cheesing.

"Alright, dancers, you know the drill!" I slipped my hand into Devon's and squeezed it, pulling him along into Room A.

THE CLASS WAS FANTASTIC; having Devon there to give additional support and confidence to the dancers was very satisfying to see. We were fine-tuning the true posture for each position—something the dancers knew, but many had been doing sloppily since they were three years old. Now that they were older, I wanted to ensure they understood the expectations.

"Fifth position en avant of the arms." All the dancers placed their legs in the expected crossed position with their feet facing different directions, their arms gently extended in a semi-circle in front of them.

"Fifth position en haut of the arms." They all raised their arms above their heads in a semi-circle. Devon walked around correcting the feet of some dancers, the arms of another, or just overall posture. Soon we were wrapping up, the class a complete success with Devon's support.

"Thank you, dancers! Please ensure you continue to practice at home." I smiled at all my students and ushered them out of the room.

"You did great!" I mouthed to Devon as he walked out with me and the dancers.

The parents all started departing with their children, but I felt a looming sensation that had me on edge.

"Ms. Mac." Knox's dry tone made me stand in attention. I had a love-hate relationship with the way I instinctively reacted to him.

"Yes, Mr. Davenport?" I nodded at him regally, going into my Ms. Mac persona where I'd be best protected.

"Can I speak with you in private?" he asked, and my heart picked up an unsustainable beat. I wasn't ready to talk to him. I knew if I was in a room alone with him, I might forget all my reasons why this wasn't a good idea.

"Oh, unfortunately, I have to brief Mr. Reid, and then we have the next class, but we can certainly make an appointment..." I trailed off when Knox's nostrils flared. *Oh my.* He took several breaths until he could speak again.

"A'ight. I'll make an appointment...even though I'm a paying customer."

The butthole. Did he really intend to throw my sex work in my face in front of everyone?

"Not anymore." I shook my head, a flush starting in the pit of my belly and traveling fast up my body. Then Trinity pulled Knox's hand. An expression of what looked like regret flashed across his face, but then he allowed Trin all his attention.

"Don't make Ms. Mac mad, Daddy. I don't want her to kick me out."

Fudge, I knew better. This was why. This was why it made little sense for us to pursue anything outside of the scenes we'd enjoyed together.

"I don't think…ok, Miss Smart, I won't," he said with a gentleness that squeezed my chest. I was really going through so many emotions because of this man. I didn't need all these extra feelings in my life.

"Ms. Mac, my apologies. I didn't mean to imply…" He ran his hand over his beard and mustache.

"Please, an appointment," I stopped him, angry at myself for letting this happen here.

He gave me a warning glance mixed with a touch of what I interpreted as contrition, then gave Trin his hand and walked out of the studio. I didn't miss the angry look he directed at Devon on his way out.

Ugh. There were no words for the mess I'd walked into all by myself.

Sixteen

Knox

Chantal called me to ask for an additional weekend, and all the conflicting thoughts about having her around Trin raced through my mind. That all my thoughts besides that were saturated with everything Ms. Mac didn't help at all.

I couldn't think straight. I wanted to follow my instincts and not allow for extra days.

Stephen felt I was too demanding and should give Chantal a chance, but Stephen had a soft spot for my ex-wife. My entire family did, but they hadn't lived with Chantal's constant unreliability, mood swings, and irresponsible, volatile behavior.

"So, what you gonna say? She's texted you twice since I've been in your office."

"I know, but she's gonna have to wait," I said, pushing Chantal's request to the side. "I want to talk to you about something else."

"Shoot." Stephen crossed his extended legs and

propped them up on the edge of my desk. I stared at him for a few seconds, and when he continued to ignore my stare, I slapped his feet off my desk.

"I've been going to Dominant classes."

'Oh, that freaky shit you like." Stephen pushed back on the chair again but avoided propping his feet up.

"Sure, whatever, but well, the woman that was training me, it's Ms. Mac."

"Ohh shiiiddd."

"Yep. And she walked out of our last session and ended the classes early. I'm...fuck, I want more time with her, and I'm pissed she doesn't. And on top of it all, she has a new teacher, and I think she might have a thing with him."

"Are you acting like a gorilla in the studio now?" Stephen asked, coming back from the relaxed pose he'd been in and sitting up straight. "Because I can tell you she ain't gonna like that."

I grumbled.

"So, you already tried to piss around her."

"I didn't. I just asked her to speak in private, then goaded her to accept even though she was clear she didn't have time."

Stephen just stared at me.

"Fuck, I know, I know I have to respect her boundaries."

"Yes, man, if she's telling you to back off..."

"That's the thing, she didn't tell me to back off. She just canceled our next sessions, but we still have a relationship as parent/teacher, and I'm her main sponsor for the show."

"Alright then, what do you want to do?" Stephen asked.

"You know the answer to that." I lifted an eyebrow, and he laughed.

"You gotta give her space."

"Do I, though? She said to make an appointment."

Stephen steepled his fingers under his chin and propped his elbows on the desk, then annoyed the shit out of me with his stare.

"Fine, she was just saving face, but I already asked for the appointment."

"Of course you fucking did."

"And she said yes, so clearly..."

"Clearly you have her in an uncomfortable situation. She is your child's teacher, and she accepted your sponsorship."

Fuck, Stephen was right: all of that fucked with our power dynamic. I had a huge weakness regarding Ms. Mac—she made me forget everything but the fact that I wanted more from her. I needed to make it clear to her that I expected nothing in return. Expected nothing, but I sure hoped I could have more time with her.

"A'ight, you have a point."

"Of course I do. Just remember to pace yourself, a'ight?"

I didn't want to pace myself. I wanted to wade deep into the waters of Ms. Aisha McKinney.

AISHA WAS TESTING ALL my buttons. She had accepted the appointment invitation just to keep me waiting an extra forty minutes while she finished a staff meeting she claimed was running longer than expected. This was her way of reminding me that outside of Q's Space, she was the owner of her time. I got the message, but it didn't mean I had to fucking like it. The woman really knew how to get under my skin, and all I wanted to do was get her under, over, and all around my dick.

I sat in the waiting area pretending to work on my

laptop, but what I really was doing was eavesdropping like a mofo'. I could hear sporadic laughter and music turning on and off, Aisha's lyrical voice and Mila's higher-pitched tones interspersed with the baritone of that new teacher and the deeper voice of her other friend.

They sure had a lot to fucking talk about. I stood up to stretch my legs and paced up and down the waiting area until finally, the door swung open, and a laughing Aisha sauntered out, looking back at the new teacher, whatever his name was. The man wasn't even trying to pretend he wasn't checking her out.

I had no claim on her, but that wasn't about to stop me.

"Aisha." I put some bass in my voice.

I grinned in triumph when her spine went through a subtle transformation, her shoulders pushed back, her eyes softening as I triggered her submissive side. I'd used the same tone of voice I employed in all our scenes, and I could see how it affected her.

"Mr. Davenport." She nodded.

"Knox," I corrected, widening my stance. Heat rolled through me as her eyes traveled from my face down to my Ferragamos. *She better stop playing with me, staring at me like I'm a snack.*

"Knox," she purred. The new teacher took in the situation, not one expression escaping his face. Was I imagining what I saw earlier? The truth was I didn't care. I wanted alone time with Aisha, and he impeded that.

"That's our cue to leave. Come, Devon, let us show you our hangout spot! It's the best bar in the area," Mila said, pulling homeboy along with her. My esteem for Mila moved up a few good notches. Behind them, Sal strolled along, not even acknowledging me, completely unbothered by the tension in the room right now. I'm not gonna lie, I appreciated her energy as well.

"You good, Aisha, or do you want us to wait?" the man asked in a lilting accent, probably from the islands. I respected that he was checking in with Aisha, but she was fine with me. More than good.

"Aisha, what would you like to do?" I asked her, waiting for her answer.

"D, it's good. I'll meet y'all at the bar, alright?" She smiled at Devon, then turned her big, beautiful eyes on me. The shine in them told me she liked the slight possessiveness I was putting out, and that made me dial it up for her.

"We might not be meeting y'all at the bar. She'll text you if she's not gonna make it."

"Okayyy," Mila whispered from the entrance.

"I know, right?" Sal said loudly, and Aisha giggled.

"Ok, clearly, these two have some history, so I'll take a step back, but my man... You make sure you treat my sister right, ok?" Devon squared up in front of me, matching my height and energy.

"I respect that. Trust that I only want the very best for Aisha, for her safety, her well-being and her...mind. So, I don't plan to test your devotion to her," I said to Devon, but I trained my gaze on her. I said that shit with my chest because I wanted her to know she was safe with me.

Devon nodded thoughtfully, then thrust a hand toward me.

"Don't make me regret this. I know people."

"Okayyy," Mila whispered again.

"Girl, get a grip on yourself," Sal admonished.

"But this is hot," Mila loudly whispered back.

After the tense conversation, they filed out of the studio, and Aisha approached the door, locking it behind them.

She turned, pushing her back against the door, her hands hidden behind her.

"Why did you take off your mask?" she accused, eyes scrunching in the corners as she grilled me with her stare. She took me aback—where was the soft Baby Doll who had demurely melted just at the tone of my voice?

"I took it off because I was tired of pretending."

She huffed and stomped her way into Room A, and I followed behind. She approached the camera system that broadcasted the classes and shut the system off.

Four armchairs sat in the middle of the room in a circle. She pushed one away from the bunch and sat on it, crossing her legs, leggings molding her thick thighs and muscular calves as she shifted on the chair.

I took my time sitting on one of the chairs opposite her, my eyes never leaving her expressive face. I admired her while her eyes spit fire at me. She had these sumptuous lines to her, thicker than your average dancer but fit and strong in the areas she needed for her art. Everything else showed off in abundance. Strong, lean arms versus overflowing breasts. Defined neck versus plump cheeks. Minimal belly for all the hips, thighs, and ass you could ask for. I let myself feast in a way I usually couldn't indulge when accompanied by Trin or the other parents.

"Are you going to just thirst?" she asked.

"No, I plan to top you soon, but first, we talk."

"There will be no more topping, thanks to you. You couldn't just pretend we didn't know each other? When did you realize it was me?"

"The first night."

Aisha's perplexed mirth kept her quiet for a few seconds as she reassessed all our interactions based on the news. That was ok—I could tell she hadn't immediately put two and two together, but by the second time... I wondered.

"I had strong suspicions before our third session."

"I thought so but wasn't a hundred," I said, attempting to keep the intensity low for now.

"I wasn't sure either, but...I felt it, and the way we interacted with each other outside of the scenes changed."

"Because we gave each other the opportunity to see who we were outside of the antagonistic roles we'd grown accustomed to." I shrugged, but that's not how I was feeling inside. This conversation... I couldn't fuck it up. I craved her buy-in; I wanted to earn her submission, her regard.

"This is all types of messy, which is why we should have kept pretending. You fucked it up, taking off the mask. You made me acknowledge reality." She crossed her arms and gave me the cutest pout. I'd work overtime on getting her to pout like that again; her lowkey brattiness was sexy.

"If we both knew, then it was already messy. If anything, I untangled it a little." I let the words settle, and the room grew quiet as she thought things through. I'd wanted to be right about her not wanting space from me, but now a bolt of unease made my stomach cramp in concern.

"Listen, I'm not planning to push up on you." That was exactly what I'd planned to do, but a man can change his mind.

"Really?" she challenged, pursing her lips. The last time I hyper-focused on those lips, they had been claret smeared around my dick. Then she'd sucked my soul out with her kiss.

"Are you looking to get kissed?" I asked, zeroed in on her mouth, unable to stop myself. I left the armchair and prowled to her. Her breath hitched when I stood in front of her, her eyes full of uncertainty, lust, curiosity, and what I wanted to believe was tenderness.

"No... Sir."

At first, I thought I heard wrong. I thought I was hallucinating, willing her to let this thing between us continue, but then she pushed out of her armchair and got herself into first position. A rush of noise overwhelmed me as all the blood inside of me increased its journey to areas below, my brain floating in amazement and gratitude as I took in Aisha in her black leggings and black crop top, no mask on her face, staring up at me.

"Are you sure, Baby Doll?" I croaked and had to clear my throat. She'd unmanned me with this gesture. I came prepared to have to fight to convince her, and here she was, honoring me again.

"Let's just focus on today, Sir," she said and awaited my command.

I didn't let that answer carve itself inside of me. I couldn't let the disappointment spread and ruin this moment.

"What's your favorite dance move, Baby Doll?" I asked instead.

"I... I love pliés. I love performing them, I love teaching them, I love being en pointe and doing grand pliés...they are basic but essential."

"Show me," I commanded, and before I uttered the last word, she rose from the floor in perfect fluidity.

"Where do you want me to show you, Sir?"

"Over there." I pointed at the bar by the mirror.

She got on her tiptoes and glided her way toward the wall. I admired her dexterity and elegant strength as she held the bar with one hand, lifted the other out, then gracefully dropped.

That this was her favorite...I was about to put the knowledge to the test.

"That's beautiful, baby girl, but I want to see you do that without those leggings on."

She stared at me for a minute, then smiled and took no time divesting herself of her bottoms.

Just a lacy black thong and cheeks for days.

"This what you wanted...Sir?" She dropped again, and this time, she made her ass jiggle, each cheek moving separately to music only in her head.

I palmed my dick over my slacks, trying to create space where there was none. It took that little with her. I might as well be fifteen again.

"Is that ballet?"

"It is when I do it for you." She dazzled me with her smile and rose again.

"Can you do that with your legs spread apart?" I asked, unbuttoning my cuffs and pulling my shirt out of my slacks. The shirt came off, then as I pulled at the white tee I had underneath, Aisha gasped.

"You have tattoos!"

"Why are you so surprised?"

"Well, maybe I shouldn't answer that. I don't want to be punished."

"You got jokes, Baby Doll. You think holding back won't get you punished?"

"Actually, I changed my mind. Maybe I need punishment." She grinned mischievously, and I had to taste that smile.

I grabbed the back of her neck and pulled her to me, our lips locking, so hungry for each other I couldn't breathe properly. She tasted like fresh raindrops on my tongue, and I wanted to lap her all up.

"Turn around," I ordered, and she presented that plump ass to me, which I tapped twice before I grabbed her by the hips and pulled her into me. She got me there so fast, I wanted her to feel my erection, how she got me there just by being herself. My dick molded into her pillow-like ass, and I grabbed a handful of her over her crop top as she rested her head back on my shoulder.

"You see what you do to me? This isn't just carnal, this is us recognizing we're kindred spirits and fighting that nature, same as we fight for our place in the world every day. I should have known when I met you... I should have known." I spoke into her ear, then flicked my tongue around the ridge of her auricle, making her grind her ass on me.

"Are you wet for me, Baby Doll?" I asked as I continued my journey down her neck, nibbling along the way. My hands hadn't known pleasure like this before. Her breasts were soft and moldable, and her nipples nestled in the palms of my hands, nudging through her shirt.

"Yes, Sir."

"Show me," I coaxed her, and she didn't disappoint. She stuck her hand in her thong and came up with a string of clear wetness from her pussy. Her fingers glistened in the mirror.

"Give me a taste."

She obediently guided her fingers to my waiting tongue, and I sucked on them. If her mouth tasted like drops of fresh rain, her fingers were what I imagined goddess tears would taste like.

I let go, surprising her as I knelt on the floor, getting eye level with that ass of hers, which I gave a chaste kiss on my way to fully lying down.

"What are you doing...Sir?"

"You're about to plié on me."

Seventeen

Aisha

Did he just say I'm about to plié on him? Is this real life?

My brain was in a fog full of serotonin as this man's presence overwhelmed all my senses.

The revelations of today, of the fact he'd always known it was me, that he wanted more, were all a lot for me to process. The list of reasons I shouldn't go down this path blared in the back of my mind, but the lust and endorphins driving me made it all seem like future Aisha's problem because present Aisha? Present Aisha was about to plié the fudge out of this man.

"Stand, placing my face between your feet."

Every time he gave me a command, butterflies tried to escape my belly. I had felt that reaction from day one, which was why I'd tried to keep him at arm's length. Here was a Dom who could mess me up emotionally yet again.

I took a second to admire how delectable he looked lying down on my polished wood floor, arms behind his bald head, wearing his black slacks, leather belt, shoes, and nothing else.

An intricate tattoo covered his entire right pectoral, a bull blowing out smoke in the center of the design, and on the other side of his chest, he had a small delicate swirl with a date inscribed in the middle. I wanted to trace my finger over the designs but knew I needed to comply. He was so *solid* with his muscular chest and thick torso, with a slight gut that made this whole view even sexier. I couldn't wait to cuddle up next to him. *Wait, already thinking of cuddling up?*

"Take your time, Baby Doll, I love when you look at me like that," he said in a lower tone, making me snap back to where his lush lips framed his smirk. He must have trimmed his beard because it was immaculate, but then again, when wasn't it? And his eyes... Shit, here I was, getting lost in him again.

Another commotion of butterflies went off as I placed myself in second position around his face. He moved his arms away to give me space, my feet perfectly turned next to his head.

"Ok then, I want you to give me ten of those pretty pliés of yours. But take your time, no rushing."

My chest stuttered as my muscle memory kicked in, performing the grand plié I'd shown him earlier with the same familiarity as getting dressed in the morning. But when I made it all the way down, that familiarity came to a crashing end when Sir dragged my thong away from my wet pussy and replaced it with his tongue.

I short-circuited as he swirled it all around my labia, then flicked the clit as if greeting an old pal.

"That's one," he rumbled against me.

How did he expect me to do this nine more times? I just wanted to park myself on his face and let him feast.

"Now, Baby Doll," he said with that tone that made me want to bend over and let him take me however he wanted.

I rose and immediately went back down, a little less finesse on this second one because now I knew what came at the end. He chuckled at my speed, and that was also a sweet reward.

This time, he enveloped my whole vulva in his mouth and made out with my pussy. The jolt of pure pleasure he detonated made my thigh muscles falter, and I almost placed my entire weight on him.

With one last suck of my clitoris, he said, "That's two."

Three to six were very indecent, and I could only hold onto the barre as this man showed me he knew how to turn me into his happy little ho. The sounds he was making as he slurped and dined on my pussy filled the room. My skin was hot, the AC doing nothing to cool down the faint sheen of sweat I'd built as I worked my way up and down.

"That's six. Let's change things up a bit," he said, beard glistening with my juices and his eyes at half-mast. The air of command and happiness emanating from him made me want to praise him.

"This is sooo good, Sir, you're such a good Dom," I purred.

His pecs rose and caught mid-breath, and suddenly, he was moving fast. Before I knew it, he'd pushed his slacks down and pulled himself up, making me shift back so that my second position now surrounded his upper legs.

And when I peered down…

I had to grip the barre, thanking all the stars it was sturdy because all I wanted to do was collapse on that dick.

A work of art, darker than his mahogany skin, with veins proving my words had influenced him, and the prettiest head I'd ever seen, perfect in its mushroom shape. The circumference promised to make me work for it, and the length... I probably didn't even need to grand plié to get to that dick.

I wanted to create a whole choreography in honor of Knox's penis.

"Seven, Baby Doll," he said, arms braced on each side of him, holding his upper body up, all flexed muscle and that glint in his eyes. He was on demon time, I could tell. That praise really worked wonders, and I was about to reap the rewards.

I took my time with this one. When I extended my right arm in a second position, I felt my pussy caress his head. I stared at Knox. He wasn't smirking now. There was an intensity to his gaze that made me wary, made me wonder if I could really keep this just about our kink.

"You know what to do," he whispered, and I complied because when my Sir gave me a command, I was a good baby doll.

I let gravity help me down, but I felt the stretch as soon as I let the head pop into my vagina.

I groaned as my juices lubricated the path down, down, down his dick.

"Fuck, Baby Doll, you're squeezing me so—fuck!" he said, still holding himself up.

"Oh..." I let out as I adjusted to him inside me, the delicious stretch making me want to bounce on him.

"That's...seven." His strained voice told me he wasn't gonna be able to keep this up for long.

I hated to stand up again, but I did, his head producing a squelch as it left my swollen walls.

"Don't you make me wait," he warned, and I trembled at

the intensity in his deep brown eyes. I kept watching him as I sank down again, and we both sighed together when our pelvises met.

I gave him a few squeezes that had him cursing low, then everything became a whirl of color, that cologne I loved filling my nose as he manhandled me until he got me on my back, legs next to my face.

God, thank you for this thick man that makes me feel like a feather and folds me like I'm fresh laundry.

With a hand next to my face and the other on my hip, Knox sank all the way inside me. The angle was so deep, I now understood when the girlies said it felt like he was touching your cervix. I mean, he wasn't *that* long, and I wouldn't want anything that lengthy around me, but I got it.

In this position, he was in charge, and he pistoned his way in and out of me, displaying his dexterity. I just held onto my legs and prayed I'd be able to teach tomorrow as he pounded into me, his balls slapping, keeping the beat of his grueling tempo.

"Oh, Sir, please, please..." I begged him, not knowing if I wanted him to slow down or speed up. Tremors erupted all over my body, and my walls were having their own party down there, stretched to their limit. My legs shook, my arms trembled, my chest thumped, and I kept begging. "Please, please. Please!"

"Baby Doll, am I not pleasing you?" he growled.

"Yes, yes!"

"So take this dick like you were made for me."

I felt my legs falter, and my pussy took over, pulsing and painting his dick with my desire.

"That's my precious slut, taking my dick like a champ," he grunted, focused on drilling me into submission.

It worked.

The pressure built around me, all my muscles contracting one last time, then I released. Light flickered in the back of my eyes as I let go of all my worries and surrendered to my orgasm and the delicious way Knox fucked me through it. He kept going with a few more thrusts, then froze and sighed as his warmth filled me up with generous spurts. I'd probably feel him dripping from me for the rest of the night.

It was worth it.

"I don't have chocolate milk here for you," he whispered into my hair as we sat flush against each other, our backs to the mirror wall. I still had my thong to one side, and his dick seemed to miss the message that he'd orgasmed, still slightly chubby after all our activities.

"That's alright. We're doing skin-to-skin, and that helps me a lot." I burrowed into him, and he gathered me closer, draping an arm around my shoulders.

Thank God Master Q had the presence of mind to have us all tested regularly at the club, and on top of that, Knox and I had discussed contraception in our initial paperwork, so he knew about my Mirena. We hadn't even thought about condoms.

"So, we're doing this." That was a statement; no lack of conviction for Mr. Davenport.

"I... I don't know. This was a moment of unrestrained passion, I..." All the doubts from before were threatening to creep up, and I knew his proximity wasn't helping. I needed to think this through with a calm brain.

"Aisha," he warned.

"Knox, I need to figure it out. This has to work for both

of us, and whatever we negotiated was just for learning. We would have to speak all over again, and you're a parent here, and I don't mix business with—"

"You're overthinking things. We have a session this Friday. I'll be there waiting; we can renegotiate then. But just in case you work yourself up in the next couple of days, just know that I want this with you. I want you as my sub outside our arrangement, and I want to explore if we could be...more."

Those butterflies I felt earlier? They just went haywire.

"Ok, listen, I hear you. I really do. I just...give me time to figure out how this looks moving forward. I mean, I don't want the other parents to think I have preferential treatment for you and Trin, and I need to make sure I'm not walking around simping for you and..."

"Again, you're overthinking things. It's amazing to me because I thought you were impulsive before..." He kissed the top of my head and stood up, bringing me up with him. He tucked himself back into his slacks, then gently fixed my thong. He picked up all the clothes around us and offered me mine.

Once we were both dressed again, we faced each other, and for a second, I wished we were going home together.

"I'll walk you to your car and let you overthink whatever you need to overthink, but I'll be waiting for you on Friday."

"I can't promise—"

He silenced me with a kiss that started gently, then when I swiped my tongue against his, it intensified until he was sucking my tongue into his mouth, and my knees gave out on me.

"Friday."

Eighteen

Aisha

Two days and I had run myself ragged thinking of Knox and his proposition of me being his sub for real and maybe more. That *more* was messing with my head, wondering how he'd gone from being my antagonist to this.

He was never my enemy—giving him that energy would have elevated him to more than he deserved—but he annoyed me a lot. And here we were, his scenes, his sex, his voice, his everything making me wonder if I could date a Dom again and not lose myself in the process.

When I was with James, I mirrored all my likes to what he liked. I craved his attention in and out of our scenes, and now I could see how he took advantage of it, never fully giving in return.

"Hi, girl, thanks for bringing me dinner as always. I don't know what I would do without you... Earth to Aisha!" Mila snapped at me. She stood by the frame of the office door with a smirk on her face while I stared at my computer.

"You know who I saw again?" she asked.

"No. Who?"

"Your girl Roxane, remember your arch-nemesis?" She propped herself on my desk and looked down at me.

"Girl, you know I had no beef with her!" I laughed.

"You might not have, but she certainly did. Hated that Ms. Brown saw all that talent in you. Well, I bumped into her in the beauty supply store when I was with my sister. She was talking to Ms. Bonita, but when she saw me, she rolled her eyes at me, then left. I didn't know she was back in town."

"Oh yeah, I forgot to tell you I saw her in the store the other day." I nodded, finalizing some of my notes for the show. Next, I would look at the medical bills for the month and pay what I could.

"Ugh, I know you never had ill feelings for her, but she never gave me good vibes. And even now, I saw her again, mala vibra. Hopefully, she doesn't stay too long and finds a ballet company outside of here."

"Nah, I think she is staying with the Miami Ballet."

"Well, I'll still wish. Oye, and you...have forgotten all about me?" She nudged my shoulder.

"I know...I know. Maybe that's what I need to zap out of all my worries. You and me tonight, what do you say?" I ghosted a fingertip up her thick brown thigh until I met her short dance shorts, then skirted the hem until my finger slipped in. She spread her legs to give me more access, the smirk transforming into a zoned-out smile. I realized not too long after finding Master Q and his club that I was a bit of a switch, but my dominant tendencies only flared up with women. And my dominant tendencies flared up a lot with Mila when we played.

"Have you been taking care of my pretty friend while

I've been occupied?" I pulled my finger out and cupped her between the legs.

"I have. You know me, I don't wait for nobody," she said and ground herself against my hand.

I had a flash of us together with Sir X dominating us both, and I soaked my panties at the thought. Ugh. Even when I was trying not to think of him and get it on with someone else, he took over things in my mind. I knew Mila would love to join us—she was the rare girl that loved being a unicorn. I loved it too, once upon a time...but now I stayed away from those dynamics, so how fair would it be for me to ask her for that? But oh, I was tempted...oh so tempted.

"Listen, how about you come..."

The chime on the front door went off. We had finished classes twenty minutes ago, so we weren't expecting anyone else. I should have been on my way home to get showered and ready to meet Knox, but I'd decided I needed more time. I needed clarity and space, and I hadn't had that these past two days. He wouldn't like it, but he'd have to live with it.

"Oh, great, just when things were getting good," Mila grumbled and jumped off the desk.

I shared her frustration because I'd been about to ask her if she wanted to join me with Knox... Maybe if I kept things strictly sexual with him, it would work. Maybe I'd still ask her.

"Oh, here we go..." Mila muttered, and I looked up to find my dad sitting on one of the folding chairs in the waiting area.

"Hi, Papa..." I said tentatively, a rush of unease taking over everything else. I hoped he'd come just to say hello, to check on me...

"Mi bella hija..." he said, and my heart plummeted to my

stomach. He always complimented me when he needed something.

"What's up? I was about to close up shop. You needed something?"

"Yeah, I did. I wanted to let you know I found a new job at a shop in Fort Lauderdale."

I breathed easier at that news. I'd been worried sick about him not having a job and just using all his time to drink. This was way better news than I expected; maybe this job would be the one to get him on the right path.

"That's what's up!" I smiled at him and rushed to give him a hug. He smelled of cigars and his Drakkar Noir, no alcohol. My spirits lifted even more.

"Yeah, baby. Listen, I know I came last time a little intoxicated, asking for stuff, but you know I have my relapses."

Mila snorted behind me. My shoulders tensed.

"Mila, please, that's not nice," I chastised her.

"Girl, please tell me you're not falling for this," she scoffed, and I bristled.

Mila had some nerve, getting all upset about my dad when she had two perfect parents that loved her. My grandparents were everything to me, but they were getting older, and I was an only child, and she didn't get it. She just didn't get it.

"This girl, she never likes me, always treating me bad when I come visit you," dad lamented, and I reached out to him.

"Nah, she doesn't mean it like that, she just..."

"Yeah, you're right, I don't mean it. I just remembered I have an appointment at my other job I completely forgot. Sorry, girly, catch you another time?" Mila's face had gone blank, her nonconfrontational mask firmly on. I wanted to reach out to her. I knew she meant well, but...I just was stretched thin right now. Who knew when my dad would be back around? I hoped I could make peace and make up with her tomorrow.

"Are you sure? I was about to ask you if you..."

"I know what you were gonna ask, but it's alright; we can chat about that another day." She gave me a polite smile, picked her dance bag up from the reception desk, and walked out of the studio.

"You need better friends," my dad said.

"Papa, I have the best friends anyone could ask for."

"They should be supportive of you and what you want. They've always been critical of me, making slick remarks. I don't appreciate that." I knew to be wary when he arrived, but I didn't know it would be about this.

"Papa, listen, why did you stop by? Because I'm about to close, and you know you're not welcome at my grandparents."

"Esos! Don't get me started with those two, they think they are better than me, fuc—"

"Let me stop you right there. They did what you and mom didn't do, so please don't speak ill of them." My chest contracted at all the nastiness coming out of my dad right now. Things could never be straightforward with him.

"Listen, I didn't come here for you to give me a lecture. I just wanted you to know I have a new job. I mean, it pays less than the one before, so I'm still struggling..." *Here it comes...* "But I can't talk to you when you get on your fart above ass attitude. I'll see you around." He abruptly stood up, and I wanted to convince him to stay and talk to me, tell me about his new job, but I knew it was futile.

"Ok, Papa," I sighed.

"Later." He breezed out of the studio, leaving me behind, as he always did.

Mila had been right to walk away. I never learned.

———

"I'M ON MY WAY," was all I said to Knox on the phone. I was thirty minutes late, but better late than never. I'd changed my mind, and I wasn't willing to inspect why. I just wanted release.

I sauntered into the Gold Room and found him sitting on one of the throne chairs, thick chest bare, black slacks attempting to contain his thick ass thighs, no shoes, drinking a glass of something amber.

"Aisha," he drawled.

Oh, he was pissed. Great. I needed him mad. I wanted a night to clear my mind. If he was half the Dom he claimed to be, he would get me there.

"Hello... Sir," I responded and opened my trench coat to reveal a see-through black sheath that grazed the top of my thighs. I'd chosen a black thong and a contraption that was just the frame of a bra holding my tits up and nothing else, no fabric on the cups.

Knox's gaze shuttered when he saw my outfit.

"Second position," he practically snarled. He hadn't gotten mad at me in any scene, but this angry Knox I knew well. I gracefully got on my knees, then arched my back until my face was on the floor and my ass was up.

"No, facing away from me," he corrected, and I got on all fours and winked at him, then turned around and showed him what he wanted to see. My pussy was already wet when I walked in as I imagined what he would do to me because I was late.

"Fuck," he said when he saw my bare pussy. I'd taken the time to shave right before coming, so it was freshly done, and the thong I wore was crotchless. I did a couple of Kegels and heard his deep intake of breath.

"You think I don't know you weren't planning to come. Were you planning to come?" he continued once he'd cleared his throat.

"No," I answered truthfully.

"What made you change your mind?"

"Are we here to chitchat, or are we here for you to dominate me?" I sassed.

"Oh, so today you got lip. Is this the real Aisha? A brat?"

"All this talking won't help you find out," I said while my face rested on the floor.

A rustle behind me told me he'd stood up. My muscles tensed, and I held my breath waiting for what he'd do to punish me.

A slow caress tickled my ass cheek, building up a shiver, then whatever he held stroked the other side, ending in between.

Holding my position, I shut my eyes, pretending to be unaffected. I wanted some impact or rough play, not gentleness.

"Oh, so you're just doing rookie stuff right now, alright," I taunted and heard him chuckle.

"Oh, Baby Doll, you don't want me on you right now. Not with how my temper keeps rising, but keep going, and you'll find out. So, what changed your mind?" he asked again, an edge to his question.

"I've never had such a chatty Dom. Would you like to sit in the corner and braid my hair next?"

I braced myself as I heard leather hit against what I thought were his slacks. Air left my lungs as I expected the hit, but it didn't come. Instead, he ran the leather strap from the top of my shoulders down to my buttocks in a sensuous trajectory that made my clit vibrate, wishing I could touch myself right now.

The tension in my shoulders and back made it hard to adapt to the soft touch. I had been expecting pain. I needed it; I wasn't a masochist, but right now, I craved the stimulation.

"Maybe this is why you wanted an inexperienced sub, so they couldn't..."

A shadow loomed over me, his cologne surrounded me, and his hot flesh met my cool back as he pressed himself against me. The unexpected feel of his finger sliding into my wet channel made my walls squeeze in greeting.

"What changed your mind?"

I stayed quiet; he'd eventually get the message.

He played around with his finger, idly sliding in and out, tormenting me with his soft touch. Dragging our lust out with his ministrations.

"You think you're driving here, but you aren't, so I'mma let you keep talking nonsense," he said into my ear, and a tremor betrayed me, giving him a glimpse of how much he was affecting me.

His other hand slid underneath me and circled my rapidly swelling clit, gathering moisture and spreading it all around my pussy. He played with me, softly tapping my clit while his fingers went in and out of me, enhancing the squelching sounds through the room.

A kiss pressed on the nape of my neck, then his tongue charted a path down the middle of my back, all the way down until...

"What changed your mind?"

"I don't know what you are talking about." I could barely get the words out.

Wetness seeped between my cheeks, his hands now holding me open for him. Before I could process what was happening, the flat of his tongue swiped my pucker, making my pussy flood with moisture.

"Aaah..." I pushed back, eager to get him to swipe his tongue over my butthole again, but he gave me a gentle tap on one cheek.

"Tell me what changed your mind," he commanded while he pushed himself inside of me, my pussy throbbing around his length. I don't know when or how, but he'd pulled his dick out without me realizing. He kept a torturously slow pace, the stretch delicious, the gentleness unbearable as he hit my g-spot with each thrust.

"Faster!" I pleaded.

"No, you're gonna be a good doll and take this dick the way I give it to you," he whispered.

At some point, my shoulders relaxed, my stomach unclenched, and I stopped anticipating his next move. Somehow, my mood shifted, and I only focused on Knox and his gentle touch and voice. Somewhere, I had left my angst behind to be dealt with another day, and I let desire take over my body.

With tenderness Knox unraveled me, and with gentleness, he accomplished what I had sought without knowing.

"Give it to me, Baby Doll, stop fighting me," he said, and the stimulation of his words and dick broke the dam. Tears ran down my cheeks without effort as I gasped in pleasure.

"You. You changed my mind. I needed your touch, I needed your support, I needed you," I blurted out, panting as I crested the summit of my want. I sobbed when he dragged his dick all the way out. I pleaded when he swirled it against my entrance, then penetrated me again, all the touches he provided me so tender, so devastating.

"Knox, Knox, KNOX!"

My body listened to his unspoken command, and I let him suspend me in a cloud of understanding and pleasure. I disintegrated in his arms and found myself aware of my surroundings again, being held against his chest as he rocked me through my sobs.

Nineteen

Knox

Aftercare hit different after this scene. Aisha's fragility demanded all my attention, softened all my hardness. Her sobs had subsided, and she lay quietly in my arms.

"Well, that was... Yeah, so short and so effective. Ten out of ten, Sir X." She broke the silence, her voice wobbling at the end.

"Will you tell me what happened?" I asked, controlling my tone. I'd been tempering myself so much around her since I'd opened myself up to the possibility of us. There was something about her approach to life that made me manage my anger in a way I only did when around Trinity. Because of everything in my childhood and then my young adulthood, I'd always had to be aware of my temper, but Aisha made me want to be more than aware, she made me want to better manage it.

I needed to keep this delicate balance and give her space to unburden herself. This wasn't something I knew how to do before...before my marriage crashed and burned in front of my eyes.

"Nothing new, same old stuff. My dad stopped by." She burrowed deeper into my side, her chocolate milk untouched next to us.

"Damn, baby, was he trying to..." I paused, hoping I'd phrased things correctly. "What was he looking for?"

"Basically, he wanted to share he had a new job, but Mila got upset. She felt he was trying to finesse me out of money, and she got mad. Then he got pissed because of her, and it all just blew out of proportion. I swear, nothing I do works for him, I just want him to..."

"Shhh, I hope you know you don't need any approval from that man." I stroked her curls out of her face, her cheeks still damp from her tears. This visit was probably to soften her up, then he'd hit her up again next time with an ask. Her father knew the kind soul she was and clearly played that to his advantage.

"He's my dad, though. He's all I got."

"Is he, though? Don't you live with your grandparents?"

"Yeah, yeah, of course, I mean in the parent department." She laid her head on my lap and kept talking into the quiet room. "You said you knew what it was to love an addict."

A trickle of cold permeated through me after her words. I hated this subject. I wanted to share her burden, but it made mine heavier, ever present in my mind. One thing I loved the most about being a Dom was lifting any weight off of a sub's shoulders, even if just during a scene. But what Aisha demanded of me right now... It was more than I'd been ready to handle.

She made me want to try to talk about it, at least.

"I told you about my pops..."

"Oh, Trin's grandpa?" she asked hopefully, probably thinking of Will. He filled the role of devoted grandpa to a T, so I got why she sounded like that. It gave her hope.

"Nah, not him, that's my stepdad. My pops isn't around. I told him to fuck off years ago." She tensed on my lap, and without much thought, I massaged her shoulder, working out some of the tension there.

Damn, she made everything she did seem effortless, but the knots in her shoulders told a different story. I exhaled and kept on. "Before that, he used to circle around the perimeter of my life, a looming threat. He's a sorry excuse for a father, even without the alcohol, but the alcohol made him reckless and meaner. For the longest time, I did so much to make him love me, make him notice me, but then I realized it was all for nothing. It messed with me for a while. I went to support groups with my moms to learn how to cope. My anger...it all stems from that."

"Oh, Knox," she said, and I didn't know how she had managed to convey so much with two words. Her commiseration, her understanding, her compassion, her empathy, all there to make the next words easier to say.

"And somehow, I clearly had a soft spot for addicts because my ex-wife...Chantal..."

Aisha sat up, turned to face me, and crisscrossed her legs. She was still wearing the outfit she'd walked in with, but now that our lust and need had subsided for the moment, it made her look vulnerable.

"You don't wanna wear your coat?"

"I'm alright, nothing I haven't worn before." She brushed me off and gestured for me to continue. Her warm palm settled on my thigh, and she chased away the cold threatening to take over inside.

"Chantal's story is different. She was a good wife, a good

friend, a wonderful mother. It just... I don't know how I missed it. We linked up in high school, and that's all she wrote. I knew that was my girl, and she claimed me as her man. We went to college, played the field so we were a hundred that we were meant to be. Once we were done with college, neither of us had felt anything stronger than lust for anyone in school. So, I knew she was it for me. Or so I thought."

I studied her face, hoping I wasn't saying too much by being candid with her, but I didn't know how else to explain everything that transpired with Chantal.

"See, her and I never had sex. We fooled around plenty, but she'd decided she wanted to wait till she was married, and I respected her choice. But when we decided to keep things casual during college, I explored. And I realized my Dom tendencies."

"Let me guess...it was a teacher?" she asked.

I peeked at her, wondering how she had guessed that.

"Mostly everyone I know in the kink community got turned by an older mentor. I mean, not always, let me not generalize. But—" She shrugged, interpreting my expression correctly.

"Was it like that for you?"

She nodded, taking her time to answer. "Yeah, but we're not talking about me right now." She squeezed my thigh.

"We're gonna come back to this, you hear? I want to know how Miss Prim and Proper became nasty." I threw my head back at her, and she laughed.

"So, you realized your Dom tendencies..." she encouraged, then took a sip of her chocolate milk.

"Yeah, I realized it with a TA, actually. I was working on some extra credit and—"

Aisha chuckled, and the melodious sound settled inside

of me, bringing a level of comfort I usually couldn't feel when speaking about this part of my life.

"I'm glad I'm amusing you. So yeah, I realized and explored. Once we married, and I explained it to her...she shot me down. She said that didn't work for her, she didn't enjoy taking orders like that. So, I kept it buried. After all, I had married the woman for me, so I could adapt." Aisha's facial expression remained a conduit to her thoughts, and right now, she was letting me see it all. I could sense she didn't agree with that last statement.

"So, we adapted, and we were good, really good. We decided we wanted to try for kids, and it took us a while. After a year of trying. I started to get worried when she surprised me one night with a positive pregnancy test after dinner. Yo... I was beside myself with joy.

"Everything I wanted, my wife, a kid on the way, my business was flourishing. Then she had a rough delivery and lots of pain after an emergency C-section. The pain meds... they helped her." I paused, downing some chocolate milk from Aisha's glass to clear my dry throat.

The warm weight of Aisha's hand on my thigh reminded me of her support.

"I missed all the signs. My business was at a critical point of expansion when Trin was a baby, so my focus was my ladies and the job, but I thought all I needed to do was make sure Chantal had what she needed to be a mom without the normal pressures. So, I hired a cleaning company, I got a catering service for the nights I couldn't cook, and I hoped for the best. She was ready to go back to work after three months of maternity leave, even though we had planned for her to stay home a year. I should have known something was off then."

"So y'all communication was off?"

"Now, looking back, we were barely talking unless it was about Trin or work. Our check-ins with each other were superficial at best. We were still fucking, so I thought we were cool there even though...well, even though I couldn't stretch my kink with her. But again, she was suffering, and I should have been paying better attention. She'd been going to her doctor, complaining about pain, and the pill prescriptions continued. I swear I should have sued that guy. Until finally, the doctor worried it was too much and tried to wean her off. That's when she started buying Perc on the streets." A dry chuckle escaped me, remembering how out-of-body I'd felt when I found out she was using.

"I had no idea; all of this was happening when she was at work. When she was home, she was present, and I thought dialed in. But inside, she was hurting. After a while, she started to really abuse the pills. When she traveled for work, she went on binges I found out about after. Things at home deteriorated. At that point, it was more than clear to me something was off, but she would shoot down any conversations I tried to initiate. Finally, I found her passed out one morning next to our toilet. She'd taken too many pills and hadn't made it to bed. We tried rehab; she came back and fell off the wagon again. Trin asked me one night if her mommy didn't love her." I cleared my throat and didn't know if I could keep going until my lap was filled again. Aisha's warm weight surrounded me, her legs around my waist and my hands filled with her soft ass. She pressed her head against my shoulder and cuddled the hell out of my hurts. We stayed like that for a minute until I gathered my thoughts again.

"That's when I realized I needed to put my foot down. Trin was almost three, and things weren't getting better. We had a heart-to-heart, and things started improving. At least her health and her relationship with Trin. Ours, though...it was still frayed. I tried stepping up; I suggested couples therapy. She deflected for a while, then agreed to it. In the middle of it, she was heavy traveling for her clients and had a weeklong trip in Vegas. I surprised her by extending her stay and flight, and I flew out there Thursday night. I found her in the hotel bar, talking with some man, flirt mode on a hundred, all dolled up. He was slipping his room key to her as I walked up to them. I will never know if she was planning to accept or not because shit popped off, and I saw red. I'm not proud of anything that happened after that. I fucked the guy up, got escorted out of the hotel, and got the hell out of Las Vegas.

"When she came back, I asked her to move out. She begged me to listen to her. She promised she'd stop drinking and the occasional pill-taking, but I knew I couldn't do anything else for her, and she needed a wake-up call. And my heart was fucking hurting, I couldn't stand the pain anymore."

Her arms tightened around my torso, and she pressed her soft breasts against my chest, bringing my pounding torso to a calmer rhythm. The echoes of the pain I felt when I got divorced still haunted me to this day.

"And you still carry that pain today," Aisha whispered against my neck, and I pressed a kiss to her curls.

"Yes, but it's not the same pain." I wanted her to understand, but I didn't have many more words to explain.

"I get it. I really do. You're not in love with her no more." I sighed into her hair, glad she understood.

"Exactly, it's just the pain of...what it should have been."

"So, when you said you understood things about my dad..."

"Yeah, I get it, and I get wanting to be there for them, and I get seeing the best of them even at their worst. See, the difference is Chantal is a good woman that was dealt a terrible hand and wasn't supported medically or mentally. I didn't support her either, not properly...but my dad, and your dad? They're in a different category. They don't care. They never will." I worried I was too blunt, and her sniffle into my chest confirmed it.

"Yeah, but I can't help but wish and hope..."

"And that's what makes you remarkable, your ability to see the good even when you're down. I wish I could take all this hurt away."

"You can't do all that, but you gave me comfort when I needed it. You did good, Sir X. You did good."

Twenty

Knox

"Good morning, Miss Smart!" I sang as I entered Trinity's room. She snuggled herself into the bed. I knew she'd pay for that last movie we watched till ten. I held back my smile, sitting down next to her on her bed.

"Come on, you asked me to take you to your grandparents, and they're planning to leave for that senior breakfast picnic early." I glanced at the clock in her room, declaring it was seven-thirty. Trin's usual weekend wake-up time was about an hour away, but I wasn't joking when I told her last night that her grandparents would be heading out by eight-thirty.

"Oh, Daddy, do I really have to wake up already?" she grumbled, covering her Bantu knots with the covers.

"Where's your scarf?" This was a rhetorical question because no matter what I bought her for her head, it inevitably found its way to the floor in the middle of the night. I'd started buying her satin sheets at my mom's suggestion to maintain her protective styles between salon visits.

I caught the corner of the bright pink scarf on the floor, flexing down to get it. Damn, I worked out and boxed three days a week, and still, these joints tried to play me every time. Ever since I hit thirty-five last year, a host of unfamiliar aches and pains had moved in to stay.

"Baby, would you rather stay home with me today?" I asked her, knowing the answer to this question.

"No! Grandma promised me after breakfast, she would take me to dance class, then to do my nails, and then we were going to have lunch together and maybe go to the mall!" she said.

"A'ight, then you better get steppin'!" Finally, she got out of bed and dragged her little feet to her bathroom.

"You want some fruit to hold you over till you get to the picnic?"

"Yes, please, Daddy."

"Let me go handle that then. Make sure you—"

"I wipe my butt real good, I know, Daddy! I know how to shower."

"I'm just saying." I smiled at her aggrieved tone as she closed the bathroom door. The morning was full of possibilities as I made my way down the stairs...

"Hey Siri, play 'Bombs over Bagdad,'" I instructed my home speakers, feeling like an Outkast type of morning.

Clementines, watermelons, and grapes cut in half for Miss Smart, then I scrambled some eggs for myself and indulged by putting some bacon to sizzle on the pan.

By the time my breakfast was ready, Trin was downstairs wearing the jumper I had set aside for her.

"Beautiful as always, princess." I grinned at her.

"Thanks, Daddy!" She sat on the kitchen stool and made quick work of the fruit I had prepped for her.

"You want some more?" I asked her, impressed by her appetite. Everything she did always had me in awe, but today, there was an additional feeling of rightness that added to it all.

"No, it's ok. Are you ready, Daddy?" She vibrated with excitement, ready to go.

"Let me just—" I shoveled some eggs into my mouth, making her giggle.

"You have me out here shoveling my food down my throat," I joked around with her as we headed toward the door.

As we got in the car, my phone rang, then quickly went to voicemail.

Chantal.

The good humor of the morning threatened to fizzle out, but nothing would ruin my mood. My daughter was excited about her day, I had one of the most rewarding nights of my life last night, and my mind only had attention for Aisha and Trin. Not even work was a priority at the moment. I'd taken Kwon out as Aisha suggested, and the conversation was going well, but honestly, things could be tanking right now, and I would still be feeling on top of the world.

"Was that Mommy? You're not gonna call her back?" Trin asked as we pulled up at my parents'. They were already in the driveway getting into my Pops's car, just waiting for Trin.

"I'll holla at her later. I wanted to make sure I delivered you on time." She beamed when I gestured at her grandparents.

"Ok, Daddy, see you later at dinner!" She threw her

arms around my shoulder and pressed a kiss on my cheek, the gesture replenishing that good humor back to its original early morning levels.

Back at home, I cleaned up the kitchen and got the Roomba going to pick up any kettle corn strays from last night's movie night with Trin. After the emotional early evening at Q's Space, I came home to Trin and just vegged out next to her, watching whatever she wanted to watch, my thoughts still swirling around how good it had felt to be open with Aisha and, in turn, have her trust me with her troubles.

Life was full of hardships, but it was easier to navigate it all if you had someone in your corner. Aisha was the type of person who would hold that corner down, give you shoulder rubs, make sure you were getting your water, and dry your temple until you had to go back to the mat to throw more punches. I found myself lured by that possibility and at the same time, scared as fuck.

The kitchen was back to its pristine form when my playlist was interrupted by another ring. This time it kept going, so I didn't have a choice but to answer.

"Morning."

"Hey, Knox, how are you? How's Trin?" Chantal asked. It was her standard greeting, always asking after Trin's well-being, something I admired in her. For a minute at the end of our marriage, I had wondered if she resented Trin or wished she hadn't had her when she decided she didn't want custody, but these last years had proven me wrong.

"She's cool, about to go to this senior church breakfast with my parents."

"Oh, well, that's why I was calling, actually. Well, not exactly, but close enough." She tended to ramble, and I knew I needed to rein her in before she went off on a tangent.

"What's on your mind?" I leaned back on the kitchen counter, the back of my neck tingling.

"I want more time with Trin. I want us to discuss me getting her every weekend," Chantal blurted out.

"I thought we had put that conversation to bed?" Fuck, I knew she was gonna sour my morning.

"*You* did, I didn't. I'm better, and I haven't used in two years. And I had a lot of shit to work through in therapy and NA. I'm doing good, and I want my baby back. I deserve my baby back."

I understood that she was deep in her own feelings and concerns, but she'd just poked me.

"Tell me more about what you deserve, Chantal?" I asked, my tone going low. Every day I worked on my temper, and even though I had a few outbursts here and there, I kept my shit in check, but sometimes...sometimes, I just couldn't help but be myself.

"Knox, I have worked hard to get where I am."

"I hear that, and I see that. But Trin isn't a trophy to be won after hard work. You gotta be sure you have your shit all the way together because Trin is starting her most impressionable years. When you have her for the weekend, she always comes back subdued. When I ask her why, she tells me she feels she makes you sad sometimes. I don't know why, and I'm not criticizing, but that shit is something that would have to change. We've been working through this in therapy, and I think we need more work. Trin needs to feel comfortable with you before we move forward."

"I... Well, I'm trying. It's just that she's so gregarious and full of life, and you know me, I'm all dry humor and can be yin today and yang tomorrow, and I don't know how to... Her and I, our personalities are different."

"You gotta think of her and her needs right now, not yours. Listen, I can't keep talking about this. We've talked about it in our family therapy sessions, and if you want to discuss it more, we'll do it there. But as of now, it's a no for me."

"Knox, you don't get to just shut down this conversation!"

"But I do. I have full custody of our daughter because when we settled the divorce, you begged me..." I said calmly, proud I was keeping things together.

"I was in a dark place!" Her tone kept rising and rising, and I breathed through my nose, controlling the simmering that was always at the pit of my stomach.

"And I understood that, and even though I didn't agree with your decision because I felt Trin needed us both equal time, I complied with what you asked. But you don't get to sweep in now and change your mind one day to the next."

"This hasn't been one day to the next, I've been mentioning it in our sessions!"

"Yo, don't raise your voice at me, I'm not your man no more for you to be talking to me like that. So, check yourself, and bring this to mediated therapy. Don't call me about this bullshit again," I said, regretting the fact that I lost the battle with my temper at the end of the conversation.

Fuck!

My fist met the hard granite of the counter, the dry thud vibrating through my knuckles. I'd pay for that punch later, but right now, I was too heated to care.

Chantal had some nerve. After all we'd been through, Trin and I, she just wanted to insert herself fully back in without any considerations as to how that would affect Trin and me and my family.

All the weekends wouldn't work, but I knew why she suggested that instead of my original plan for one week at each place. She was still extremely busy and traveled a lot, so the weekend was when she could focus on Trin. But life didn't work that way, and weekends were quality time for our family. This needed way more conversation, as I had said the two times she'd tried to slide that shit in at the end of therapy.

A headache threatened to settle in the front of my skull, and I fought the urge to succumb to my bad mood. I'd planned to do some yard work and chores, but now all I could imagine doing was reaching out to Aisha and seeing what she was up to. I wanted to tell her what happened today and hear her point of view, but the thought of that made my mouth dry. Suddenly, the reality of Aisha felt more pressing, and I wondered if I was ready for any step beyond the physical.

I FOUGHT the urge to see Aisha until about six when my parents told me they were surprising Trin with dinner and a ballet show. When they said they hadn't gotten me a ticket assuming that I wouldn't want to watch all the dancing, I took it as a sign to call Aisha.

Once I made the call, she made me work for her yes. I enjoyed every second of the call. There had been no reason to punk out earlier, and I regretted letting the day pass without contacting her. But I had rectified that, and now we were meeting at this little bistro close to the dance studio that made some fusion of French and soul food.

Aisha didn't keep me waiting long. She met me outside the restaurant wearing a long black maxi wrap dress, one of those that made you want to figure out how to unravel the ties and discover what lay beneath.

"Hey, Knox." She leaned into me and pressed a kiss to my cheek. The clean lotion-like scent of her enveloped me, and I let the smell remind me of the times I had her thighs around my face.

"Hey, Baby Doll, how are you?" I searched her face, hoping she felt better after what she'd been through with her dad. Fuck, I should have called her, checked on her. Instead, I had stewed in my anger for hours, wanting to be in a better frame of mind before contacting her.

What a waste of time.

"I'm good, Sir." She cupped my face and winked. She seemed so much better, and I marveled at her bounce-back ability.

The hostess sat us down at a corner table that had natural privacy away from the hustle of the dining floor. A waiter right behind her got our drink orders and left the menu for us to decide. We took our time exploring the menu, catching up as we studied the dishes.

"But for real, are you good? I should have called you, checked in."

"I thought you might bring Trin to class, but it was your moms. But I figured work probably had you tied up, and you'd reach out later." She shrugged.

"So, you were expecting my call?" Fuck, I messed this up bad. I held my palm up, and she placed her hand in mine as the waiter brought us our drinks.

"I did because you seemed very adamant that you wanted to pursue this, and you are very bullheaded..."

"Man, insults and all." I reared back, clutching my chest with my other hand as she laughed at my theatrics.

"Am I lyin'?"

"Cold-blooded. Here I am thinking of you the whole damn day, and you were over here cataloging my faults."

"You have a weird way of showing you're thinking of me." She gazed at me with skepticism. I debated telling her about what happened with Chantal earlier today, but she didn't need to hear my ex-wife drama.

"Listen, I might have slightly fumbled the bag today, but don't get it twisted; I'm all about you, Aisha."

She gave me a bashful smile and sipped her wine. I didn't break eye contact with her—I wanted her to feel how intensely I meant that.

"Alright, Sir. We aren't in school no more, and to keep a sub like me interested, you need to be about your business. And *I* should be your business."

Oh damn, she told me.

"I'll make sure you feel every inch of my regard," I told her and tasted my whiskey.

"Are we still talking about your intentions?" she chuckled, breaking the intensity of the moment.

"I love that you have a kinky mind, but tell me how, with all the kinky stuff you must have done, you don't curse?" The waiter came back to get our order.

"For the lady, the onion soup gratin, and for the entrée, the shrimp and grits with spicy tomato. For me, the gumbo to start, then the spicy pasta Orleans."

"Right away." The waiter left the table, and Aisha's eyebrow curved delicately upward.

"So...you're ordering for me now?"

"Yes. How did I do?"

"You got what I wanted, so how did you know?" She leaned forward in her seat, her eyes searching for the trick.

"I paid attention. You read a few out loud, but when you read those, you paused and then reread them quietly. I'm observant like that." I raised my whiskey to her health and took another drink.

"Ok, I'm impressed. Usually, Doms ask me what I like to eat. Never had someone actually deduce it via observation."

"There's always a first."

"Ain't that right?" She played with the stem of her wine glass until I pressed my hand against hers.

"Are you good, though? For real?" I said, attempting to deduce what her facial expression wouldn't give.

"Oh, that? Yeah, I mean, it's what I'm used to dealing with my dad. I'll be alright." She shrugged, but I noticed something was on her mind.

"Baby Doll, for this to work—" She flipped her hand from under mine and placed it on top of the table.

"What is this?" she asked. There. That fleeting eyebrow twitch. She was bothered.

"What do you want it to be?"

"I was perfectly fine just leaving it in the Gold Room." At that precise moment, the appetizers arrived, and they settled the plates in front of us. Once the servers departed, I cleared my throat.

"Were you fine, though? You didn't wonder at night after our sessions how it would be to have aftercare in your own space? What it would be to acknowledge our mutual attraction? What it would be like to go on a date? To figure out how to take what we did in that room and apply it to our daily lives? And I'm not talking about the kink. I'm talking about the way you and I connected, even on the first day. How we couldn't help but open up to each other."

Her eyes shone as the usual intensity between us built, an intensity that didn't allow us to hide behind our polite society masks but made us be ourselves around each other.

"I... Yes, you're right. I wondered, and I fantasized, but I also tempered myself."

"Why did you do that?" I asked, my palm still touching hers.

"Because...it's a long story, but the short of it is I can be reckless with my heart. Just give it away without thinking about the consequences. What if we don't work out? Do you leave the school and affect Trin in the process?"

"You were thinking all of that?"

"You weren't?" she challenged.

"Nah, I was thinking how good it would feel fucking you in my bed, waking up next to you instead of having to walk away at Q's Space. I wondered how it would be to taste your tears and laughter. I pictured us doing scenes in my kitchen, at your school, in the car..."

"So, you were just thinking horny thoughts?" She shook her head.

"No, I also was intrigued by you, wanted to understand you better. Then when I saw *you,* the real you, I wanted more. Why do you think I offered to sponsor, then to do the dance?"

"Because you wanted to annoy me?" she said, then hummed happily, her tongue sliding over her bottom lip to capture a last drop of soup that had threatened to fall from her lips. Damn, she had me here thinking of her lips in verse.

"No, because I wanted to help keep Trin happy and you close. That was my goal."

She laughed at my earnest expression, then shook her head.

"I don't know if I believe that. I mean, you hated me before."

"Baby Doll, you know better than that. The energy I put out to you was never out of hatred."

"So then why, Knox? Why rile up the parents and broadcast your concerns and nitpick everything I do?" I could sense her frustration right now, how our past hadn't fully been erased by our scenes together.

"I wasn't nitpicking. It's just the way I talk."

"Come on now."

"Fine. Something made me want to ruffle you...you reminded me of me when I was seeking approval from someone that wasn't capable of seeing beyond their own nose. And then I noticed your quiet strength, and I think something in me wanted more of that, but I did a fucked-up job of showing it." I gathered a spoonful of soup and offered her some to taste. That pink tongue made her return again, distracting the hell out of me. She savored the soup and gave me a mischievous grin. She'd let me have it just now, and I got it—we needed to have it out before moving forward.

"Ahhh, so you're a fifteen-year-old spoilt kid. That's what that was." She grinned, and I dropped her gaze, regret flooding me at the memories of our many encounters.

"I want to apologize; I thought I was doing Trin and you a service by being *that* dad, the challenging one. It was an asshole move, and I am so sorry I made you feel anything but my appreciation for how great a teacher you are."

"Thank you. Thank you for acknowledging you did wrong. Now that I know more about you, it doesn't excuse it because we don't need to be a product of our parent's mistakes, but I get it." I flinched at her words and took the message, knowing I sometimes used my parental trauma to justify my behavior. Aisha, with her perseverance and her kindness, made me want to be better.

For the rest of dinner, we kept up the flirty banter, enjoying each other's sense of humor now that we had laid our antagonism down and allowed each other to see new aspects of our personalities.

I found out she used to dance on Broadway. Even better, she'd danced in a show I went to see the last time I was in the city while I was still married. To think we were so close and didn't even know what would come in the future for us.

I told her about my love for boxing, and we talked about some of our favorite pastimes when off work.

By the time the server brought us dessert, Aisha's eyebrow tic had subsided, and we were having to temper our laughter as it carried through the rest of the dining room floor.

"And then my moms just looked at me, dusted off her dress, and told me to meet her at church for second service. All of that hard work for nothing," I told her while she dissolved in laughter.

"My grandparents would have given me two weeks' timeout for that nonsense. The plotting it took you to leave the talc powder close to your church suit so you'd be able to stay home, you were doing too much. You want to try my pie?" She split a piece and presented it to me to taste. She hadn't even tasted it herself. I don't know why that gesture moved me, but my chest felt a little tighter as the sweet cinnamony puree melted on my tongue.

"You want to try my ice cream?" I offered in return.

"Of course, you got it chocolate just for me, didn't you?" I'd seen her eyes hesitate between the pie and the three-scoop chocolate ice cream, so I picked that for me.

"I did, just so that I could do...this." I presented her with a spoonful. Her mouth parted, everything going in slow motion like those ice cream bar commercials where everyone is moving at half speed. Her eyes closed before her lips did, and she wrapped her tongue around the scoop, the sensual licks causing enough heat for the concoction to soften on her tongue. My mouth watered at her display, then she closed her lips on the spoon and opened her eyes again, winking at me.

"You know you're gonna pay for that, right?"

"Pay for what? Enjoying my ice cream?"

She kept taunting me as I settled the bill to the point things were getting tight in my slacks. I stood up, doing a quick swipe to adjust things, then pulled out her chair.

She smirked, missing nothing.

"Who would have thought you were just this bratty little sub? You kept that under wraps real well. We definitely have to negotiate again," I whispered in her ear as she sauntered in front of me. My hand found its way to the small of her back, and I guided her around the tables to the exit.

Humidity greeted us outside, heavy in the warm night air, as a faint breeze attempted to foil the heat.

"Did you drive or order a rideshare?"

"Rideshare. I had such a long day with the dance team getting this show right that I knew if I drove and had one glass of wine, I'd had to leave the car here."

"Let me take you home." My hand itched to drag further down, but the valet guy was standing right next to us.

"It's ok if you want to squeeze it." Her breasts pushed against my shirt, and she hooked a manicured finger in my Cuban links. Her chocolate-scented breath made me brick all the way up.

"You're lucky I have to pick up Trin," I responded and accepted the dare, my palm getting lost in the softness of her hip down her lush ass until I had a handful. I squeezed her into me and let her feel her effect on me.

"You're gonna pay, Baby Doll."

The trill of her laughter wrapped around me, easing all my concerns if just for tonight. Being with Aisha made me hopeful. I'd grown so jaded from my previous experience that being in her presence felt like Christmas morning back when I was a kid.

I escorted her to my car once it pulled up and drove out. Aisha's scent of lotion and woman made the car ride a new experience as if this was a new vehicle and I was leading a different life.

"Baby Doll, what are you wearing underneath that dress?"

"Panties, Sir," Aisha responded, her giddiness clear.

"You know what to do. I don't need you wearing panties right now." I made my command implicit, knowing she'd comply. I kept my hands on the steering wheel, eyes ahead, while my peripheral vision captured her lifting her hips to slide the panties off her hips and legs. A warm lump hit my lap as I stopped at a red light.

Her lace panties.

"Open up," I said, enjoying the scent of her pussy filling the car as her thick legs spread under my order. I wished I could taste her, run my lips over her, then open my mouth to gorge. But I also needed to get her home safely, so I focused on the road.

"Play with that pretty pussy," I urged her, and my dick throbbed at the sound of her wetness as her fingers strummed on her.

"Mmmm." Aisha's hips pushed up the seat, the dress

opening revealing her sumptuous inner thighs glistening with her cream. Her hand picked up speed as she amped up herself.

"Slow, Baby Doll, there's no rush."

"We're getting close to my house, though," she whined but slowed down.

"You trust me?" My hand gravitated toward where it truly wanted to be. With one hand on the steering wheel, I lost myself in the silky touch of her pussy, gliding my index finger in tiny circles around her clit.

"I don't. You...you told me this was payback," she grunted out. I chuckled; she wasn't wrong.

I slapped her pussy three times for her sass, then went back to driving her breathless.

"Ahhh, ahhh," she moaned as we approached another red light. She hadn't noticed, but I had circled this block twice already, prolonging our time before I had to drop her off. I wished I could bring her home after picking up Trin, but the thought of that made my palms sweat. It felt too soon.

I took advantage of the red light and pulled out my erection, which, at this point, was ready to drill into her. After drenching my fingers in her wetness, I brought my hand to my length.

"Fuck, Baby Doll, you're so wet, I coated my dick with one touch."

Cream coated my skin as I jerked myself while driving slowly onto her street, the noises coming from her all I needed for this to be a quick-ass nut.

"Ohhh, can I go faster?" she pleaded.

"No, Baby Doll. Is this your house?" I asked after following the instructions she'd given me to get here.

"Yeahhh," she whined, and in a desperate move, yanked

the fabric of the dress off her left tit, then started plucking her nipple.

"Goddamn, I didn't tell you to do that," I said, and she laughed.

"What are you gonna do? Punish me?" she taunted, starting to move her fingers quicker in and out of her pussy, while she played with her breast, her flesh vibrating to the beat of her thrusts.

"If you don't slow down, you won't get this dick next time we're together."

"Sir," she whined but slowed down. She'd made a mess of herself, so juicy between those thick thighs of hers. My hand flew up and down my dick as I watched her edge herself. I knew how close she was. How much she wanted to come for me. I also knew what she really truly liked, and I wanted to test how far she'd go for it.

"Stop touching yourself and watch me."

Her breath hitched, her hand stilled, and her heavy-lidded eyes zeroed right on my length.

I gave her a show because I'd figured out another thing about her.

"You like to watch, don't you?"

Pants filled the car as I beat my dick for her enjoyment.

"You don't have to admit it, but I know you do. Because you're my dirty little slut, aren't you?"

"Oh, my goodness," she moaned, her hand hovering over her pussy but complying for now.

"You want to come for me?" I asked her.

"Fuck yes, please, yes." She licked her lips, and her hips gyrated in the air, searching for the release I was denying her. My nut was imminent; the power she honored me with was the best aphrodisiac, and I was weak for it.

Her deep brown eyes followed the path of my hand up

and down, focusing on how I pulled my balls out of my boxers and tugged at them, shining with want as precum leaked out of the tip of my penis.

And when her pretty little tongue slid out as if tasting that chocolate ice cream again...

"Fuuckkk." I spurted all over my steering wheel; my pants, hands, and seat all got it.

"Oh, oh, please let me come," she begged as I struggled to catch my breath. The way she was looking at me right now would stay with me the whole night. I wanted to jerk off again to the image of Aisha spread open in my car seat with one tit out, eyes wild with lust.

"No, you know what's coming next. This nut, it's mine. And you're gonna hold it for me till I tell you to let it free. Ok?"

Heavy breathing lifted her chest with repressed need, but she nodded in understanding. I knew I needed to bring her down from her high, but it was late, and I needed to get to Trin.

"Baby Doll?" I gripped the back of her head and pulled her to me, kissing her with all the passion I couldn't unleash on her today. She mewled when I tried to slow the kiss down, which was how I found myself with a lap and hands full of Aisha as her wet pussy teased my dick, making it rise again.

Fuck, this girl played dirty. If I had the time...

I disentangled her off my lap, bouncing her back onto her seat. Thank God for the AC, but I probably would have to ride to my parents with the windows down to air out the scent of our passion. And the sight of her right now? There was no way I was getting rid of that mental picture. There was no way I'd ever air it out of my brain.

"Call me when you get in, and I'll walk you through

what to do next," I told her as I tucked away my protesting dick and cleaned everything with the ever-present wipes I had in my car.

"Yes, Sir," she said to me with eyes full of unshed tears, a gift of her submission to me.

"Don't worry, Baby Doll, you'll get to come...when I say so."

I waited until Aisha walked up to her house and took a breath to settle the tightness in my chest. I'd gone into this looking for a sub to play with occasionally and was now knee-deep in feelings, hopes, and wistfulness.

I was in trouble.

Just when she was about to enter the house, she turned around and raised her voice. "My actual safe word is Coupe," and with a grin, she sashayed inside.

Twenty-One

Aisha

Death by edging.

That's what my epitaph would say if I didn't get to come soon. Four days this man had me waiting for him, sending flirty text messages. Some of the texts were downright nasty. In between that, he'd checked in with me, asking how the choreographies were going, telling me about his day, inquiring about mine. Asking after the health of my grandparents...then bam! Another nasty text telling me how he was going to slut me out the next time he saw me.

Whenever I felt like dismissing his order and started masturbating, he found his way into my messages, telling me he'd know if I had come. It was like he had a sixth sense connected to my pussy, and I didn't like that.

He also had a sixth sense for when my mind went into overdrive, wondering if I was making a mistake letting things get deeper between us. But it had all happened so organically that my reasons for not messing with him seemed like excuses.

I hated excuses.

Whatever I had gone through with my ex-boyfriend, it was in the past. There were no rules about me dating parents in the studio outside of the ones I made on my own, and I just wanted to have fun, not overthink things for once. Let myself enjoy everything Knox had to offer. So, every time he texted me a sweet nothing out of the blue, I took it as a sign I had made the right decision by just going with the flow.

Then yesterday, after some tame text messages, I received a video.

Knox's dick dripping water in the shower, heavy, thick, and veiny and... My entire being shivered at the beautiful display. I was the odd woman that enjoyed dick pics and videos and had told him that, but only if solicited, and the sender needed to put some effort into it. Knox had gotten a full A for what he sent me—just the dick swinging between his legs, wet from the shower, then he stroked it just once and laughed at the end of the video.

He'd just sent me another text, this one of his dick print in his gray slacks, with the message, *thinking of you,* and I was throbbing, considering going to my office and putting myself out of my misery.

"Are you even listening to me?" Sal asked.

"Ahh...if I say no, will you be mad at me?" I sat next to her at the reception desk and paid attention to what she was pointing at on her laptop. She ignored my question about being mad.

I felt bad. I had been the one to ask her to help me search for clues as to what could be happening with the students leaving the school, and I knew she had a new commission she needed to focus on, and here I was, daydreaming instead of paying attention to her findings.

The mass exodus had subsided lately, and I hoped the worst of it had passed, but I still had a nagging feeling something was off, and I couldn't figure it out.

"I think this is the school that is poaching your students. It opened a month before you lost your first dancer."

The website for the school was very simple; a white background with gray and black cursive letters spelling out the name Dance Pride Studio. The slogan was "Serving the community through art and dance."

Sal clicked around, and we saw some stock photography of dancers of different ages. The hours of operation were in there, including a phone number. The about me section only had a school email, asking the viewer to contact the studio.

"It doesn't have much info, does it? Oh, look at this! That's one of the new shopping centers around west of Miramar." I quickly popped the address into my map app and showed Sal my findings.

"We should stop by," Sal suggested, lounging back on the office chair.

"And do what? Accuse them of stealing my students? We aren't even sure this is the right place."

"You know it is." Sal shook her head, disappointed in my non-confrontational stance.

"Listen, let's at least figure out who runs it. How would we feel if someone came over here snooping and asking weird questions?"

"Fine, you got a point," Sal said. "I'll keep digging."

"It's ok if you don't have time, you know? I know you have a lot going on right now with the new software commission."

"Aisha...you're good. You already know I got you, babes."

My chest expanded, and I started thinking of something I could surprise Sal with for a snack later today when Mila walked in, announced by the chime, Knox walking in behind her.

"Look who I found in the parking lot!" she presented Vanna White-style.

"Hey, Knox," Sal greeted him, then went back to her laptop. Knox smirked, touching his well-groomed beard, amused at her dismissal. His deep chuckle did things to my insides. And did he have to dress so fine? He had on dark gray slacks and a jacket, with a wine-colored shirt that was open at the collar. His shoes gleamed like he was wearing them for the first time, and his cologne... He had worn my favorite one, even though it was daytime.

"Aisha..."

"Sir," I responded, letting him know I needed his attention and my release asap. Then I realized I had my older ballet class and said a few choice words in my head.

"I came to invite you for a late lunch."

"Oh... I wish, but..."

At the exact moment I was going to decline, Devon walked out from the back in his rehearsal tights, no shirt on.

Three sets of heads turned from one end of the reception to the other to admire Devon. One head quickly dropped down to laptop level, but I'd caught that.

I also made a quick adjustment to find Knox's eyes squinting at me.

Oops.

"What's up, man? Didn't know you were here," Devon greeted Knox amicably, offering his hand to dap. Knox reciprocated Devon's gesture.

"Yeah, I came to get Aisha to take her to lunch."

"But I can't go. I have the advanced ballet class coming in less than an hour."

"I can take it. I know what you're teaching them, and it's one of the classes I'm gonna take ova' so..." Devon shrugged, rubbing his chest while smiling at me.

"Are you sure?" I searched Devon's eyes, wondering if he felt any type of way about me leaving the class in his hands, but Mila interrupted my thoughts.

"Yes, stop overthinking it. Devon was just telling me yesterday how he's ready to step in," Mila said. *Oh*, when had she become Devon's spokesperson? I peeked a look at him and saw his slight smile and shrug.

I widened my eyes at him, and his dimple popped in amusement.

"Aisha?" Knox called my attention again.

"I'd be delighted to go with you," I said, giddy at the thought of what he would do to me on this lunch break.

"Aisha, I just sent you an email about that new dance studio that opened in West Miramar. I'm going to keep digging," Sal said as if no interaction had happened between anyone but her and me.

"What dance studio?" Knox paused as he offered his arm.

"You know that new strip mall that has the Orange Theory and the PetSmart?"

Knox tensed at my description, and I wondered what was wrong with him.

"Yeah, that one, I know it."

"Well, there's a new studio there. Sal has theories about it. But nothing we can prove, so it's alright." I shrugged, knowing I'd be back to sleuthing with her soon enough. For now, I just wanted to enjoy his company.

"Go easy, Aisha, I got it." Devon nodded.

Knox stared at Devon, then offered his hand to me, and when I placed mine in his, he pulled me into him. It was imperceptible to anyone but us, but I knew that was his way of staking claim. So possessive, and I was just the girl to lap it all up.

"Alright, man, good to see you. Ladies." He half-nodded at Devon, then nodded at Mila and Sal, who were both looking at us with amused expressions.

He pressed his hand to the small of my back and guided me out of the dance studio, and I basked in the way he took control.

Going with the flow was the right decision.

"This is a cute spot. I've never been here before." I glanced around the small Mexican restaurant as we waited for our meal.

"Yeah, this is one of our shopping centers. We have them all around Pembroke Pines and Miramar."

"I love that. I love to see us thinking big and strategically." I nodded, impressed at his business reach.

"You're strategic too. Listen, I might not have always understood your goals because I was being hard-headed, but what you've done with your studio since you opened it? You more than quadrupled your student roster, and starting this Christmas show was smart."

"Yeah. Now, if I could only figure out who's actively poaching my dancers," I said while the waiter placed our meal in front of us.

I took a bite of the rice and did a happy dance.

"Oh, it's that good, huh?"

"Yes, it is. Here, taste it." I offered him some of my rice.

He'd ordered steak salad, and I teased him about watching his figure.

"That shit is hittin'. So, have more dancers left?" he asked as he enjoyed his entrée.

"No, not anymore, but we might have found the place that is poaching them."

"That's Sal's theory?"

"Yeah."

"Mhm." He stared beside my head, then back at me. A frisson of unease ran through me, but I dismissed it. Why would he know anything about this situation? That was just my overanalyzing nature kicking in again.

"Yeah, Sal wanted to go confront them, but we have no proof."

"And that would be dangerous. Going to accuse someone without proof? Promise me you won't do that." Our gazes met, and he held it there, his intense regard making me take notice of his earnest concern. I had imagined his discomfort earlier, or maybe it had been this overall worry about my situation.

I slid my hand over the table, offering it to him, and he immediately grabbed it.

"I won't do anything reckless."

"Thank you, Baby Doll. This is why you're such a good, good girl." His voice rumbled through me, making my pussy lips twice as heavy. I was so engorged down there just from being in his company. He didn't have to do much.

"Listen, we haven't renegotiated our D/s dynamic," he said, then wiped his lips with his napkin. My eyes were lured by his immaculate beard and lips and stuck there.

"Yeah."

He chuckled.

"Do I need to put you out of your misery before we negotiate or after?"

Glancing around the restaurant, I realized it was empty. "After is ok."

"Ok, good, because I don't want to take things for granted. How much of what we discussed before during our sessions was correct?" he asked.

"All of it. I think the only thing we really didn't discuss is that, as you guessed, I'm a voyeur, and I can be bratty in the right circumstances."

"That's what's up. I don't mind brattiness under the right circumstances. Does the protocol I shared work for you? Do you like scenes only in the bedroom, or are you ok in other locations?"

"I'm ok with having some type of word or signal to indicate you want to play, and it's up to me to agree if I'm down for it or not if we're in public. I like playing like that, but in the right place at the right time."

"So, if I were to say 'Baby Doll'...and you answered 'Sir' back, would that work?"

"Yes." I squirmed in my seat. "That would be sufficient."

"Baby Doll, I want you to go to that room in the back. It's for private events. They don't have it in use right now. Go and wait for me there."

Oh...

"Yes, Sir."

I stood up and took my time walking to the private dining room, aware of his gaze on me. I felt that heat, and I strutted my hips a little more just for him.

My heart was racing as I entered the darkened room and found a wooden table with about twenty chairs around it. My blood was pumping so fast I could hear it in my ears.

The door behind me opened, then closed again, and I dropped to my knees.

"Good, Baby Doll, but I want you to get into second position on the table there." He pointed to the dining table. "But with no pants or underwear on."

I glanced back at him as he palmed himself, his brown eyes as intense as ever.

"Yes, Sir." No bratty behavior from me right now; I needed to orgasm too bad. My leggings and panties were off in record time.

The cold dark wood kissed my knees, and the air conditioner soothed my wet warmth as I assumed the position for Sir X.

"Mmmm." His deep groan insinuated itself in my ears, traveling deep into my core, and I quivered in anticipation of what he would do next.

"This pussy is so ready for me. Look at how it throbs hello." He pinched my labia, and I gushed in response.

"What a slutty mess you are. Now I'm gonna have to take care of it." He growled before the heat of his tongue swiped across my pussy all the way up to my entrance.

Exhibiting amazing dexterity, he licked and lapped my vagina, extracting some of my juices with his expert licks. My legs trembled, and my thighs spread further open, my position bringing most of my body flush against the table apart from my ass, thighs, and pussy.

"Fuck, baby, I really had you suffering, didn't I?" he murmured into my pussy, then gave it one last lick, making me moan in frustration. The slow road to my climax was four days long and one second too late. I was losing my famed control, and the edging was becoming too hard to manage.

"I'mma do right by you," he said, and the melody of his

belt hitting the floor was all I needed to hear for my entire bottom half to contract to the promise of his dick.

My pussy pulsed, my clit vibrated, and tears trailed down my face as his dick thrust inside of me with slow precision. I gripped every inch of him, and when Knox bottomed out, a detonation went off inside of me. No amount of cajoling or reminders that we were in a public place and people were outside kept me from keening as one of the longest orgasms of my life took over my entire body. I felt the hairs all over my skin raise in attention, my nipples felt like diamonds cutting against my bra, and the keening continued until Knox covered my mouth to keep some of the noise muffled. I bit into his palm in desperation because he had started to move, and each thrust created a new explosion inside me.

"Fuck, are you coming...fuck, again..." Knox's thrusts faltered as my pussy cosplayed as a boa constrictor around his dick. I felt the tears wetting his hand as my orgasm became two, then three as he kept up his relenting pace, his other hand on my hip in a bruising hold. I would cherish the bruises tomorrow; they'd be a reminder of such extraordinary orgasms. I felt lightheaded as Knox jerked inside of me, and liquid warmth filled me as he repeated my name over and over.

Well, my panties were ruined.

Knox sat across from me, drinking his cup of coffee, not one hair out of place. I, on the other hand, felt as if I had danced for fourteen hours straight and needed a bath and a bed, in that order. The waiter had given us a knowing look, and Knox slid them a bill, so clearly, he'd arranged that private room just for us. I wasn't mad; that's how badly I'd needed to come.

"You're not gonna drink your hot chocolate?" he asked. I'd excused myself to the bathroom to get myself in some type of order after our fuck session in the private dining room, and when I returned, the cup of Mexican hot chocolate and an order of sugar cinnamon churros had been waiting for me.

But what had really melted my heart were the earnest eyes that greeted me when I met his gaze. He looked so tentative and excited for my approval; I couldn't help but plant a big kiss on those sexy lips.

"Yes, Sir, of course, I will." I took a sip of the rich concoction, savoring the sweet, slightly bitter flavor.

"Davenport, fancy meeting you here." A voice took me out of my food porn experience, and I opened my eyes to find the gentleman Knox had introduced to me at the networker.

"Hey, Kwon, what brings you to this neck of the woods?" Knox stood up and shook hands with the man.

"Oh, I was driving around looking at your properties and what opportunities we might have if we do the merger and decided to stop in and get a late lunch. Sorry, I'm being rude, Ms. McKinney, is it? We met at the networker?"

"Hello, Mr. Kwon, good to see you again." I shook his hand, touched by his formal regard.

"Remind me again, how do you know Ms. McKinney?" he asked Knox, Mr. Kwon's gaze alternating between both of us in polite interest.

"Oh, this is the teacher at my daughter's dance school," Knox said, then cleared his throat. "Our company is sponsoring the Holiday Dance show, and we're meeting to button up some key items."

I stared at Knox while he continued to speak with Mr. Kwon.

Static interference grew louder in my ears as my mind raced to understand why Knox hadn't introduced me as his date. At this point of the game, he had told me he was into me, that he wanted something more than a D/s dynamic, and had proceeded to kinky court me through dates, texts, and calls these past few days.

And I had been falling for each moment and each word. It was all very early, I knew that. It was all very new and delicate, and I had baggage, and he had an oversized suitcase of past hurts, and we hadn't even spoken about Trinity. What did this all mean?

I went through the motions after Mr. Kwon left us, saying goodbye to him like an automaton.

Knox probably assumed I was still in subspace, so he gently guided me with his warm hand on the small of my back out of the restaurant into his car.

We drove in silence, his hand on my thigh, my eyes trained on the window as my mind imagined a thousand and one scenarios for why Knox had introduced me as just a dance teacher.

And when he dropped me off with a sweet kiss and the promise of a call, I knew no matter how much I analyzed it all, I would still be waiting for his call.

Twenty-Two

Knox

The gym smelled of sweat and leather, and the noise of a full Saturday morning resounded across the space. Four boxing rings sat in the middle as different people trained in each of them, with stations around the perimeter for punching bags, speed bags, and assorted boxing equipment.

The guys and I had agreed to meet here for our weekly session. We were waiting for our hour of reserved time at one of the boxing rings.

Usually, I was champing at the bit if we had to wait for any equipment, but today, that wasn't even registering. There was only one reason for my chill behavior—my mind was full of Aisha. Not even Chantal's constant texts stressed me out.

"Damn, I've never seen you this zen," Stephen joked as he held a heavy bag while Denzel hit it with some quick combos.

"I can be chill." I leaned against the wall while Toño hit the speed bag with his usual flare.

"Nah, you aren't chill, but that lady got you chill," Toño said without breaking concentration.

"So, you aren't gonna update us?" Stephen asked.

"It's going good, we spend a lot of time together. We feel like teenagers with her living with her grandparents and Trin with me, but I'm trying to take my time, though. I don't know if I need to be jumping into a serious relationship so soon after the divorce..."

"You've been separated for four years, three of those years divorced. You trippin'," Denzel managed to say between hits, sweat running down his face. He stayed doing the most, so by the time we went up to the ring, he'd already be tired.

"Yeah, but I gotta think of Trin. Introducing her to a new woman when she's only known me to be with her mother..." I shook my head, my stomach twisting at the thought of what Trin would say.

"Again, that's just what you've been using to hold yourself back. Trin was three when y'all split; she's known you longer single than married," Toño said, stopping to focus on our conversation.

"What is this, an intervention?"

"Nah, bruh, we just can tell Aisha is making you happy. You're in a good mood all the time now, you take the time to disconnect from work...we see the difference." Stephen shrugged, then grunted when Denzel threw a very fast hook.

They weren't wrong. I felt the good influence of Aisha in my life but still, moving too fast could have an adverse reaction on Trin. She loved Aisha, and the dance studio had been a constant for her. I needed to protect that for Trin, and that probably meant Aisha and I needed to move slowly.

I just didn't know the definition of that word when it pertained to Aisha.

My phone vibrated just as our ring opened up.

"I'll be right with y'all," I told the guys, expecting it to be Chantal, who had been hitting me up periodically as she had Trin for the day.

It wasn't her weekend, but I had reluctantly allowed Chantal to take Trin to one of those ice shows and have a girl's day. The compromise was that Trin would sleep at my spot, and she'd bring her to me before bedtime.

It wasn't Chantal, though; it was Aisha.

"What's up, baby? How's the day at the studio so far?"

"I'm alright. Listen...this has been bugging me for days, and I wasn't going to say anything, but I want things between us to be as transparent and open as possible."

No good conversation started like this. I strolled out of the main floor of the gym and found a quiet nook in the hallway that led to the dressing rooms and showers.

"What's wrong?" I asked, cutting to the chase. My stomach was in a vice, awaiting her concern.

"When we were at lunch the other day...you reintroduced me to Mr. Kwon as Trin's teacher." She paused, and my mind cataloged the exact moment she was referring to. I hadn't meant to make her feel any type of way. I knew she valued her privacy, and that had been my top priority.

"Yeah, because my first instinct had been to introduce you as my Baby Doll, as my sub. I don't play in public without your specific consent. We hadn't talked about it."

"Oh." I could hear Mila's loud ass talking to someone, but no noise was coming from Aisha. My stomach couldn't relax until she relaxed. How had I missed that this was bothering her? I thought she'd been worried about her school, and I'd already been moving things along to alleviate that worry.

"And I could have introduced you as my girl, but we were still talking and figuring things out, and you had recently told me you didn't even want to do all of that with me. So, what's a man to do, go out on a limb and be left out there in the cold?"

"Oh, Knox, I told you during lunch I was open to trying. I can't be living life based on my past experiences." I could hear her exasperated affection, and I breathed easier. She hadn't particularly said she was good, but she had implied it. It felt good hearing it, though.

"Alright then, you my girl?" I asked, trying to ignore the sweat that had gathered on my palms as I awaited her answer.

"Yes, you know I am." My heart leapt in my chest, and nervous energy gave me the urge to go punch some shit. This felt good...right?

"Ok then, that's settled. You're my girl. We'll talk more about how we let Trin know. Because that's the first person I need to tell before we go out here printing couples business cards and shit."

"What are you talking about? Who knew under all your grumpiness was a whole fool?" She laughed.

"Chill, you know you've been enjoying getting to know all my facets."

"That I have. Hold on... Who is it? Papa? What are you doing here?" Aisha's voice grew muffled as she stepped away from her phone, and I let out a curse. She had a lot going on today; she was teaching all the small children's choreographies to some of the older teens so they could assist with the last weeks of rehearsal. She'd told me the idea to incorporate that experience for the older dancers in her dance team, and

I thought that was brilliant; a great way of giving them access to leadership skills. She didn't need her dad's destructive behavior around her when she needed to be harnessing positive energy.

"Aisha. Aisha. Baby Doll!"

"Yes, Sir." She was back on the line and sounded a bit breathless.

"I know your dad is there, but you're gonna do something for me, alright?"

"Ok...Sir."

"You're gonna focus on you today and the commands I'll be texting you until I see you tonight for the dad's rehearsal."

"Oh...ok, Sir."

"Don't let anyone disturb your peace today, you hear me?"

"Yes, Sir."

"Ok, Baby Doll, stand by for more instructions."

I felt good about that. I couldn't command her not to speak to her father, no matter how tempted I was to do that, but I could offer her something else to focus on. In the end, she was her own woman, and my dominant tendencies were not to overtake her own agency.

I went back to the guys, my mind saturated with thoughts of Aisha.

"Who's ready to get a beating?" I asked as I slid into the ring.

"I'm sure the beating won't be worse than that whipped simp face you have on right now," Denzel trolled me, but I let that shit roll off my back. After all, there were worst things than being infatuated with Aisha McKinney.

Twenty-Three

Aisha

> Sir X: Did you let your father get you in a funk?

I stared at the text message as my dad swaggered out of the dance studio. According to him, he was just coming in and checking how things were with me. In conversation, he let it slip that his job was shorting his pay, and he was worried about next month's rent.

My guts had curdled at that news, and right away, pictures of my dad on the streets started flashing in my head. At the same time, a little voice in the back of my head reminded me that I had been down this road with him before, that he always landed on his two feet with or without my financial help. So, while my dad complained, I found a zen place inside of me. I still loved him and wanted to help whenever I could, but I wasn't going to let him rob me of my peace. I wanted recovery for him, but he didn't want it for himself. So, I could only offer my love and support—the non-financial kind until I was in a better place.

Just as I had arrived at that decision, I received a text from Knox reminding me that I had control of my thoughts.

How timely.

The man seemed to have a direct connection to my thoughts and emotions. Who would have thought that the same man that loved to annoy me would be the person that saw me for all I was?

I texted him back: I didn't get in a funk, he's just leaving. Same old same old Sir.

> Sir X: Good Baby Doll. Do you have any toys at work?

I poked my head in Room A while anticipation gave my steps a bounce. Our dancer volunteers from our advanced class were learning the jazz choreographies with Mila that the tots would be presenting.

I checked my watch and calculated I had about an hour before we started working on the ballet and the African dances, and I was leading that part of the class. Enough time to play with my Dom.

I breezed through the studio, excitement coursing through me, as I wondered what he had waiting. The foresight of having my office in the back and away from the reception seemed inspired as I entered the small office and locked the door.

> Me: I have one of those lipstick vibrators in my dance bag.

> Sir X: I approve, and for the future, you should have a dildo, a g-spot massager, and some vibrating plugs in your bag at any given time. I'll buy you some.

Yes, Sir, please go ahead and fill my toy chest with goodies.

The small device looked innocuous as I pulled it out of my purse, but it packed a mean punch. I loved using it on my clit for quickie climaxes.

My phone buzzed on my desk, and I rushed to read his instruction.

> Sir X: Take off whatever you're wearing waist down. I want you bare.

I wanted me bare too.

I had on a leotard today, so I got myself all the way naked, my blood rushing through my veins as fast as I removed my clothes.

> Sir X: Send pic as confirmation.

A flash of heat went through me at the thought of him seeing my picture on his phone, not expecting to see all of me.

I took my time, putting the same effort into it as I liked to receive.

After some internal deliberation, I decided to pose spread-eagle with my thighs hooked on the arms of my office chair and the lipstick vibrator nestled between my breasts. With my watch, I set a timer for my phone and held my breath.

My arousal was evident in the picture, glistening wetness between my legs and a sultry look that I knew would make him want to be here with me instead of whatever he was doing.

I sent the photo and waited.

Less than seconds later, my phone vibrated again. It was a wall of text, and I scoffed at him sending me so much to read when I was needy for him.

> Sir X: Goddamn Baby Doll, you must warn a man. You're making me want to drop everything and show up for my rehearsal five hours early. You know I wanted you to come with the vibrator but now I changed my mind. I want that orgasm all for me once everyone leaves. So, you know what to do: edge yourself for me. Every hour on the hour until I'm inside you tonight. Ok?

Compliance.

The beauty of D/s relationships is that the people who want to be in the dynamic have agreed upon a set of parameters and boundaries that, if followed, will bring untold pleasure to all parties involved.

I understood that in theory and practice, but there were days like today when I wanted to say the hell with rules and commands and just do me. Again, this man had me on the edge of my climax, denying me release.

Every hour after his first text, he commanded me to go to my office, take off my clothes, send him a pic, then place the vibrator on my pussy until I felt I was about to come.

Then I had to stop.

Somehow, he'd managed to time me well, and his texts telling me to put my clothes back on were almost exactly when I was about to orgasm. The second-to-last session before his rehearsal had me considering just giving up.

In the middle of it all, I had to go and check on my grandparents to find Pops's scooter was malfunctioning and wouldn't reverse properly. I'd been postponing the purchase, but that told me I couldn't do that any longer.

That news was a splash of cold water on my smoldering heat. It meant another trip to the doctor I needed to schedule with urgency so that Medicare would cover the replacement scooter. I knew I didn't have enough to pay for the repairs of the model Pops loved, which was one of the most expensive ones.

I'd lost some of the edge after that exchange at home, and when Knox texted me for my four p.m. assignment, I was a little out of the game, my text response lukewarm.

Right away, he picked up on it.

> Sir X: Change of plans. I need a video of you edging yourself for this session.

My attention span immediately snapped back to his command as I divested myself of my leotard.

I made this one different than the ones before and propped my phone down on the floor to lean against the desk and pressed record, then I got into my second position just for Sir. Even without him here, I felt the pull of his control as I pressed my upper body to the floor, sliding the vibrator over my clit. I clenched at the thought of Sir X with me, guiding me through with his words and his touch. I imagined his deep rumble as he corrected me for something I was doing wrong. I got lost in thoughts of his dominance and how much I wanted to come just for him. I jolted at the reminder that I wasn't supposed to climax. With one last circle of the vibrator on my nub, I turned it off, then crawled toward the phone.

"I hope you liked that, Sir. See you soon."

An hour later, after my last edging session, I sat next to Mila while Devon regaled us with some story about a cousin in Jamaica.

My blood hadn't stopped its speedy passage through my veins as I hovered slightly off the ground in my cloud, everything feeling fuzzy and soft around the edges.

"Girl, are you alright?" Mila asked when I didn't join in the laughter after Devon's story. He'd excused himself to the back, and she was staring at me as if I had a horn or something.

"I'm a bit high... I've been receiving commands from Sir the whole day."

"Ahh, that's why you're acting like a crew member of Apollo 13."

"Damn, that reference is older than you."

She shrugged. "Mari." As if her older sister's name was all the explanation needed. "So, you're enjoying your relationship then?"

"Yeah, I am! It's good. Earlier, I was stressing about Pop's scooter breaking, then Sir texted me and..." I paused, a sense of déjà vu making the earth tilt for a second. I stared at Mila as her mouth moved, everything progressing in slow motion, and the soft edges from earlier dropped into nothingness.

"Girl, damn, are you in subspace, and that negro is not even here?" she asked, amused.

"Mila, am I doing what I did with James?" I whispered, still spooked by the out-of-body feeling.

"What do you mean, bebita? I don't get... Oh, do you mean when you felt you 'lost' yourself in him?"

"But I did. I was just a walking, talking, kinky sexual being. Everything he wanted to do, I was down for. I almost didn't do the last show because I wanted to be down and ready for anything he wanted, and he had gotten that job..."

"Wow, wow, you were in love with that man, and you're simplifying what happened with him down to your kink. It wasn't about the kink, it was about him. And not for nothing, you've done the same thing with your vanilla boyfriends in the past. You let them become your everything, but now you've learned not to do that. All through your time with Knox, you've been present for the kids, on point with creating the choreographies, not missing any doctor's appointments with your grandparents..." Everything Mila said made sense to me. I had found better ways to find my center since the last time I got lost in my kink; I didn't fully agree with her about what caused me to lose my center, but I didn't feel like arguing right now.

"All the times you've been deeply in love, you've confused heartbreak for obsession." Mila shook her head. I wanted to push back, but at that moment, the chime went off, and Knox walked in.

He wore a black t-shirt and black sweatpants with a black beanie.

"Hey, Mila. Aisha..." he said with the way he had of lengthening the s and h, pursing his lips around the sound. It made me want to lick his bottom lip.

I stood up to hug him, and before I knew it, I was kissing his bottom lip, capturing it between my teeth. I took advantage of his gasp and slid my tongue inside his mouth. My worries seeped to the edges of my brain, not gone but not urgent any longer.

The fuzzy feel enveloped me as we lost ourselves in each other. When we separated, Mila's eyebrows were all the way up her hairline.

"Listen, y'all know I'm down for the threesome whenever you're ready, right?" she said wistfully, and I buried my face in Knox's chest, inhaling his cologne, laughter fizzing out.

"Aisha told me about her idea the other night, and I mean, as long as your friendship stays intact...I'm down," he said, his deep voice rumbling inside of me.

I pushed away from him and gave him another kiss on the cheek.

"Thank you, Sir!" I said, smiling, and he winked back.

"Yeah, any time!" Mila said, walking into Room A, fanning herself.

"Don't tell her that too much, she won't forget." I giggled as he hugged me to him.

"I don't want her to forget. Come on, let's go and get this rehearsal going."

An hour later and we were deep into the choreography.

It was adorable; we had mixed some easy hip-hop moves that would be accessible for all the participants, and thankfully, most of the dads had rhythm and a sense of direction.

They were already looking like a somewhat cohesive unit after an hour of practicing the first half of the dance.

Knox impressed me with his rhythm and natural sense of music, even suggesting some moves. He was one of the front performers, and my eyes kept straying to him as he naturally took his leadership role seriously.

He'd confessed to me that he hadn't wanted to dance, but Trin had been so excited, and he wanted to make her happy.

These were the things that made me dissolve into a puddle of happiness. The way he dedicated himself to his daughter, to his loved ones... I wanted that for myself as well.

I sat on a stool, offering helpful suggestions, when Knox met my gaze, then gave me a slow nod.

I checked my phone and saw a text.

> Sir X: It's time.

What did he mean by that? I stared at him, and he raised an eyebrow. Then his eyes traveled down my fuchsia leotard, creating a path of flames down my body, and he smirked.

"Ah."

He crossed his muscled arms over his chest while Mila and Devon demonstrated the next eight-count of choreography to the group. All the while, Knox and I were locked in a duel of stares, and I already knew who would win.

Both of us.

I hopped off the stool and gestured to Mila that I would return.

I sped up, almost floating to my office, where I quickly shed my leotard and dropped to my knees.

Seconds later, the door swung open. At the same time, my heart tripped a beat as Knox sauntered inside.

"Is your office soundproof?" he inquired.

"Soundproof enough." I nodded.

"Good." He grabbed me by my neck and yanked me up, crushing his lips against mine.

He must have performed a magic trick of multiplying his hands because I felt his touch everywhere; at the back of my neck, the side of my breast, my belly, between my legs. He ignited every single cell in my body, and I was already heated.

"This is gonna be quick, then later tonight, I'll take you slow, alright?" he asked, but really, he was telling me. And where could he take me slow? We were constricted to these stolen moments until he spoke with Trin.

Pressed against the door, he positioned himself between my legs, the fabric of his t-shirt caressing my hard nipples, making me chase more. I braced myself against him, holding onto his shoulders as I undulated my body up and down him. Maybe if I rubbed fast enough, I'd put out the fire he'd started with his first edge session today. Maybe if I opened wide enough, he'd take me swift and hard, just like I needed. Maybe if I bit his ear, he'd growl his need.

I was correct in all these assumptions.

One stroke, and he was deep inside of me. My walls gathered around him, welcoming their King and Lord. My wetness made things messier and easier for both of us, the glide of his shaft in and out of me exquisite torture.

I pressed my nose into his neck, inhaling the cologne I so loved on him, my mouth watering at how delicious he smelled.

"Baby Doll, if you keep doing that, I'm gonna come faster than I want to," he said, clenching my behind as he plowed into me.

"But you smell so good, Sir." I whined into his neck, then dragged my tongue over the same spot I had sniffed before.

"Fuuck." Knox faltered, then slid me down the door.

"Hands on the desk." He followed the command with a slap on my ass. Happy to comply, I spread my legs, arching my ass, so he had full access to my pussy, and held onto the desk for whatever he had to give me. The choreography track started over again, telling me they were inching toward the end of the rehearsal, and I worried we'd be caught.

"They're gonna wrap up soon. What did you tell —Ooh."

He thrust his dick in me with no preamble, my flesh stretching to accommodate him again. For a moment, it felt as if he had never been inside me, and I needed to figure out how to accommodate his girth all over again. But then my body remembered, and I yielded to the relentless pressure as his hips slapped against my ass, making it wiggle with each pounding stroke. I squirmed at this new angle, his length knocking on things it didn't need to knock.

"You better stop running from this dick, or I'll put you on a dick diet for the rest of the night." He punctuated each word with a thrust inside me.

"Ahh, Knox, I'm trying," I promised as my knees grew weak, the pleasure of us together seeping into my pores.

"Don't try, Baby Doll, be a good girl and take all this dick." His hard strokes deserved a poem to describe their perfection. I didn't have such tools, but maybe I'd dance to this tempo he'd created. My huffs grew louder as we heard the music outside start over again.

"I need the nut now, Baby Doll."

"Yes, yes!" All he had to do to get me to that space higher than the clouds was tell me what he needed. His needs were mine. His desire fueled mine. His orgasm was equally mine, as his warmth filled me as he reached his release, triggering my own uncontrollable quivers.

"Come stay tonight with me. Have dinner with me and Trin," he whispered into my hair, and I melted into the desk.

How could I keep centered when this man kept tilting me off-kilter?

In a day, he'd taken me for a full ride, and I didn't want to get off. He protected me from my own destructive thoughts and offered support regarding my father.

Whatever concerns I had...they couldn't compete with my deep yearning to be close to him.

"Yes, I'd love that," I said, not letting this opportunity pass me by.

Twenty-Four

Knox

Did I make a mistake moving this fast? I'd been so taken with Aisha, so enthralled seeing her in her element at the rehearsal, I'd just gone ahead and invited her home. Her submission to me during our scene had been a siren call.

I'd been separated for four years and divorced for three, and I'd never brought a woman to the house. My home was a sanctuary for Trin and me, and I didn't let anything or anyone disturb that.

I wanted to believe that Trin had a good childhood so far, and one of the ways I'd provided that was by being laser-focused on her. Since Aisha, I'd found myself making that focus expand more. I'd forgotten how it felt to care so deeply for the well-being and happiness of someone as much as I cared for Trin. I mean, I cared about my parents and my friends, but this visceral need to know Trin was always good... Yeah, I felt that for Aisha as well.

So, I had to figure out how to calm my nerves because this was happening. As I still had to get Trin, I'd invited

Aisha to come through after she got home and situated her grandparents for the night.

"Trin?"

"Yes, Daddy?" she asked as she sat on the sofa in our family room. Her eyes were half-mast, with a loopy grin that told me she was exhausted. I was so glad she'd had fun with Chantal. No matter my issues with her mother, I knew Chantal was striving to be a better parent to Trin, and that's all we could do. I respected that attempt.

"You had a good day with Mom?"

"Oh, yeah, I did! The show was so much fun! And we had lunch together, and then we got our nails done, look!" She flashed her fingers at me, the pink and purple sparkles shining off her small nails, proud as can be. Damn, my little girl was growing up, and I was so in my feelings about it all.

"That's what's up, Miss Smart, I'm glad you had a good day with Moms. I ordered some pizza, and I'm steaming some broccoli for dinner," I told her while I moved around the kitchen, pulling plates and cups to set the table. If Trin paused for a minute, she'd see the nerves evident in my jerky moves, but she was clearly on the way down to Snoozetown.

"Ok, daddy," she yawned.

"Oh, and we have company tonight," I dropped as casually as I could muster.

"Really?" Her puffs bounced as she popped her head on top of the back of the sofa, facing me at the kitchen island. "Who's coming?"

"Oh, Miss Mac. She'll be having dinner with us."

"Ahhhhhh..." She nodded as if it all made sense. "Why?"

"Well...listen..." Shit, I was about to fuck this up. I needed to cut the crap and level with her.

Wiping my hand with the kitchen towel, I approached

Trin, sitting on the sturdy coffee table across from the sofa so we'd be at eye level. Her gaze was curious as she waited for me to gather my thoughts. I took deep breaths as words crystallized, only to be discarded for a better approach. I wanted this to go well. I *needed* this to go well.

"See, Ms. Mac and I... We're seeing each other."

"What you mean, seeing each other? I see her too, every week." Trin stared at me as if I was making zero sense, and for a second there, I agreed with her.

"Nah, Miss Smart, I like Ms. Mac. She's my...my special friend."

Trin's eyes widened, and she clasped her mouth with her hands, the pink and purple sparkling as she squealed.

The sound soothed my worries, and I let out a sigh of relief.

"I love Ms. Mac! So, is Ms. Mac your girlfriend? But you're so mean to her, did she like that?"

Oh shit, I hadn't been ready for this.

"Umm, well, I haven't been mean to her in a while."

"Mmm, that's right, but you used to be. If you were a boy in my class—"

"Listen here, you don't let no boys..." Fuck, I was fucking this conversation up. Just as I tried to regroup, the bell rang.

"Oh, can I open the door, Daddy?" Trin hopped off the couch with impressive skill and was by the door before I could blink.

"Now, what have we said about that?"

"No opening doors, only grown-ups do that," she chanted.

"Exactly. It's for your safety." I opened the door, and there she stood. Aisha wore a big T-shirt with a Black ballerina in the middle and leggings, her hair in a high ponytail and no makeup on with a warm smile on her face, the aroma of the pizza in her hands trying to overpower her clean lotion scent. She'd never looked more beautiful. She stirred something long dormant in me—hope.

"Hello!" she chirped, her cheeks blooming to redness. Her eyes darted down, away from my face, and her smile widened even more.

"Miss Trin!"

"Miss Mac, please come on in. I don't know what my Daddy is thinking, keeping you waiting by the door," Trin said, sounding like a replica of my mother. Damn, those two needed to stop hanging out so much. Trin was sounding like a sixty-year-old auntie. But I was grateful; she was cutting the nervous energy emanating from both of us with such ease.

Aisha's laughter followed behind as they chatted and Trin showed her the kitchen. I trailed behind, seeing how well they got along, as the pressure on my chest eased, and my movements went back to their regular smoothness.

Aisha already had a great relationship with my daughter; the introduction to us as a couple had gone seamlessly on the foundation of their teacher/student relationship. Warmth settled in my chest as I leaned against the kitchen counter, and Aisha followed Trin's instructions as she pulled plates and placed pizza slices on them.

"I should be serving you." I raised an eyebrow as she opened the pot with the steamed broccoli.

"Really? Well, Miss Trin here told me to feel at home, so that's what I'm doing. So how about you both go wash your hands, and we'll sit down and have this yummy pizza?"

Both of us filed away because Aisha had her teacher voice on, and there was no arguing with her. We came back to the dining room to find plates on each setting and iced tea in our cups.

"This is my favorite pizza in the city, and I love that it's thin crust," Aisha told us after Trin said grace.

"Mmmm, you're right, Ms. Mac, this is delicious," Trin said, a piece of cheese trailing out of her mouth.

"No speaking with your mouth full, Miss Smart."

Aisha met my gaze and gave me a bashful smile that hit me right in the chest. We ate while the three of us chatted about our favorite food joints in the area, and Trin regaled us with stories of the show she had seen in the morning.

The pizza hit the spot, and Trin ate all her broccoli, so I considered the dinner a resounding success.

Before I knew it, Trin's loopy smile slowly morphed into a spaced-out gaze and repeated yawns, which told me I needed to get her to bed with expediency.

"Ok, Miss Smart, it's bedtime. You have to shower and..."

"Can Ms. Mac read me a book before bed?"

Aisha's eyes widened, an emotion I couldn't fully pinpoint making them shine brighter.

"Of course, Trinity, it would be my pleasure!" she said, and I wondered why I'd bothered being nervous at all.

"And the ballerina bowed to the claps of all her friends. The End," Aisha whispered to a conked-out Trinity. She turned off the lamp, then met my gaze with a delighted smile.

"Should I turn off the night light, or does she need it for a good night's sleep?"

"Once she's out, she's out, night light or not. But I usually leave it on in case I need to come in and get any clothes ready for the next day or just to check up on her,"

My hands were in my sweatpants pockets, and as we exited the room, Aisha slid her hand in and interlaced it with mine.

This felt right. When I wasn't in my head and just let things vibe, it all flowed so well.

"You were good with her...do you want kids?" I asked, wondering how her answer would affect me. I'd always wanted at least two kids, but since my divorce, I'd stopped hoping for more.

"Oh yeah, one at least...maybe two. How about you?" she asked hesitantly.

"I'd love to give Trin a sibling. You'd be good parenting a stepkid?" I smiled, and she returned the gesture, the current between us stronger than ever.

"You know, I never thought about it in such concrete terms, but Trin...she's amazing, I'd be honored. She's such a good kid, Knox, you've done good." Her words shone on that space that always wondered if I was doing good by Trin, filling me up with light.

"Thanks, baby, that means a lot."

I sat on the sofa and patted my lap. Aisha curled herself up on me, her warm ass cradled by my thighs. It would soon be cradled by something else, but for now, I just wanted to hold her.

"You know you're a good dad, right? I might have been annoyed at you, but one thing that has always been clear to me is how attentive and present a dad you are. Parenting ain't easy; I teach children, and some days, even with my happy-go-lucky self, I can barely string two words together. And you're doing it practically on your own."

"Well, that might change soon..." The words came out without thought. I stiffened under her, not sure I wanted to bother her with my worries.

"What happened?" She slid herself away, making her back meet the arm of the chair, draping her legs on my lap so we had better eye contact.

"My ex... Chantal wants to have Trin every weekend."

Silence.

"Can I ask you something?"

"Of course, baby, you can ask me anything. At any time."

"Why doesn't she have Trin for more days?"

I paused, searching for a way to explain the situation without putting the mother of my child in a bad light.

"She realized that her addiction and her mental health were impeding her being dialed in for Trin. When we went through the divorce, she asked me to take full custody on paper. Only one weekend a month for her. She travels a lot for work, and she did rehab for a while, wanting to truly go deep into the roots of her addiction, so she knew she wouldn't be there for Trin like she needed to be. At first, I was pissed. I wanted Trin to have both parents equally present, but after a while, I got it. Then I got used to it, and now..."

"And now she's trying to change things, and you don't like it."

"Exactly."

"But what's best for Trin?"

"That's the million-dollar question. I think that it'll be hard for me to do leisure things with Trin if she's at her mom's every weekend, but I get that she travels. I just wish she wanted to be involved in the everyday hustle and not just be the fun weekend parent. I probably need to sit down and talk to her about how I feel in detail in our family therapy, but I haven't wanted to even go there... You know? I haven't been able to sort through this without getting mad before tonight."

"Huh, what changed?"

"The weight of your booty on my dick, probably."

"What?" she spluttered, her cough melding into laughter. "Here we are, having a real conversation, and you come out of left field with that."

"I'm just stating the truth," I said and hoisted her by the waist and got her ass right back where it was at the beginning. Where it belonged.

"Here, let me rub it a little bit," I cajoled as she swatted my hands away from her side while gasping with laughter.

"Can you be serious, please?" She laughed harder as I tried to tickle her.

"Serious for what, baby? I'm serious—some would say I was grumpy before you—but that's just my outer layer to protect myself from bullshit. And you? You're such a calming force for me. You make me want to work harder on my own bullshit. But this, my goofy side? This is me too."

She studied me as I spread my arms on the sofa.

"I see you, Knox," she whispered.

"I see you too, baby." I chased her whisper and gave in to the kiss I'd wanted to give her the moment she walked into my house.

"Stay. I want to enjoy you the whole night, just us."

"Oh, umm... Yes, I'd love that, but are you sure? I mean, Trin could wake up." I stopped her worries with a kiss, then another. Then another for good measure.

"I told you she's a deep sleeper. And this feels..." I paused, doing a gut check and coming back sure. "It feels right."

Her eyes shone with deep emotion, and I wanted to surround her with all the love and care she deserved.

"I gotta see if Sal can stay with my grandparents. But if she can, I'll stay."

Drawing strength that surprised me, I stood up, pulling her so her legs wrapped around my waist, her arms automatically joining behind my neck.

"You wanna see my room?" I asked, feeling again like my first time.

"Yes, Knox, show me," she said, her solid weight working just as I imagined a weighted blanket would. The only things I felt with her in my arms like this were safety, care and lust. I also felt a lot of lust.

The trek to my room was record-breaking. I entered, my hands full of Aisha.

"Please dim the lamps," I asked her, and she complied, giving the room a similar feel to the Gold Room.

"This ain't Q's Space, but I hope you like it."

"Are you serious? This is gorgeous! You have great taste. Your whole house is beautiful." I thanked her with a kiss, pride brimming out of me at the homey but elegant vibe I'd tried to foster in the house.

My dark gray walls had white framed photos of special places I'd visited with Trin. I loved black, and my furniture reflected that, but I had added splashes of color all over because Trin had asked me not to make my room boring, and she was the princess of this domain. Now here was someone who could be the queen, and my hands itched to caress every inch of her body on my bed all night long.

"Thanks. I'm glad you like it because I see us in this room, making memories."

"Oh, Knox."

I laid her in the middle of the bed and enfolded her with my body.

Words caught in my throat as I witnessed the emotion overflowing from her eyes. Not wanting to speak anymore, I showed her instead with actions what resided in my heart.

A soft kiss to her mouth transformed into a passionate embrace, our tongues tangling as we rolled around the bed, making space to remove our clothing. Soon, I was naked, and she only had her top on, but I didn't want my lips apart from hers, so ripping her T-shirt made the most sense.

"Knox!"

"What? I'll get you another one, I promise." I trailed kisses down her neck into her trembling mounds as she laughed.

"I love how you look at me," she whispered as I shifted my body next to hers to lay on my side, leaving no space between us. I wanted to better admire all her beautiful tawny skin, flushed in her arousal.

"How do I look at you?"

"Like I'm everything you ever wished for," she said, taking a deep breath to calm herself.

"That's an understatement, Baby Doll," I said, propping my face up on my fist to better see her, and gave in to the urge to play with her tits. The silky feel of her breast under my finger made my dick rise in anticipation as I caressed her with delicate touches along the line of her cleavage.

I lifted the lace just enough for my fingertip to slide under the fabric and found her nipple, the hard nub the evidence of her excitement. Her soft breathing with the cute little hitches whenever I touched her a way she especially liked would probably make me orgasm way before I planned, but I didn't care; I loved to hear how needy she got for me.

"You like it when I touch you here?" I hovered my finger right over her left nipple, gazing at her as she closed her eyes.

She nodded.

I pinched it, and her eyes flew open, her flesh trembling

at the sensation I created. The look of outrage morphed into soft eyes.

"Yes, Sir, I love it when you touch me here."

"Good, Baby Doll, I love how needy you get for my touch," I whispered in her ear, then ran my tongue in the swirl, a soft sigh emanating from deep within her.

I tasted her salty skin, running the tip of my tongue as if it were my finger around her ear and the side of her neck. Letting my baser instincts take over, I yanked the lace cups down her breasts with my free hand until both nipples were free. I left the bra on, loving the way it propped up her tits for my viewing pleasure.

Proof of my need painted the soft skin of her thigh as my dick searched for any friction as relief. I rubbed it against her softness, my hands tingling as I massaged her breasts. The tingling traveled from my fingertips and connected directly with the nerve endings in my dick and tongue, all of it working in tandem to drive her as wild as touching her made me.

"Oh, Sir, please," she begged.

I bit her neck, then sucked and licked to ease the sting. I needed to touch her everywhere; the underside of her breast, her stomach, her cute belly button down to where she needed me the most. The delicacy I managed while touching her at first was slowly seeping away from me as I pressed my entire hand against her pussy, reveling in the way the simple touch made my palm wet.

"Oh, you're such a little greedy slut, look at how you're wetting my hand."

I showed her my palm, and her eyes glazed over with lust. She was so responsive to me that I felt my chest tighten, and again, the words that wanted to tumble out earlier threatened to escape me now. To avoid saying what I was feeling, what I was sure was showing in my face, I ravaged her with my lips instead, tasting her sweetness, enjoying her mewls of pleasure as I sucked her tongue into my mouth.

I slid a finger inside her tender wet flesh as our tongues tangled, our breaths melding to the beat of our hearts. I slid another finger in as my tongue dragged from her chin down her chest, and I captured her areola with my mouth, suckling her as she clenched my two fingers.

I rubbed my thumb over her hard clitoris as I smothered myself between her tits, inhaling her sweet scent, coming up for air to watch her eyes flutter closed when it got too good for her.

Now three fingers drove into her while my palm cupped her pussy, and I stimulated her clit, making her buck and shudder, getting her just where I wanted her.

"Are you gonna give me that nut, Baby Doll?" I bit her nipple, then laved it with swipes of my tongue, pressure building in my lower back the harder my dick got. At this point, I was nudging her with my length, my dick having no give left in it. The solid rock between my legs needed her soft wetness to soothe me.

"Yes, it's yours, Sir," she moaned as her walls gripped my fingers, her earthy scent permeating the room as I thrust in and out of her.

"Good because you can only come when I tell you you can," I growled into her ear, then bit the lobe, her hitch in breath making precum leak out of my dickhead.

The first of many memories solidified in my brain as I admired her, mouth parted, eyes half-mast as she rode her passion against my hand. Her pussy seized my fingers with such force I had to close my eyes for a beat hoping she wouldn't make me spill outside of her.

Before that happened, I pulled my fingers out of her pussy, the sound of her not wanting to let them go music to my ears.

"Ok then, let me give you all you need," I said as I braced myself above her, her parted legs the best welcoming committee for my needy dick.

My words...they could be interpreted sexually, but I meant differently. I just didn't have the courage to tell her yet, so instead, I joined her warm haven in one stroke, grabbing one of her thighs to hold on.

Then I let it all go.

I fucked her hard, my dick drilling into her wet pussy, her clenching driving me to move faster. She started panting as my dick worked her walls and my balls contracted, and I felt lightheaded, my orgasm a few strokes away.

I needed her to come first, though. I needed to feel her gripping me so tight I forgot all my worries and all of hers.

"I need that nut now, Baby Doll." I relaxed my arms on each side of her, wanting to erase any space between us. When her flesh cradled mine from the top of my chest to the tip of my toes, I realized we were no longer fucking.

We were making love.

Even my actions betrayed the one thing I wasn't ready to tell her.

So, my body took over as we undulated together, sweat slick between us.

"I need you to..." I grunted, bottoming out, holding still for a second.

"I know what you need." The connection between us stretched and lengthened as it tangled us together. I felt the ties pushing me further into her until I felt a flutter, then a full pulse around my dick and so much wetness.

"Fuuck."

All through her orgasm, we never broke eye contact as she came silently, her body seducing the climax out of mine.

Without delay, trembles started in my legs as I jetted out in her in long strokes. My brain glitched, and my entire body shivered as the best orgasm of my life happened with the woman I was falling inevitably in love with.

I need to tell her, she needs to know flashed through my mind as I succumbed to a deep slumber, cradled in Aisha's arms.

Twenty-Five

Aisha

When's the last time I slept past six a.m.? It's probably this bed. It's nice, real nice. Makes me not want to open my eyes.

Is Knox still next to me? Maybe I should check if he's hard... Ugh, my legs feel like I'be been dancing en pointe for three days straight, that fourth time last night was one too many. I'd do it again.

I'll need a plan when I sleep over cause I need me more of this. Sal is a doll for sleeping over so Momma and Pops weren't on their own. I wonder what she'd like for lunch.

I think I need to change the ending of the dads' choreography, it needs something unforgettable. Why is my mind racing? I should sleep another twenty minutes.

My musings were cut short when I sensed a presence next to me. I tentatively stretched my hand to the opposite side of the bed; it was still warm, but Knox wasn't in it. I pried my eyes open to find Trinity hovering next to me with a curious look on her face.

"Uhhhh..." I pulled the sheets all the way up to my neck

even though I was wearing Knox's t-shirt and boxers. We'd had the presence of mind to change the sheets after our last time, showering and putting some clothes on when Knox explained that Trin sometimes woke up early and would sneak in his room and get into bed.

He hadn't felt comfortable locking his bedroom, and even though this standoff was uncomfortable as hell, I understood his hesitation.

"Hi, Ms. Mac." Trin waved at me.

"Hi, sweetie, did you...um, sleep well?" I asked her, my mouth dry. *I hope I didn't drool in my sleep.*

"Yeah, how about you? Did you like my Daddy's bed?"

Suddenly all my training went out the window as I gaped at Trin. Words failed me. Knox strolled into the room from the bathroom, and I'd never been so happy for someone to interrupt a conversation.

"Good morning, Miss Smart," he said.

"Hello, Daddy, can we have pancakes?" Trin batted her eyelashes at her father, and he melted right in front of my eyes.

Oh, he was putty for his daughter.

"Of course. Aisha, would you like some pancakes?"

Our eyes connected, and that tenderness I'd recognized just seconds ago still filled his gaze. My cheeks heated, blood rushing to them as I nodded, not having the words to express myself right now.

He winked, then held out his hand to Trin, giving me a moment of privacy to get myself together.

After I collected my thoughts, I waltzed into the kitchen, ready to help Knox with breakfast, but he shooed me away, to Trinity's amusement.

"Alright, alright, I know when I'm not wanted," I said,

walking over to the other side of the island to sit next to Trin.

A slight sting on my bottom made me jump.

"Did you just swat that towel at me?" I turned to find a smirking Knox with a rolled-up kitchen towel.

"Yeah, just so you stop talking nonsense, talking about not being wanted." He shook his head and went back to pouring batter on the griddle.

"You see this, Trin?" I stared at her in mock outrage, and she dissolved into giggles.

That's how the morning continued, the ease with which the three of us interacted with each other sending me higher than my best company ballet days. I let the fuzzy feeling of our morning envelop me, and for a second, I let myself imagine how it could be long-term with Knox. I realized I wanted it so bad. I hadn't let myself think too much ahead— I knew I wanted to be with him, but I hadn't tried to frame or define it in my mind. But this morning had me rethinking what I wanted from him.

I wanted it all.

The pancakes were delicious, and after a bit of a tug of war, I won and convinced Knox to let me clean up. I had just turned the faucet on to rinse the plates when the doorbell rang.

"Mmm, I don't know who'd be here at this time on a Sunday. Maybe it's your grandfather, Trin." Knox sauntered to the door.

"Hi, sorry for coming unannounced, but..." A voice I didn't recognize got louder as someone walked into the open area where the living room, dining room, and kitchen were located.

I put the plate in my hands down, a sense of foreboding passing through me.

"Who's this?" The voice went from friendly to inquisitive.

"Oh, hi!" I turned around and waved at the woman.

Wow, she was a beauty. Just seeing her made me realize who she was. Chantal.

She was shorter than me, with a petite, curvy body, and I could see where Trin got her gorgeous hair; she had a mane of black curls almost to her waist. Right now, her eyes were cold, judgmental, and trained on me.

"Who are you?"

"Uhh…" I searched for Knox's gaze as he walked in behind Chantal, but all his attention was on his daughter.

I did the same and saw Trin chewing her bottom lip, eyes swiveling between both of us.

"I'm a guest of Knox's, and Trin's dance schoolteacher." The fact that she didn't know me was something I still found flabbergasting, but I now had a better understanding of their situation.

"Trin's teacher? Really, Knox?" Chantal said in disgust.

Trin's eyes shifted between Knox and Chantal, and I wanted to go and hug the little girl, but I knew it wasn't my place.

"To what do we owe the pleasure of your visit, Chantal?" Knox asked, and in that moment, I realized that even at the height of our antagonism, Knox hadn't really disliked me. The tone he'd just used…may he never use it with me.

It was indifference mixed with dismissal and a deep-seated annoyance. It wasn't hate, that would be worrisome, but this tone… It meant co-parenting was probably hell for them both.

"Ugh, I'm sorry for interrupting this idyllic scene, but you weren't answering your text messages, and Trin left her bag with her schoolbooks at my house. I figured she needs it for tomorrow." She thrust the bag into Knox's chest, and Knox's jaw tightened.

"Sorry I didn't answer. I was occupied."

"Oh ho, I bet you were," Chantal lashed out. Tension gathered in my shoulder blades, and I could only imagine how Knox was feeling. And Trin... Blast it all, I dried my wet hands with the kitchen towel and approached her. Her little shoulder was shaking when I placed my hand on it, wanting to offer her comfort.

"You want us to go to your room?" I whispered in her ear while her parents argued.

"No," she whispered back, and I knew I should probably press the issue when the door swung open and Knox's parents walked in.

"Chantal!" Mrs. Jameson embraced her, cutting some of the tension away.

"Hello, sweetheart. We came to get you. We're going to a dance festival in Plantation, and we thought you'd like to see it," Mr. Jameson said to Trinity.

I felt horrible. I needed to leave and let Knox and Chantal figure things out. I knew they'd been separated for four years and went to family therapy for Trin's sake, but there were some unresolved sentiments here.

"You should go, that sounds like fun," I whispered in Trin's ear, and she nodded.

"Come, honey, let me help you get ready." Mrs. Jameson extended her hand to Trin, whose face twisted with worry.

The moment Trin was out of the room, Chantal whirled on Knox.

"Why would you call your parents like that? What do you think I was going to do to Trin?!"

"Lower your voice. You forget Trin is seven; she understands everything that's happening. Sometimes you operate around her like she's still three." Knox hurled his words at Chantal with a precision that made my chest tighten.

"This again. Only *you* are the father of the year, only *you* know what's good for Trin. But you didn't hesitate to bring your who—"

"Watch your mouth, Chantal."

"I think I better leave," I said, making my way to his bedroom to get my things.

"No."

"Oh, Ms. Mac, you don't have to."

"Yes."

All those answers came at the same time from Knox, Mr. Jameson, and Chantal, making me pause.

"This is not your house, Chantal."

"Oh, you never stop reminding me that... Oh, forget it. I told you I want more time with Trin, and you deny me, but at the same time, this woman gets to spend time with *my* daughter. I'll do what I must to make sure I get my time."

Chantal stormed out after that ominous comment, slamming the door, leaving Knox pinching his nose in exasperation.

"That spiraled out of control." He sighed. "I can understand her being taken aback. It's been four years, and she's never had to deal with me dating anyone seriously enough to bring home."

"Well, son, there's no manual for handling divorces, but maybe you should discuss this at family therapy."

I rushed to the bedroom. In there, I let the tears that had gathered stream down my face. There was no reason to cry; this wasn't about me, but I felt responsible. I could have just stayed home, talked things through with Knox so he could take this step in a more concrete, planned manner. We rushed into things, and this is what happened.

The door clicked shut, and I felt his presence behind me as I gathered my clothes from the day before in my bag.

"You don't have to leave."

"We should have thought this through with a little more foresight."

"Nah, I should have given Chantal a heads up that you and I were serious in our last session, but that's all I owe her. You already know Trin, so things are special with you," he said, pulling me closer to him. His arm slid around my waist, and I rested my head on his chest, my back to his front.

"I feel bad...for Trin, for you. Even Chantal, even though she wanted to call me a lady of the night."

The snort against my hair had me contorting myself to see Knox's face.

"Are you laughing at me right now?"

"Lady of the night? You really do the most not to curse."

"I teach children for most of my day. If I curse out of school, it'll bleed into my language in the studio, so I just don't do it," I said defensively but couldn't avoid the smile that came through. I turned in his arms and hugged him, enjoying the moment of stillness after the drama of the morning.

"Are we moving too fast?" I mumbled into his chest.

"I don't know...but my parents want you to come to Thanksgiving."

"Oh...wow."

"And they want you to bring your grandparents, so I think the car's left the starting line regardless," he said, squeezing me into him. "Are you sure you don't want to stay? Trin will be out for a few hours."

"Nah, Sal did me a solid staying with my grandparents, but I have to go."

I didn't say the rest—I needed space away from him to think straight. This day had been a lot, and I needed to figure out how tomorrow would look with Knox Davenport and all the responsibilities that came with being in a relationship with him.

"Ok, Baby Doll, but don't you go overthinking things now, alright?" He kissed my forehead, then bent down to steal a kiss, our lips dancing together with a tenderness that threatened to make my eyes fill again.

"I can't promise that." I shook my head, dazed after his tender kiss.

"Damn, I wanted to spare you this. I can't promise not to overthink things either," he confessed, and I bit my cheek to keep myself from asking him what that meant.

If I'd planned to even try not to fret, that plan incinerated in front of my eyes as I exited Knox's house, hoping the light quiver in my belly went away.

Twenty-Six

Knox

Thanksgiving morning started with Trin jumping on my bed with a big smile on her face.

"It's Thanksgiving, Daddy! Come on, we need to make our food!"

We weren't expected at my mom's until midday, but Trin loved waking up early and baking the pies with me. The house looked like the Michaels Thanksgiving display. Trin had gone overboard with the fall décor she'd selected during our trip to the store.

I was glad for this moment just for Trin and me—a lot was happening lately between Chantal and me trying to work things out with our co-parenting and things getting serious with Aisha. That didn't touch the surface of how busy things were at work and all the preparations for the Holiday Show for the studio.

Once the assorted pies were ready, we packed everything up and headed to my parents' house.

"So, Daddy, is Mommy coming to Thanksgiving?" Trin

asked.

"No, she's spending it with her family. But you'll be spending Christmas with her like we both explained to you." I knew this from previous conversations, but I hadn't heard from Chantal since she stormed out of my house.

Trin stayed quiet as she processed the information.

"Alright, but Ms. Mac is coming for Thanksgiving, right?" I tried to read into her tone, wondering what she thought of all of this, of me dating Aisha, of what Chantal had said that Sunday at my house.

When I'd asked her how she felt after she returned home, she said she was ok, and she understood that her mommy was upset, and she knew she'd feel better once they spent more time together.

After that, every time I checked in with her, she just nodded along, saying she liked Ms. Mac and she loved her mommy. Trin was such a sensitive and highly intelligent child I didn't know if she was bottling things up or if she truly was ok. It was all messing with me.

"Yeah, she is, but are you good with that?" I asked her.

"Yes, Daddy! You asked me yesterday too, and I told you I like Ms. Mac," she said, showing a little of the temper she unfortunately inherited from me.

"Ok, I just want to make sure I'm not doing anything that makes you uncomfortable."

"I'm fine, Daddy."

"Alright, baby."

The aroma of turkey, stuffing, greens, and bacon greeted us the moment my dad opened the door for us.

"Son! Trinity! Happy Thanksgiving!" He wore a turkey hat on his head and made a gobble-gobble sound, making Trin giggle.

Just as we placed the pies on the table, the bell rang again.

"Welcome! Welcome!"

Aisha's shy smile hit me straight in the chest. She was gorgeous, with her hair all in a bun on the top of her head, eyes shining with excitement as she introduced her grandparents to my father.

"Who's—oh! Welcome!" Mom's loud voice reverberated from the kitchen door as she rushed to greet Aisha and her family.

I stood rooted to the spot, feeling Trin's hand slip away from mine as she also went to the door to greet everyone.

Aisha's exuberance was contagious, and her grandparents hit it off with Trin right away. She searched for me and met my gaze. Lifting an eyebrow, she winked and turned to answer a question my dad posed.

The sight of her hugging my mom and shuffling the pan in her hand, all the while making sure her grandparents were good made everything feel right.

The stream of doubts cleared up like the sun coming out after a rainy afternoon, and I let her magnetism pull me in.

"Hey, baby." I bent over to steal a chaste kiss.

"Hi," she responded, breathless.

"Here, give me the mac and cheese. Do I need to put it in the oven?" Mom asked, taking the pan away from Aisha.

"Not right now. Depending on your schedule, this just needs twenty minutes right before dinner."

"Daddy, do you think this mac and cheese will taste better than Auntie Roxane's?" Trin asked. Before I could answer, my mom laughed at a joke from Aisha, and Trin joined in the chat.

I interlaced my hand with hers, and on my other side, Trin did the same.

Yes, this felt right.

———

STEPHEN and his family arrived a little after one, and the house was a cacophony of laughter, music, and TV.

Shelly was spending Thanksgiving with her boyfriend so we facetimed her in, and Aisha and her grandparents got to meet her. Instantly Shelly and Aisha clicked making plans of meeting once Shelly was back in town.

Aisha integrated with my family seamlessly, and her grandparents were a great addition to the group. Her Pops had a great sense of humor and had all us guys cracking up in the family room as we watched the game while the ladies played cards in the living room.

"Ok, everyone, it's that time!" Mom announced.

We all shuffled our way into the dining room, where my parents had added additional tables to make one long one for the day.

"This smells delicious. I'm telling y'all right now, don't wake me up when the 'itis kicks in!"

"Pops! I told you that's not good to say no more!" Aisha groaned as my niece and nephew guffawed.

"Oh, please, we all Black here, y'all know I mean no harm." Pops dismissed her and zoomed his way to his seat.

"Amos, stop it, you're embarrassing Aisha," Aisha's Momma admonished.

"You embarrassed, cupcake?"

"No, Pops." She laughed, then blew a kiss at her Momma for looking out for her.

We sat down to eat, the dinner a fun experience, everyone trading stories and jokes.

Aisha radiated happiness, and I snuck my hand underneath the table to hold hers. Her eyes dropped down as her shy smile bloomed, and if we were on our own, I'd steal a kiss and more.

We all helped with the cleaning, making the process quick. Pops fell asleep in his scooter just like he promised.

As I rounded the corner back to the family room, Momma took the opportunity to pull me aside, and I braced myself for whatever was coming. Momma looked like she didn't suffer any fools, and I wanted to make sure she knew I was serious about Aisha.

"You know that girl there, she's our everything. She doesn't talk about it much, but having lost her mother to her addiction so young in her life and her father being a good-for-nothing, she's starved for love. So she goes out of her way to show everyone how much she loves them. And some people take advantage of that." She gave me a side-eye. I don't know what gave her the impression that I'd ever use Aisha, and I fought not to bristle at the implication. I knew where she was coming from, though. I hadn't been the best to Aisha in the beginning, and that was a deep regret.

"Momma...can I call you Momma?"

"If you love my granddaughter, yes, you can."

"Then Momma it is." I said it with my chest, my heart pumping twice as hard even though my stomach swooped down at the confession. I hadn't said anything to Aisha, but I knew how I felt. I knew what I wanted with her. I just needed to fight through these doubts that told me we were moving too fast.

"Ok, son, you make sure you keep making her smile the way she was smiling today. If not, her Pops and I'll come get you. Don't you think we can't take you; we knew some moves back in the day," she warned me, and I fought the urge to smile, knowing Momma probably got down in her youth.

"Listen, I'm looking for this to be for the long run. As long as your granddaughter lets me love her, I'll do it with my whole heart."

———

AFTER A COUPLE of rounds of dominos, where Stephen and Pops got very competitive, we called it for the night. I tucked Trin in at my parents', and together, Aisha and I drove her grandparents home.

I helped her settle them in, making sure they had all they needed for the night. After they took their meds, we said our goodnights, Momma giving me a warning glance on her way to her room.

Aisha and I walked together to her living room and stood by the door.

"Thank you for the invite. Today was a dream," she said, sliding her arms around my waist and pushing up to give me a sultry kiss that had me wishing I could take her home with me.

I told her as much, and she bit her lips.

"Why don't you stay here with me?" she whispered.

"You know, I was hoping you'd invite me, Baby Doll. I'll run home to get some clothes and a bag and be back in a second."

I stayed true to my promise, returning to her in less than thirty minutes. She opened the door in a long silk robe, her hair down, her face free of makeup. I could feel her excitement, and my dominant side clawed inside me.

"Fuck, you're gorgeous. I love you all ways, but this way, I love you best."

Aisha's eyes widened, and I froze for a second, then embraced what I said.

"You know I had to tell your grandma first? She teased it out of me, but yes, I love you, Aisha. I don't know when it happened, and I know we still are very new, but I trust my gut, and my gut tells me you and I were meant to go from annoying the shit out of each other to driving each other wild with lust to end up here, filled with love..." I trailed off as her eyes brimmed with tears.

"Come on, we're standing in the door like we're sixteen and my grandparents don't let me have boys in the house. Come." She tugged me in and upstairs to her room. I was glad her grandparents' room was downstairs with their own en suite bathroom because I didn't know if I could keep civil with her tonight.

I tried to push away the need to hear her tell me she loved me as we walked into her room, and I sensed her right away in the décor, with gray walls and purple and pink touches. She had abstract drawings of dancers pinned up and a few photos of her performances on and off Broadway, with the ballet company, and with her friends and her grandparents.

Her bed was all white and full of pillows, and I wondered how long it took her to move them before going to bed. She was what I called neat-messy, with piles of clothes all draped nicely on a chair in a corner and a tower of books on the floor.

"So, I want to start by telling you a story," she said, sitting on her bed and patting for me to sit as well.

"When I was in New York, I had a boyfriend. He was my first true dom. I had been in the lifestyle but hadn't been collared, as they say. He was the choreographer for an off-Broadway show I was working on, and it was lust at first sight. When James found out I was a sub, it was on." She smiled, and I felt my gut twist at the thought of her smiling like that for another dude.

"We got on so fast, and I got lost in the kink of it all. I loved submitting to him, and combined with my love for him...I think I lost myself a little. I think I was a fantasy come true for him, looking back on it all. He'd found the perfect girl with the type of body he loved, and she was into kink. But I don't think he found me emotionally compatible.

"There were signs. He'd only want to fuck and hang out at his place or mine, but when it came to going out with friends, unless they were from work or going out with his family, he'd pass. But still, he swore up and down he was in love. And I believed him. I dismissed the signs. He asked me to marry him after one of our performances on stage, and I melted right there, I was so happy. I still don't know why he proposed..."

What the fuck? She'd been engaged? I had to calm myself. I...I knew something had hurt her in the past, but I hadn't been ready for this.

"It didn't last for long." She shook her head, interpreting my look. I realized she was starting to get nervous due to my reaction, and I had to comfort her.

"Why don't we get ready for bed, and you keep telling me?"

She smiled and dropped her robe on the floor, and again, my chest tightened at the honor of being here in her room, where she was the most vulnerable.

Aisha swiped most of the pillows to the floor, answering the question I had before, and got herself under the comforter, then waited for me to remove my sweatpants and t-shirt. I slid into the bed in my boxers and pulled her to me, inhaling her lotion scent. With our backs against the headboard, she rested her head on my shoulder.

"I saw your face, and I can tell you're surprised I hadn't shared this. But it was a low time in my life. After some soul searching, he realized he wasn't ready for marriage, or at least not with me. He got married the year after he left me to the most vanilla of people."

Fuck. I clenched my fist, and if I ever met that nigga, I'd make sure to make him rue hurting my Baby Doll.

"I got depressed because I had linked my submission to our relationship, and I couldn't access it like I used to before. When I moved here and presented the idea to do hired sessions with Master Q, I realized that I had the tendency to fall for my doms a little, probably because of my experience with James. So, I started putting additional boundaries on my sessions, and right before starting with you, I'd been on a break." She paused.

"All this is to say that I've been through some stuff with my submission and getting my wires crossed. But with you, it's all been so natural. The annoyance to lust to love, it all happened without me overthinking anything. If anything, I tried to fight it. I tried to keep you behind that black and gold door. But you and your way of making sure you take care of my well-being and making sure I see all of you and the way you see all of me... I—" She choked up, making my heart skip a beat. "I'm so happy to take a risk again, and I know my heart is in good hands with you."

I couldn't wait any longer after those words. I gently nudged her face up, pressing my knuckle under her chin, and touched my lips with hers. I didn't have any more words in me. Outside, the rain started to fall as I deepened our kiss, our tongues loving each other. I sucked her tongue, and she moaned in pleasure, and soon, my hand was lost inside her boyshorts, and my dick pulsed in her hand.

Undressing became its own act of foreplay, the silky white sheets caressing my back as I hoisted her up on me. Our declarations of love aroused us. I tasted her soft skin, that spot between her neck and shoulder, and felt her shudder.

"I want to make you feel like this every single day, all the time," I whispered in her ear as I lined up my dick with her entrance. The heat of her body pressed against mine, and she surged over me, seeking our pleasure. I entered her with exquisite slowness until I was deep in her.

"Oh, Knox."

Aisha bit my bottom lip, and I grabbed her lush ass, ready to punish her for making me lose myself in her.

I held her still and flexed in her, my strokes making her walls tremble.

"Oh, Sir, right there...don't stop."

"Never, Baby Doll, never."

I kept my promise, not slowing my pace until I felt her telltale flutter, her orgasm milking my own. I felt my legs tingle, then go numb as I emptied myself inside her, cum and heart all hers.

"I love you, Baby Doll."

"And I love you, Sir."

Twenty-Seven

Knox

"So, guess what? Five of my dancers returned!" Aisha jumped into my arms as I entered the studio for our daddy dance rehearsal.

The studio shone with Christmas lights twinkling over green wreaths. She had decked out the space, and the holiday feeling snuck up on me.

"For real?" I asked her, happy to hear that—it meant my actions were bearing fruit.

I hadn't wanted to worry her too much, but I'd found out that the studio poaching her dancers was in one of our properties. We had a clause in all our contracts that we provided half-price rent for six months or until we deemed the business ready to pay full rent, whatever came first. I activated the ready clause after realizing the competing studio was at capacity at the expense of cheap rates obtained through my fifty percent discount rent program.

The program was meant to help the community prosper and give a leg up. I'd applied the discount out of a sense of responsibility to my old family through Chantal, but I was regretting things now. I knew I had to talk to Aisha soon and explain my connection to her poaching situation, but managing it all without poisoning her against Chantal was a magic act I wasn't sure I could perform.

Was it too much to wish my co-parent and my girlfriend got along?

"Hey, where did you go just now?" Aisha asked as she pulled me into Room A. "I want to show you the new end of the choreography."

She'd changed the end to make it more organic. After the last eight-beat count, she had us in a formation of two lines to then break out jumping and just vibing for the last minute of the song; the idea was for us to freestyle till the stage went dark.

"That's an amazing idea, Baby Doll," I said and pressed her to me, searching for the calm only she gave me. My chest still felt tight at the thought of what I'd inadvertently put her through.

As I kissed her, some other parents started to come in. I hastily pulled away, and she frowned at me, her hurt look punching me in my gut.

Being official with her meant she was now comfortable being open with the other parents. She'd gone from reticent to wanting things to be official, and I remembered her Momma's warning. I squeezed her hand in apology, unable to help the reflex to keep things under wraps. My need for privacy and my conflicting feelings about us moving too fast kept me in a state of overwhelming confusion.

"Ok, parents, this is one of the last rehearsals, so let's make sure we leave everything on the floor. Remember, whatever facial expressions you're making while dancing, you want to really exaggerate them so everyone can notice them even if they bought the nosebleeds, ok?"

Aisha pressed play, and we started our rehearsal. Lowkey, I was proud of how well I knew the steps and how much fun I was having. Most of us were in our thirties, and the song selections were all music we loved when we were in our young adulthood.

Aisha sat in a corner, amping us up as we went through the steps over and over.

"Ok, ok, gents, you're killing it! Let's take ten, so y'all can hydrate. I don't need anyone passing out here!" She laughed and handed out bottles of water.

I checked my phone to see if I had missed any communications. Chantal had gone radio silent after the situation at my house and hadn't shown up for our co-parenting therapy session after Thanksgiving. I was worried I wouldn't be able to bridge the gap with her, so I kept hoping she'd reach out. I'd tried reaching out myself to no response.

Instead of a text from her, I found one from Liam Kwon asking me to call him. That was odd; we had just met yesterday, and everything was going well. Kwon had asked us for time to make the final decision, which I appreciated; there was no real rush, after all. I had so much going on in my life, I'd started to reprioritize things at work—another consequence of Aisha's good influence.

I quietly stepped out of the room into the waiting area and dialed his number.

"Davenport, how's your evening?"

"I'm alright, Kwon, good to hear from you. I know you asked us for time to decide, so I'm surprised to get your call today."

"Yeah, well, I received an interesting email today, and I didn't want to wait till tomorrow." Kwon's tone was always formal, but there was something in his voice that made my muscles tense.

"Tell me."

"I got an email from an anonymous source with some compromising pictures and video of you and your friend, the dance teacher. It seems to be her studio, and in there, you have her bound and gagged."

What the heck? God, being with Aisha was rubbing off. How could someone possibly have photos and videos of that night? Shit was fucked up to have our privacy violated that way... My ever-present simmering temper radiated through my veins. Pain shot through my head, threatening a relentless headache.

Aisha and I'd had a fun night right before Thanksgiving, where I had explored some of my bondage kink with her. We'd both loved it. It had been for just us, though, no one else. I couldn't wrap my mind around why someone would want to violate us like that.

"I...I don't even know how someone could get that."

"Is her establishment accessible to the public?"

"Well, yeah, but... She's been searching for a receptionist, and..."

"Well, I don't know what your relationship is with her—"

"Oh, we're...friends." It slipped out of my mouth so easily I immediately felt ill at the words. I don't know why I even said it, I just knew that I couldn't afford this marring my business or hers or Trin. My kink was private, not something for people to consume and mock. Someone out there was trying to hurt me through my sexuality, and that shit pissed me off.

"Listen, Kwon, thanks for letting me know. Can I call

you back, though?" I said, knowing I couldn't keep a civil conversation right now.

I liked Kwon, and I wanted to partner with him, but if this meant we were done, then maybe we weren't meant to work together. This should have no bearing on business, but someone thought it would.

Fuck. Who could be trying to sabotage me or Aisha?

In my reverie, I didn't notice that Aisha had come out to get me.

"Hey, Sir, are you alright?"

"Hey, Baby Doll, I'm fine," I said, trying to fake a smile. The lie tasted sour in my mouth. The grimace she made told me I was unsuccessful.

"What's wrong, Knox?"

"Nothing that doesn't have a solution." I nodded and draped my arm around her shoulder, dropping a kiss on top of her curls. I didn't know how to even begin to explain everything, but before I did, I needed to see this video with my own eyes and talk to Kwon, understand what the email said.

"Are you sure? Your expression right now..."

"Nah, Baby Doll, don't you worry about anything. All you need to focus on right now is your show. This..." I waved my hand the way I wanted to wave away my anger. "Is nothing to worry about. Do you trust me?" I asked her and smiled, knowing this one was more genuine.

"Of course, I do, but...I don't want us keeping things from each other, alright?" she asked, stopping me right outside of Room A. Her big princess eyes stared at me, making me shift on my feet. There were things I was keeping from her, but not for long.

"I promise to tell you what you need to know," I said,

making sure I kept it 100% with her, even if it was a bit muddy.

She squinted her eyes at me and pressed her hand on my chest.

"I only need a Dom in my bed and in my kink. I don't need a Dom for anything else. This isn't a 24/7." She shook her head.

I understood where she was coming from, and I was going to tell her everything. I just needed to sort things out first because something told me there was more to it than an anonymous email. When I talked to Aisha, I needed to offer facts.

"Ok, Baby Doll." I pressed a kiss on her soft mouth.

"Why do I feel you're just trying to appease me?" she said.

I forced a laugh and pulled her into Room A, knowing I needed to get a handle on this situation right away.

Twenty-Eight

Aisha

"Girl, what is that?" Sal asked as my heart beat so fast, I felt it was loud enough for her to hear.

This morning I'd found a cryptic subject line from a weird email address in my business inbox. Years of being friends with Sal told me not to open it without her being present.

She came through immediately, her urgency making my nerves jump. Mila and Devon had been in the studio and heard my call to Sal, so both expectantly waited to see what the email was all about.

"That's Knox and me playing."

"Y'all play here?" Sal asked, and Mila stepped on her toe, making Sal grunt.

"If you don't move your feet off mine," Sal grumbled, stopping the video to protect our privacy. My skin crawled with the thought of someone accessing my space in such a violating way.

"Well, you're not helping with your judgy voice."

Sneaking around like teenagers had clearly made us more reckless than we should have been, and now here we were, paying the price.

"How the heck did they get in here, though? Whoever this anonymous source is?" Mila asked, putting into words one of the main things making me want to toss my breakfast. "Whoever it is, they had a good-ass angle. Damn, Aisha, you really do like fu—" Mila started, and I placed a hand over her mouth.

"Be careful," Sal warned, but it was too late; Mila had pressed her tongue to my palm.

"What's wrong with you?!" I asked her.

Mila just shook her head. "I can see you're about to lose your shit, so I tried to defuse things."

"Not helping." I brushed her off, the unease of weeks becoming a deeply embedded discomfort I couldn't shake.

"Sorry, I'm feeling as sick as you are. Who the fuck would come in here and record y'all? That's some intrusive shit. That door needs to be locked moving forward. I know you feel the chime is sufficient, but..."

Just as Mila was talking, Devon stepped out of Room B and came over to us. The moment he'd heard the three of us gasp when we opened the email, he'd stepped away from behind us to give me some privacy and rushed off.

"Look at this." Devon showed us a little wireless webcam. "I found it in there."

"Fuck. How long has that been there?" Mila asked, rushing into Room A to come back out with another camera.

"You need more cameras," Sal and Devon said simultaneously. They both looked at each other, Devon with an assessing stare, Sal with a scowl.

"I do," I said, walking away from the desk and sitting in

one of the waiting room chairs. My hands shook, my body growing cold as what had happened fully settled in my brain.

The cameras I had installed only pointed toward the dancers for the parents to see them practicing. They didn't cover the front of the rooms, so none of my footage would show who snuck in unless they decided to walk toward the back.

"This is ridiculous, why would someone want to film things in here?" I wondered, feeling my space despoiled. My stomach threatened to empty at the thought of never feeling safe here again.

"I don't even know how I'm going to tell Knox. All along, he's been insisting on me getting a receptionist..." I felt defeated.

Finally, things were looking up with the studio. Students were coming back, and no one went into detail about the other school.

The parents all acted as if nothing had happened, and I was wary of rocking the boat. I could ask up front, but I knew from some of the whispers that whoever it was had been mean, and they didn't want to upset me or my grandma and were just happy to be back. They didn't owe me the information, and if they didn't give it freely, I didn't want to push. In the end, they'd returned. I had to remember many of the families around were making the best of their finances, and if they'd found lower prices, I couldn't fault them for exploring other options, no matter how much it hurt.

The show was ready, we had final dress rehearsals in a few days, and my grandparents had all they needed medically for now. I had even been getting along with my dad. And Knox...

"Girl, he's your man now. He better be supportive instead of being a dick and pulling an 'I told you so'," Mila said, and Sal nodded along.

"I'm sure Knox will be supportive," Devon said, and Sal frowned at him.

"I should go talk to him. I just...ugh, this is bad. The anonymous person is threatening to send the video to the dancers' families unless I cancel the holiday show. Like who is this, and why are they acting like a movie villain?"

"I know, it's blackmail, and it's punishable by law. You could take them to court, are they reckless?" Sal wondered.

"That's why it's anonymous," Devon said.

"Yeah, but they didn't count on me," Sal said ominously, and I knew she was going to put her considerable skills to use to find my blackmailer. I felt my stomach calm a bit at the comfort of knowing I didn't need to deal with this by myself.

In the meantime, I needed to go and talk to Knox and warn him of what was happening. After all, these were his photos and video too. And then I'd have to spend a pretty penny upping the security here to feel comfortable again.

Knox and Stephen's office was a two-story building with all the modern touches you could ask for. The main doors opened to a wide open lobby with a large glass reception desk, where two people sat, busy on their computers.

When they heard the door shut, both the man and the woman raised their heads and smiled.

"Welcome to Davenport & Jameson, how can we assist you?" the man asked. I hadn't visited Knox's offices yet, but I knew both were recent college graduates in architecture.

The panic that ran through me earlier had subsided to a dull state of worry, Sal, Devon, and Mila having calmed me enough to be able to get behind the steering wheel to take the twenty-minute drive.

"Hi, Joshua, is it?" I asked, and he cocked his head, meeting the gaze of the other lady, who I imagined was Ebony.

"I'm Mr. Davenport's...girlfriend, Aisha." I extended my hand across the glass desk as Joshua stood up and enthusiastically shook my hand.

"Nice to meet you."

"We've heard wonderful things about you, Ms. Aisha, and the boss is working less on the weekends because of you, so that's a win for us all," Ebony confided with a smile. I returned the smile and glanced around, wondering where I could find Knox.

"Here, let me show you where the offices are."

"Call me tomorrow, I'll hook you up—" Stephen approached the desk from one of the hallways leading to the reception and stopped when he noticed me. I tried to keep my expression relaxed as I gripped the papers with the email where the blackmailer asked me to drop the show.

Every time I thought of it, I wanted to pinch myself. What the heck was this, a Tyler Perry movie? I couldn't believe this was my life right now.

"Hey, Aisha, you good?" Stephen asked with a concerned expression.

"Ahh, I need to see Knox."

"For sure, let me show you his office. Come this way." He gestured to the hallway he'd just come from, and I followed behind.

The hallway had pictures of different projects they'd developed through the years, with a cool color palette of whites, grays, and light blue that would usually be soothing. It wasn't doing the trick on me, but I could see how any other time it would have.

We passed several doors that led to other offices until we got to the end of the hallway. Stephen pressed his finger on an electronic pad that read his biometrics, and the door clicked open.

"Knox...he's a stickler for safety," Stephen explained, which made sense after the hard time he'd given me about having a receptionist. And he'd been right.

The door opened to a cozy waiting area with gray sofas and a coffee table with three iPads docked into it. Across from it was a large conference room with glass walls and tall windows facing a man-made lake. On each end of the waiting area was a door, one with Knox's name and the other with Stephen's.

I took a moment to take it all in and breathe.

"What's up? You look flustered," Stephen asked, a thread of concern in his voice.

"Yeah, you're right; I'm worried. I don't know who, but someone is trying to blackmail me, and it involves Knox, and I need to warn him right away." I flashed the printout in my hand, Stephen's curious eyes following it.

"I see. Well, let's knock on his door."

We walked over to Knox's door, which was slightly ajar.

As we approached, a voice trailed off—he was on a phone call.

"I hear you, Liam, I got it under control."

Pause.

Stephen frowned and stopped as I continued walking. I knew he was on a call, but I just wanted to knock on the door lightly so he'd know I was here.

"Listen...yeah. Well, now you know. I mean, I said that

yesterday, that Aisha and I are just shooting the shit, nothing serious. But...exactly. You understand why? Yeah, no, she doesn't need to know yet. But I appreciate you coming to me."

My hand froze midway to his door as his words registered.

He was just shooting the shit...

And he knew something he didn't think I needed to know. I stared at the door, then at the printout in my hand. I met Stephen's gaze, which seemed to widen in alarm.

"Knox, Aisha is—" I stopped him, shaking my head as I heard Knox inside.

"What? Let me call you back, Liam."

The door swung open, and Knox appeared wearing his glasses, beard immaculate, his eyes searching mine. I could tell he wondered how much I'd heard.

Everything seemed to be moving in slow motion. How reckless could I have been? This man, this made-for-me Dom had shown up in my life and given me a glimpse of what it could be like with someone that understood the whole me. But all along, he was just, what, stringing me along? Shooting the shit?

I should have trusted my instincts when he had those moments of hesitation about moving forward. I excused them all, giddy in our lust, in our love.

Old me would stop and want to hear his side, be understanding, even apologize for eavesdropping, but I wasn't about to get hurt again by a man like him. A man making me believe he felt what I felt when instead, he was on a completely different plane.

"Oh, I heard it all. The fact that you and I are just shooting the shit."

"Aisha..." Knox started, then stared at his brother. "Do you mind giving us some privacy?"

"Sure can do. Good to see you, Aisha. Hear him out," Stephen said with pleading in his eyes. Of course, he'd say that. This was his brother, and he wanted to make sure his brother was good.

'Thanks, Stephen, for showing me the way," was all I replied.

"Listen, you only heard part of the conversation, not all of it," Knox said, gently pressing his palm to my elbow. I hadn't realized my arms were crossed, and I stepped away from his touch, waltzing into his office.

"Right. So, tell me, what did I miss?"

I sat on the armchair in front of his desk as he walked over to his chair. The gentle touch to his beard told me he was assessing how much to say.

"Say it, Knox, don't hold back now."

"I feel you'll misinterpret what I have to say."

"Only one way to figure it out." I shrugged, my stomach swan-diving. I'd come here for support; I'd come here to warn him, and this was what happened. I should have known better than to trust this D/s connection could be more.

"Well, that was Liam. He called me yesterday."

My breath caught in my chest. Knox's gaze rested on me, then he removed his glasses and rubbed the back of his neck.

"I...he'd received some photos and video...via email."

"An email like this?" I threw the printout at him, and the two papers swooped down in front of him, landing perfectly.

His eyes quickly scanned the message, and he swore under his breath.

"Listen—"

"No, get straight to the point, please." I sat taller, bringing in my posture, holding my core so my heart wouldn't spill out of me in the process.

"I... Listen, I thought I could handle this without having you worry right before the show. I didn't know she'd come for you too."

"She?" *Who was she?*

"I've had my suspicions who's behind the dance thing. Not sure yet, so I can't confirm, but all—"

"But I'm your girlfriend, you can confide in me without... Oh no, right, you're not my man. We're just shooting the shit." I laughed, the sound turning to dust in my mouth.

"That was a mistake; you heard one side of the conversation. I had called Liam to tell him I was wrong for saying that yesterday, minimizing what we had. See, he got a similar email, but it was more like, 'this is the person you want to do business with?' He was calling to warn me."

"Yesterday, during the rehearsal."

"Correct." Knox nodded, chewing the corner of his mouth.

"So, you lied to me to accomplish...what?"

"I don't know." He pushed his chair back and stormed around his office. "I wanted to seem in control, I guess."

No matter how good my posture was right now, my heart was still disintegrating the more I heard what Knox had to say.

"Ok, so you denied me. And?"

"Don't sound like that, don't get mad at me." He rushed over, sitting in the armchair across from me, his hands resting on my knees. He looked worried, but there was a tinge of annoyance behind it all.

"You don't get to dictate how I feel right now."

"Ok. Well, I called him today to let him know you and I are serious, and I was wrong to..."

"Lie."

"I didn't—fine, lie. Ok. Yeah, and Liam understood I'd just been caught off guard. He just wanted to warn me. He said what happens between two consenting adults wasn't his business, nor did it impact his view of my company. I was glad he said it because that was exactly what I was gonna tell him, and fuck him if he didn't see it that way."

I stared at him, deeply hurt by the fact that he'd lied about us even if he tried to rectify it the next day. It wasn't the first time this happened with Kwon, and it did not make me feel any type of secure with him.

"You do this—deny what we have—when things get rough." I nodded.

"That's not true." He shook his head.

"Well, that's how I feel."

"Great, so what I feel doesn't matter. The fact that I feel like shit for saying that, and the fact that I tried to fix it, doesn't matter?"

My breath stuttered as I considered his words. Should I be more lenient? I don't know. I'd been understanding my entire life, and what did I have to show for it?

"You get to feel whatever you feel."

"You're shutting down on me, Baby Doll."

"Do not call me that right now." I stood up and paced the length of his office. "So, what is it that you know that you didn't plan to tell me? Who is she?" I shifted my attention back to that small tidbit he'd tried to gloss over.

"I'm not ready..." Static went off in my ears as Knox tried to rationalize why he couldn't share everything that was happening with me. I don't even know if he realized keeping me out of it was another way of telling me he wasn't ready for this.

The door felt so far away, but I reached it in quick strides. I thought I'd have someone to rely on in this situation, but as always, I didn't. The difference now was I wouldn't stay, even though all the signs told me I needed to slow down, to assess.

"Aisha, you're overthinking this. Please listen to me before you jump to conclusions," he said, and the thread of desperation in his voice made me pause by the door. Then I thought again about the fact that he hadn't planned on telling me a thing, and my stomach contracted.

I knew what I needed to do.

"No. I'm not overthinking anything. You don't need to tell me a thing. Whatever this is about, if it's because of you...fix it. Fix it, and after that, don't talk to me no more."

"Aisha." Knox overpowered me with his presence, his cologne, which he now used day and night, making me weak in the knees. How could I say goodbye to this? To him?

The brush of his knuckle under my chin singed my skin, and I jerked my head away from the heat he created.

"Baby, please," he urged. I closed my eyes and felt my pulse pick up his heartbeat and mimic it like a slap to my face. My body, as always, betraying me when I needed it to stay the course.

"No. Fix this. You and I don't need to hurt each other. We have plenty of hurt surrounding us. We were supposed to be each other's oasis. This...what you did, what you planned to do...you were never going to tell me." I stopped, my breath hitching.

"Fuck." He softly cursed and hung his head.

"Fix it and leave me alone. Trin... Trinity is always

welcome, but you are not. Drop her off, don't come in. And I'll find a way to refund your money."

"Stop. Don't do this, we can fix it together."

He reached for my arm, and before he could convince me, I stormed out of his office.

"Aisha, stop!" he bellowed, his steps echoing behind me as I power walked through the waiting area. Stephen came out of his office, took one look at both of us, and stood between Knox and me.

"Move out of the way!" Knox warned him.

"Let her go," Stephen said calmly. Knox's face crumpled, his desperation palpable. I couldn't look at him one more second, or I would stay and hear him out.

Thankful for Stephen's intervention, I left Davenport & Jameson, my heart shattering in the process.

Twenty-Nine

Knox

How COULD things go from perfect to wrong in a second?

"What the fuck was that, bruh?" I asked Stephen. He let me go, raising his hands.

"Listen, I don't want no problems, but...she was asking you to let her be." Stephen didn't break eye contact with me, and I understood where he was coming from.

This was essential code. When we were younger, we always promised not to overpower a woman to the point we weren't listening to what she was saying. We had witnessed a nasty encounter between my mom and my biological dad while my stepdad was away at work that marked us both.

"Fuck." I went back into my office, Stephen following me.

"What happened?"

I didn't feel like discussing anything with him, but Stephen was worse than the FBI when he wanted to know something.

"Someone is blackmailing Aisha and trying to ruin things with Liam. They snuck a camera into Aisha's studio and got some photos of us in a scene."

"So, when were you planning to tell me?"

I started to answer, and he raised his hand to stop me. "Never mind, you probably were on your 'I can fix the world' shit. I won't kick you while you're down, but you should have talked to me the moment you found out our business was on the line. Do you have an idea of who it could be?" Stephen wondered and plopped himself in one of the armchairs, placing his shoes on my desk. I didn't even bother telling him off.

I felt bruised and battered, my ribcage and chest bearing most of the brunt besides my heart.

"I think it was Chantal."

"What the fuck?! Never mind. Listen, you've managed to villainize her, and I get it. After your Pops, I can only imagine how it would have felt being in that situation. But that's not Chantal." Stephen shook his head, and I knew I'd made a mistake sharing this with him.

Of course, I didn't want to believe the mother of my child would stoop so low, but hadn't she warned me she'd do anything?

And hurting Aisha... Well, that just felt like a bonus. This was why I wanted to understand everything that happened before telling Aisha. Chantal was part of my life regardless of what happened next, and I knew Aisha needed peace of mind when dealing with her if we ever got past this. Co-parenting was hard as hell, and I didn't want Aisha hating Chantal...or Chantal hating Aisha.

"Nah, you need to go and speak with Chantal, clear this shit up. Then go and apologize to your woman and fix this shit." Stephen stood up, spearing me with a look of disappointment.

"You want this picture-perfect life where you and Trin have nothing around you that messes up your flow. But you're gonna have to detach yourself from that idea if you ever want to live your life to the fullest."

And with that, he left me in my office.

"May I please speak with Chantal Davenport?" I asked at the reception desk of the talent agency Chantal worked for. As I was escorted to her office, I saw the person I knew had been behind the sabotage, probably at Chantal's behest.

"Roxane." I felt my gut roiling at the shit she probably pulled.

She smirked and waved. "Hey, Knox. Be good to my cousin in there, alright?"

I restrained myself from going after her. Nothing good would come of a conversation with her. I'd asked her to stop calmly and removed her discount, and still, she pulled this shit. Better to speak with Chantal—after all, she was her cousin.

Chantal sat behind her desk with pictures of different Black celebrities lining her walls and furniture, eyes wide with worry.

"Why?"

"I didn't— I'm sorry, Knox." She didn't pretend not to understand my question.

"Do you hate me so much that you'd hurt my future, both professional and personal, like this?" Dealing with Aisha these past months had taught me to check my anger and investigate what lay behind it.

Having her in my life and seeing how she could manage so much without losing her composure had made me want to step up my game. So right now, I stood with all the hurt in the world, letting the anger go.

"I didn't listen. I...I don't want you to get mad, but..." she stuttered out.

"I'm not mad." I sighed and sat on the sofa in her office.

"You're not?" She stared at me as if I'd sprouted wings.

"No, I'm hurt and confused and feeling a bit helpless, but...I'm not mad." I shook my head, letting all those feelings rush to the top.

"Oh, Knox. I was angry and felt like you weren't listening to me, and I vented to Roxane... I mentioned Aisha, and she told me she'd heard Aisha was into some kinky shit through some of the dancers she knew from New York, and she'd take care of things for me. I told her not to do anything that would hurt you or Trin... To be honest, I didn't include Aisha, but I figured she understood Aisha was included.

"Next thing I know, I'm being blind copied in those emails she sent, and I lost it with her. She completely dismissed me and told me she did it for me but also her. She's trying to get Aisha's studio shut down. Apparently, she's having a hard time starting hers and feels Aisha's is a threat to her success."

I stared at Chantal, wondering how shit had gotten so out of hand. It pacified me to hear her say that she didn't want to harm me or Trin. I didn't miss the Aisha omission, but I couldn't fault her. But Roxane was on some Cruella shit, and I had no time for her bullshit.

"I'd suspected as much. I realized she'd been poaching Aisha's students for months, so I stopped her half-off discount on her rent, and she lost some students back to

Aisha. It seems she was offering dirt cheap tuition because of my discount. When I agreed to help your cousin, I never expected it to be to the detriment of Aisha's studio." The throbbing headache I'd tried to keep at bay intensified at the thought of what I'd inadvertently put Aisha through.

"Oh my God, she... I didn't know, I swear I didn't know. She asked me to move Trin to her dance school, but when I asked Trin if she'd like to change, she was adamant that she loved her school and was looking to audition for the dance team next year, so I let it be. I didn't...I made a mess of things, didn't I?" She looked so forlorn, and I didn't have the energy to be upset at her.

"I mean, you can't control your conniving cousin...but I can, and I will. She came for me and mine, and I really can't stand that. I asked her to step back when I removed her discount, and I explained why I did it. I thought we agreed, but now she's come and trespassed in another space and is threatening to blackmail me and Aisha. I can take her to court for that."

"Hold on, hold on, court? Aren't we taking things a little too far? I mean, I'll tell her to step down, I..." Chantal's eyes widened in panic, and she got up and sat next to me in the other guest armchair.

"She took things too far, I didn't. Just sneaking that camera into Aisha's place is a felony, never mind her putting things on paper threatening Aisha's livelihood and my business deal." Every time I thought about it, it got me even more fired up.

"Oh God...I'll fix it. I'll talk to her, I promise. Please don't get her in trouble, she just— Never mind, I won't make excuses, but I'll make sure she deletes all the pictures and video. I'll send you proof!"

"A'ight. Fix it, Chantal, or I'll do what I need to do." I got up, leaving her with tears gathering in her eyes.

"Will you make things hard for me with Trin?" she sniffed.

"No, we'll talk." I heard her crying behind me as I left, worried this wouldn't be enough to fix things with Aisha.

Thirty

Aisha

The dance team performed their hip-hop choreography as if they were already on stage. Something needed to go well in my life, and if it was work, then so be it.

Last night, I'd tossed and turned until the wee hours of the night, pissed off at the blackmailing email, putting all my brainpower into what I could do to minimize the impact if the blackmailer went ahead with their threats.

Trusting Knox... I didn't even want to think of him, but I knew he was working on straightening things out.

He'd send me a dozen text messages, some promising nothing would happen with the pictures, then others asking to talk. I ignored them all. I couldn't articulate all the hurt I carried inside from what he'd done to us.

The fact that he denied me to his prospective partner wasn't the biggest issue, but it certainly stung. It was the same behavior I'd seen him project here and there when everything seemed to be progressing well. It was like he couldn't allow himself to imagine a life where he wasn't a divorced dad.

It was all he knew.

I understood he needed to provide stability for Trin, but I'd never shown him anything but understanding.

Letting someone in the way we had done... It took courage, it took guts, and sometimes, I feared he lacked some of that courage. My eyes watered at the thought, the black, pink, and brown leotards a blur of movement as the dancers took it from the top again under Mila's tutelage.

And the fact that he knew who was hurting my business and had kept it to himself? Now that was the lowest of blows. This studio was everything I'd fought hard for, something I could give to these young dancers as a foundation to hopefully catapult them to success. He didn't get to mess with that. He didn't get to keep me in the dark. Our D/s relationship was not an excuse.

Even Knox knew that was the case. Earlier on, I had received a text from Master Q, telling me Knox had reached out for advice.

> Master Q: Why are you making your Dom suffer like this?
>
> Me: This is beyond our D/s dynamic Master Q...
>
> Master Q: He said the same, but still I thought to check in with you. You know I'm here if you need to talk.

Master Q, always there for his tribe. I just didn't have the words to convey all my feelings right now.

I'd compromised before in my life; I'd always been understanding of other people's journeys, sometimes to the detriment of my own. But today, I was pulling a Cookie—I was putting me first.

"Psst. Psst. Yo! Act alive," Mila whispered, then turned to the dancers. "Alright, y'all doing good, but I want it to sink in so well you can do the routine in your sleep!"

I stared at her, wondering what she meant when someone knocked on the door.

Sal, our standby receptionist, didn't play games about people interfering, so I wondered who'd gotten past her defenses.

I wandered over, slowly opening the door to find myself face-to-face with Knox.

"What are you doing here?" I hissed.

"You aren't answering my messages. I needed to update you." His voice... Just his voice, and I felt my resolve cracking.

"No, I don't need to talk to you. I asked you to fix it, period. There's no need for a status report."

"Damn, you've always had all this fire in you, and I had no idea. You really were holding back before everything, weren't you?"

"We need focus," Mila said behind me, and when I turned around, a dozen inquisitive faces were staring at us.

"Yeah, sorry, team. I'll take this in my office."

I pushed him out of the room into the reception.

"Yo! What's this betrayal?" I asked Sal, who was face-deep in her laptop.

"He said, and I quote, 'If you let me knock, you'll be my favorite friend of Aisha's.'"

"Since when do you care about that?" I threw my hands in the air. "Besides, he already considers you his favorite." I shook my head, shocked that it took that little for Sal to crumble—she didn't like men like that.

"He's different. And you know my radar is stellar," she said to her laptop, reading my mind.

"Judas," I grumbled and stalked down the hallway to my office.

"You love me," Sal reminded me as I rounded the corner.

"Are you gonna give me a chance to explain?" he asked, his contrite tone registering in the midst of my anger. He really was serious about this.

"I'm not certain there is a lot of space to explain."

"What you mean, there's no space to explain?" he said, a note of exasperation creeping into his voice.

Yep, there it was.

Tension brewed in my body as I fought the urge to let my rational side take over and calm my anger.

"I don't think you really get why I'm mad."

"Baby Doll..." He reached out for me, his hand caressing my arm, but I pulled away, pressing my back against the wall of my office.

"No, listen. You're asking me for what, for me to hear you explain why you've kept me in the dark? Why you knew better for me?" I asked, my head pounding as my brain and my body fought for supremacy.

"No, I don't think I knew better, I just wanted to protect you," he started, his expression open and pleading.

"Protect me from what? There are very few people, four actually, that have my best interests at heart," I said and felt the shift in temperature as his face closed off.

"That's fucked up for you to say that." He reared back, giving me the space I needed.

Take it back. Take it back, he's hurting.

"Well, that's how I feel." Hurt slashed across his face, then nothing.

"What do you want to hear from me?" he whispered.

"I want you to fix this, and then I want you to not come here again."

"Are you sure that's what you want? Are you sure you want to turn your back on us?"

"What *us*? According to you, there is no us. According to you, this is you making the decisions and me being the cute little sub that—"

He put his palm up. "Alright, Aisha, let's not keep saying things we'll regret," he said, and my stomach cramped at the thought of hurting him. Outside, though? I kept my composure.

"I'm gonna leave…grant your wishes…for now," he said, the promise lingering between us, refusing to let go of what we had.

He walked out, head high, my heart racing as I wondered if this was truly it for us. If I was making a mistake. But no…I needed to think of myself.

I stormed out of my office, hoping against hope that this day would be over, but just as I approached the reception, I found Knox standing there with my father while Sal stood with her arms crossed by the door.

"Hija, you still fucking with this… You're not as smart as I thought." My dad nodded his head toward Knox, and Knox's jaw clenched as he expelled air out of his nose. The uncertainty that I felt before bled away, a sense of resolve taking over.

"I'll ask you not to speak ill of your daughter. She's a great woman," Knox said.

"Listen, hija, I need some money, 'dis people are trying to kick me out my apartment! They say am missing two months' rent but they just tryin' to steal my money…" Dad said, gesticulating, waving alcohol fumes all over the reception.

I gave a quick thanks the dancers were in the room with Mila.

"You need to leave." I pointed my finger at the door.

"Who, him? That's right," Dad jeered.

"No. You. Leave. Don't come back until you're clean and in AA. There's nothing I can do for you until you want to do it for yourself." Every word filled me with a sense of peace I never knew before. I glanced at Knox and tried not to let his proud expression get to me.

"Que carajo!" my dad screamed, spit coming out of his mouth. "You don't get to tell me to leave. I'm your father, so all of this is also mine!" He gestured around, and Knox moved closer to him. I shook my head at Knox, knowing it was all bluster. I'd seen this before when my grandparents had banned him from our home.

"Do not come here again. If you do, I'll make sure to make things hard for you." I pointed toward Sal, who gave an eerie smile.

He had been around enough to hear and see what Sal could do with a laptop and some time.

"Fuck you. You're no daughter of mine anyways," my dad said with one last hurtful parting gift, slamming the door after him. The barb hit its mark, my heart crumbling at his dismissive comment. I knew that was the addiction talking, but I also knew I didn't deserve this type of treatment anymore.

Knox smiled at me, the pride in his gaze threatening to disarm me. I kept my impassive expression, holding onto the threads of adrenaline that had pumped my courage these last minutes.

His smile dimmed as he realized I wasn't reciprocating, then he nodded once.

"I'll see you soon, Aisha," he promised, following my father out of the studio as I let all the emotions of the day seep out and let the tears move in.

Thirty-One

Knox

Step 10: Continue to take personal inventory and when we are wrong, promptly admit it.

I'd fucked up on this one.

I sat in fellowship at a Nar-Anon Family group meeting; I hadn't attended one in a while. When Chantal and I reached a point of no return, when communicating was near impossible, I started attending these meetings, a desperate attempt to work on myself to be able to fix her. During the program, I realized that my job wasn't to fix Chantal, and in taking personal inventory, I realized how I'd held onto a perfect view of our marriage without putting in the work. Then I worked on trying to forgive myself for failing Chantal, not in her addiction but in dismissing and not understanding her pain.

Work like the kind you do in twelve steps is ever-evolving and transformational. But I'd stopped making the effort; amid work, life, and parenting, I'd forgotten to take personal inventory. And in failing to do so, I'd missed what I'd started to do to protect myself.

I let the words of others wash over me—mothers, brothers, wives, children, all of us united in loving someone that was an addict.

The emotional work of taking stock had taken a toll on me. I sat in my car after the meeting, contemplating where to go next. My parents had Trin for the week; my mother had quickly realized I wasn't doing all too well and had gently suggested the idea of Trin staying with them.

Driving aimlessly, I took a detour to Ms. Brown's, noticing Aisha's car in the parking lot.

The urge to park and try to make her talk to me had me tight in its grip, choking me until I exhaled again, the sense of realization hitting me hard. Here I was doing some stalkerish shit, missing her so bad that I needed a glimpse of her car outside the studio to be able to keep on with my day. A volcanic stream rushed from my gut to my head when I realized I might lose her...

Familiarity saved the day, taking me to my parents' place without much thought.

Not one muscle moved as I sat in my car, contemplating what to say to my parents. The house door swung open and out walked my mother with two travel mugs. The sight of her soothed me, reminding me of the times when my biological father would disappear for days, and it was just her and me holding each other up.

"My boy," she said in greeting after claiming the passenger seat and placing my cup in the cup holder.

"What you bring?"

"Irish coffee." She shrugged and took a sip of her drink, closing her eyes.

"You know, I'd been with your father since before I

turned twenty-one...and because of his addiction, I didn't drink a single drop of alcohol until after we separated." One corner of her lips lifted as she got lost in thoughts of the past.

"Your dad...his needs made me focus on him so much that I forgot myself for years. And when we separated, I felt so guilty... I felt I had abandoned him." She took another sip of her coffee. "You should try it before it gets cold."

Following her recommendation, I sipped the sweet yet bitter concoction, the alcohol packing a punch as it traveled its way down to my stomach.

Taking stock sucked. I knew exactly what my mom was trying to say, but I currently didn't have the words to explain how I'd just realized that I had carried guilt for years without really confronting it.

"When I met William, and he started courting me—"

"Was that 1896?" I said, wanting to break the air of contemplation that permeated my car.

"Humor won't save you from the thoughts in your head. I wasn't gonna say, but you're looking a bit rough...when was the last time you shaved your head?"

My hand prickled as I rubbed my head, which I hadn't groomed in more than a week.

"Sorry, Moms. You were saying when you met William?"

"Yeah, when I met him, it took us six months to get to a place where I could trust myself to love him and for him to trust me with meeting his kids and family. See, I kept breaking up with him every time things progressed and got serious. So, he didn't want to meet you nor for me to meet Shelly and Stephen. I would cry myself to sleep, so frustrated, but I just couldn't shake off the guilt..." She nodded, then stared at me.

"It took my support group in Nar-Anon to realize I had forgotten to forgive myself."

No light bulb turned on, no aha moment materialized. I'd stopped doing the work, but in restarting, I'd realized what my mother was saying right now. I'd never forgiven myself for my failed marriage, for not seeing the signs earlier with Chantal, for making it hard for her at times to restart her life as a mother and co-parent. But most importantly, I hadn't forgiven myself for failing, so how could I start over?

The choked feeling returned, and I let the burn in the back of my eyes do what it must.

My mom walked the path with me, of silence, forgiveness, and acceptance, her hand warm on mine as I shook quietly, silent tears streaming down my face.

Many minutes later, after the worst had passed, leaving me exhausted and cleansed, I ventured a few words.

"I want something new, something more than just this."

"And you deserve it, Knox. Don't let the people that have hurt you in your life dictate your limits; only you should do that."

I nodded, grateful for her company and her insight. She'd gone through so much in her younger years and somehow hadn't let the scars sour her view of life.

"Now I have to convince Aisha I'm serious about us."

"I'm sure you'll find a way. You're bullheaded if nothing else." She smiled and pressed a kiss on my cheek.

Thirty-Two

Aisha

> *You are the only person that has made me relook at the world with a different lens. I'm back at Nar-Anon Family meetings, I'm doing the work. I want you to know that I'll respect your boundaries, but I won't stop reminding you that we're meant to be together. I'm sorry for not making that absolutely clear to you in the past. I'm going to do better.*

I'd been receiving these handwritten notes for the past week. They came my way via Trinity, his parents, Sal, Mila —even Devon had handed me one this morning.

Why was he testing my resolve? I'd felt so sure that

walking away was the right answer for me, but these notes... And that didn't even touch on the gifts.

He'd sent me new nipple clamps with our initials engraved; a g-spot massager with a note that said, *I can't wait to try this one on you*; a bouquet of daffodils, delphiniums, freesias, and marigolds that had me rushing to google their meaning; a beautiful pair of diamond earrings; a deep brown leotard and tights with another note that read, *for the next time you dance for me*; and the one that had me ready to break my silence and call him—an empty velvet box that seemed perfect for storing a collar.

Knox promised the world through his gifts and soothed my worries through his notes, but I couldn't shake the uncertainty that had clouded my thoughts about the two of us. My mind worked overtime to analyze each gesture he sent, every word he wrote, trying to find an alternative meaning to what he'd clearly stated.

"How many times are you gonna read this last message?" Sal asked as her fingers sped over the keyboard.

"Sorry, I thought you were deep in sleuthing mode. Do you really think you'll be able to figure out who's trying to blackmail me?"

"I am, and yes to your question, but your thoughts are so loud I had to say something." Sal shrugged, never breaking eye contact with the screen.

"Should I reach out to him?" I hated how hesitant I sounded. It reminded me of my old self with James when I wanted him to love me so much that I bent over backward to make it true.

"How does it feel when you imagine that?"

I closed my eyes, taking stock. A warm sense of rightness laced with passionate need surrounded me as I pictured talking to Knox again.

"Yeah, that face tells me all I need to know. I give you a couple of days," she drawled.

"What?"

"You love him, he made a mistake. He's making amends. You're a good soul. I know how this story ends." Sal beamed at me, and that was such a rare occurrence I was struck speechless.

"Oh, you like Knox?"

"For you? Yes, he's right for you. He challenges you, dotes on you, and gets that you have a need to give and don't do a good job at replenishing. And you know me and men." Sal shrugged, then went back to her laptop as if she hadn't just rocked my world with her swift assessment.

Before I could say anything, the chime went off, and Mila walked in and gave me a wide-eyed look that had me shifting focus.

"What?" I asked.

"Girl, guess what I just found out!" she started, but the chime went off again, and a storm of blonde braids, pink clothing, and strong perfume hit me.

"Roxane?" What was she doing at my studio? I stared at Mila, who in turn gawked at Roxane as if she'd just sprouted out through the floor.

"You bitch!" she spat, pointing at me as if I was the source of all her ills.

What in the world?

"You got that boyfriend of yours to fuck me over. I hope you're happy, all that talk about being glad for me and my future the other day at the groceries was bullshit, wasn't it?"

"I have no clue what you are talking about?" I said, but my brain was one step ahead of my mouth, and the picture of what had happened these last months started gaining color.

"You always hated Aisha during our dance classes, and she never even did a thing to you," Sal accused, while hidden by the reception desk, she wrote on her laptop SHE DID IT.

"But you decided to mess with her livelihood, and now you're mad?" Mila had recovered from her shock, and she'd squared up, a menacing expression directed at Roxane.

"Fuck off, this does not involve you two. Oh, the poor, sweet orphan always needed these two to defend her. Your boyfriend fucked me over. He kicked me out of my establishment. Now I need to find a new place, and with all the students leaving, I had to postpone my holiday show."

"Which you had planned on the same day as hers," Mila said, and everything fell into place.

"Roxane...why? I was nothing but kind to you back in the day."

"Oh, please, you were so full of yourself. I hated your fake ass self then, and I can't stand you now. But this wasn't about that, it was plain business. Your dancers are the best in the area, and I always get the best." She shrugged as if that nonsensical statement explained how her wrongness could be excused. Some people just were too hurt to even realize when they were being destructive.

"But you aren't getting anything right now. My dancers are back at the studio, and you got kicked out of your studio and have no show. And you know the saddest part? You helped me level up. I was able to create scholarships out of this experience, and I created a new holiday show. And what do you have to show for all of this?"

"That's alright, I'm sure my cousin being all good to Knox and telling him my business will probably bring them back together. That's what I came here to say. Right now, because of me, Knox is reconsidering custody and rethinking how his family dynamic should look, so it seems I still managed to fuck up your life." She shrugged and smiled while Mila and Sal watched me for any reaction.

In Roxane's world, a man making the moves that Knox was making meant he wanted back with his ex-wife. I wouldn't even fight her assumptions, but what she'd given me here was a gift.

Between the decisive gesture to kick Roxane out for hurting my business and reassessing things with Chantal, this all told me he was looking at things differently, and that gave me hope. I wasn't done being mad, but I was ready to hear him out. So I matched Roxane's smile. I beamed at the news as her smile faltered at the strength of my satisfaction.

"Whaa...why are you smiling?"

"Have a good day, Roxane, you've been nothing but the bearer of good news." I looked down at Sal, who winked. Great. "Oh and, that anonymous email you sent me? We traced it to your account, thebaddestdancerbitch@gmail.com, right? And I can tie it directly to you and your business through the IP you used, which matches your home. If you fuck with me and mine again, I will take this information and sue you for blackmailing and defamation. Do you understand?"

I noticed when the blood drained from her face, realizing she'd messed with the wrong one.

"Have a good day, Roxane." I showed her the door while Sal and Mila high-fived.

"Girl, are you ready to forgive Knox? 'Cause he did that shit!" Mila said.

She might be right. It might be time to let things go and start anew.

Thirty-Three

Aisha

"Trin, can you call your dad in?" I asked Trinity as she walked out of the studio. She turned around with a hopeful look, her little face glistening from the exertion of today's rehearsals.

"Ok!"

It was our last one before the dress rehearsal we were gonna have in the venue tomorrow, and nerves were running high. This holiday show had sold double the number of tickets than our main May show, which put pressure on all of us. We owed our audience a great performance.

It had been so hard to focus on the show and choreographies and intricacies of it all while my mind continued to wander with thoughts of Knox.

He'd reached out with a letter today via Trin, where he explained his faulty reasoning for keeping me in the dark about Roxanne and Chantal. He'd felt personally responsible and wanted to fix things before saying anything to me.

The discount adjustment on the rent had been his attempt at fixing it without hurting me or Roxane, but he hadn't counted on her retaliation.

Reading the letter made me miss him so much, I wanted to curl up against him as he explained it all to me while I enjoyed a glass of cold chocolate milk. Instead, I walked over to Room A and rehearsed with my dancers, session after session, until I couldn't feel my legs anymore. Now here I sat behind the reception, my stomach a nest of enraged wasps.

"You called for me?" His voice was velvet and smoke, and I wanted to burrow inside of it and relax all my nerves away.

"Yes. I wanted to talk to you." I stood up. His tired face, the bags beneath his eyes, and the slight stubble on his head told me how hard these past days had been on him.

"Oh, Sir," I sighed.

"Hey, Baby Doll." He gave me a cautious smile, which I returned gladly.

"I know you probably have Trin tonight—"

"She's been staying at my parents' while I work on some things."

"Oh, ok."

"You wanna drive with me? We can drop her off, check on your grandparents, then go to my place?"

With a knot in my throat, I nodded, agreeing to his plans.

We dropped off Trin, then headed over to my grandparents, who shooed us away, assuring us they'd been taking care of themselves before we were born. They could be so stubborn. The exhaustion of the day crawled over me, and by the time I opened my eyes, we were in Knox's driveway.

"Are you alright, baby?" Knox asked me, the tentative way he spoke to me making me sadder than I should be.

"No, but hopefully, after we talk, I will be?" I asked, not really expecting an answer.

"Hopefully, we both will."

We walked into his house, the familiar scent of him and Trin enveloping me as I entered their space.

"Do you need dinner?"

"Nah, a snack will be fine." I took off my shoes and relaxed in a corner of the sofa.

Knox padded back with a plate of cookies and chocolate milk for us to share.

"I'm sorry, Aisha." He sat down on the other side of the sofa and studied me for a second after he delivered his message. I nodded, waiting to hear him out.

"I've been writing to you as I worked some things through, and I can see where I went wrong. I wanted us to be serious, you know this, but I did a poor job of showing you that. And you didn't need uncertainty from me. After all, that's all your father and not having your mom created in your life. So...at first, I thought you were overreacting." I scoffed, and he reached out and held my hand. "But I can see where I went wrong there too. It wasn't an overreaction on your part, it was a mirror response to the uncertainty I was creating in you, so when you were confronted with the knowledge of me denying you and keeping things from you... Well, we know what happened next.

"I've explained why I did the things I did, but I want you to know that in the end, I understand those explanations don't really matter because I was missing the big picture. I should have been more in tune with you and let myself be vulnerable so you would be more in tune with me. What happened could have been a stumble rather than a complete fallout between us. Because the reality is, I can't promise I won't fuck shit up in the future, but what I *can* promise you is that no matter what, you'll always know what's in my heart."

"I...ok..." I said because words failed me right now. Somehow, I hadn't had to explain my anger and disappointment to him. He'd seen more than I realized.

"Yeah, I...I can't continue to give my all to people that don't do the same for me. I've spent so much time doing that for my dad and hoping my mom was still around...it's just taken a toll on me," I whispered.

"I know, baby. Can I hold you now?" he asked, and I agreed. In a flash, he grabbed me and had me on his lap.

"When I realized the true connection we had in those sessions, I wanted things to be more between us, but I didn't realize all the walls I was unconsciously putting up between us as well. All the little hoops that were unnecessary. My divorce fucked me up some, but that's no excuse." He shook his head, and I nuzzled into him, kissing his neck, love beaming out of me now that we were talking to each other, letting our guards down.

"I know. I understood that and felt it but didn't have the bravery before to show you how it was hindering us."

"You know, I don't think I've ever had this type of heart-to-heart before, not with a partner, at least." His deep voice rumbled, his hands incapable of staying still as he held me, making me vibrate under his touch. Fullness and calmness surrounded us as we showed each other how needy we were for each other's touch.

"I don't think I've ever felt I could do that before. Just say what was on my mind with an open heart without worry of being hurt." A tear escaped me as Knox massaged my hip, his chest rumbling like a big cat expressing his satisfaction.

"I hope I'll always be the person you can unburden yourself to without fear," he whispered in my ear, then bit my earlobe, the slight pain traveling right to my pussy.

"Same here, Knox, same. I love you."

"And I love you too. Will you do me the honor of making love with me?"

"Always."

He carried me straight from the couch to his room, laughing when I made him stop so we could bring the cookies and milk.

Pressing me gently to his bed, he stripped me of all my clothes, his linen smelling like softener, but then I remembered I'd been sweating the whole day.

"I...need a shower."

"Can't it wait? I want you so much." He spoke the words into my belly, triggering a swarm of butterflies and giggles.

"Yeah, but things are a little...musky," I said, closing my legs, but he was having none of it.

"Nah, don't be shy now, Baby Doll, I don't mind a little seasoning on my dinner," he said in that deep voice that triggered all my subby instincts.

"Oh, my word, Knox you're so nasty sometimes." I covered my eyes, laughing as he nuzzled the inner corner of my thigh, his beard tickling me before he gave me a sensuous lick from my entrance all the way to my clit.

"Only sometimes? I have to rectify that."

And he proceeded to do just that, feasting on my pussy until he had me gasping, begging him to put me out of my misery.

"You can't come yet. I'm sure you've been masturbating and being a bad baby doll without me telling you what to do." He speared me with a look of disappointment, then went in again, doing just enough to make me gush in anticipation but not nearly enough to make me scream in release.

"I didn't... I didn't touch myself once," I confessed between pants.

He stopped what he was doing to stare at me.

"For real?" he asked, his unkempt beard glistening with my juices. I shook my head in desperation, needing him back between my legs.

His eyes softened, and a tear gathered in his eye.

"Me either. I didn't want to do anything if it wasn't with my Baby Doll. I really missed you, Aisha." That hollowed feeling in my chest had been obliterated during our conversation, but now, with his earnest gaze and quiet admission, he filled me all the way up past any level he'd ever done before. The bed disappeared from under me, and I was held up by his love, the lightheaded feeling taking me higher and higher.

"Oh, Knox," I sighed.

"Don't worry, I'll have you saying that like it was the only word you've ever known," he promised with a glint in his eyes that made me want to rub my legs together.

And just as he said, he took me there several times until all I knew to say was his name as a plea, a prayer, a promise.

Thirty-Four

Knox

The dress rehearsal had my baby so stressed, I wanted to haul her into my arms and take her somewhere where she wouldn't have to worry. To imagine, I had criticized her and her business skills in the past, but now that I was on the other side of the curtain, I understood how much she took on with little support.

Mila and Sal were her right-hand women, and I was never happier to know she had people in her corner. But this type of production probably took an army of people to put together, and she was here doing it with a team of five if you included me. I'd asked Stephen and my parents to help out backstage for the show, realizing that any extra help would be beneficial and give Aisha a break.

She needed to be at the sound booth making sure they understood the cues, on stage making sure the dancers knew their marks, on the side of the stage, directing the tots who, no matter how much they practiced, needed visual cues for their numbers, and in the dressing rooms making sure all the dancers were changed and ready for their turns. There was only one Aisha, though.

"Let's run that again!" She directed the dance crew with a very intricate modern dance choreography, a mix of African dancing, hip-hop, and jazz that I knew was one of the routines Aisha was the most nervous about. The crew were all very talented and were doing a terrific job, but for some reason, Aisha wasn't entirely convinced.

"Why are you so nervous?" I whispered as I passed by her with some pieces for the backdrop and props.

"Well, I... Don't tell anyone, but I got a few of the top dance schools to come and see this show. Jan, Calista, and Tim are looking for college scholarships, and I figured it wouldn't hurt. This is essentially their audition, but they don't know that. I figured I would surprise them with the good news once they responded. It'll be their decision to make if they want to go that route, but at least they'll have choices." She shrugged as she discreetly pointed at the two seniors and junior in the crew.

"Oh, wow...that's amazing. That would be a great break for them and their families." Pride and awe surged in me at all the moving pieces she'd kept together as she continued to build upon her legacy. I dropped the prop in my hands and gathered her in a hug. I could feel her vibrating in my arms with pent-up anticipation.

"Do you need some correction to get you through the day?" I kissed the top of her head.

"You're so nasty, Sir. How do you know what I need?" She laughed into my chest.

"A'ight, after this run, make everyone take a fifteen and meet me in the last dressing room in the hallway."

"Yes, Sir."

She turned and got back to her drill sergeant mode,

giving them a few tips to further enhance the choreography. I kept focused on my job building the backdrop with the other dads until I heard her announcement.

"Ok, everyone, take twenty minutes. We're gonna be running the entire show again. Parents, this is a good time to make sure your kids are hydrated and have snacks. We set up tables in the lobby for everyone to sit and relax."

The hubbub of voices and laughter as everyone made their way out of the theater made me brick up in anticipation. I planned to keep things simple, but there was nothing simple about the need I had for Aisha's submission right now.

The dressing room I mentioned was the largest one, with chairs all around white dressing tables with large mirrors surrounded by those showtime light bulbs you saw in movies.

The click of the door and the changing pattern of my heartbeat announced Aisha's entrance.

I turned around, and she was in first position, wearing her T-shirt and panties, her leggings neatly folded on the side.

"Sir," she said, gifting me with her smile and her big brown eyes shining with excitement.

"You're doing so good, Baby Doll. You've had me hard this whole day watching you give orders and direct everyone. You're a gift I never thought I deserved."

"Oh, Knox." She sighed, her gaze melting, making my chest tighten with emotion.

"Shhh, you're gonna get me out of my zone, then we'll just end up fucking."

"I mean, there's really nothing wrong with that." She shrugged, giving me a little taste of that brattiness that sometimes shone through. Now I knew that brattiness came out when she was entirely comfortable.

"Don't tempt me," I mumbled, loving the sound of her laugh bouncing off the walls. "Stand up, Baby Doll. Drop your panties and stand against that mirror over there." I pointed to the dressing area next to me.

Swan-like in her movements, she complied, pushing her butt out for my touch. I gave into her silent demand, sliding my hand from the top of her ass down to where she was slick for me already.

The button of my jeans clanked against my belt as I dropped them to the floor, my dick trying to burst out of the opening of my boxer briefs.

"I want you to list ten ways you've felt loved by me today. For each one, I'll give you five strokes; at fifty strokes, you get to come. If you can't think of ten ways, then you get to punish me tonight."

Her gasp was loud in the room.

"What...Sir?"

I dropped my briefs, my dick ready to be inside of her, our eyes connecting in the mirror.

"If I haven't made you feel loved, then I'm not doing my job as your man," I said, my voice dropping as emotion threatened to overtake me. I didn't plan to take one day for granted with Aisha.

"Oh, Knox, you're nasty but oh so sweet too." She sighed, then cleared her throat.

"I felt loved this morning when you came to pick me up and sat down and had breakfast with Momma and Pops and made them both smile."

My dickhead glided into her wet entrance, the heat of her enveloping me making me doubt I'd be able to keep up this scene. Aisha's moan made her entire body vibrate as I gave her five shallow strokes, avoiding bottoming out yet. Her flesh squeezed me, greeting my dick with so much enthusiasm I almost lost it on that last stroke.

Our ragged breathing merged in the room until Aisha spoke again.

"I felt loved when you held my hand all the way to the studio, then when we drove here, your little finger caresses making me so..."

I didn't let her finish, giving in to the pleasure of her slickness and the sound of her voice as she expressed herself. The five strokes went by too fast, and I cursed myself for the torture inflicted upon us both.

Panting, Aisha continued.

"I felt loved when the other dads showed up ready to work."

"You deserve all the help in the—fuck, Baby Doll, squeeze me like that again," I pleaded as I fucked her, slowly giving her more of my length but holding back. Her walls tightened around me, making it twice as hard. She was probably doing it on purpose.

"I felt loved when you hugged me as I shed a few tears when I saw the three-year-old class do their ballet," she said at the same slow pace I was stroking her.

I increased my thrusts, the last one bringing me all the way in her.

"Yesss..." she moaned, her delicate sounds making me want to go wild inside her.

"Fuck," I groaned, pressure building in the back of my spine.

"Ahh...I felt...loved. When I saw the note you snuck into my purse, telling me how proud you were of the show and me."

These next five, I gave to her hard and fast, afraid if I

didn't pick up the pace, I'd lose myself in her and fuck the scene. The silky touch of her hips under my hands made me shake with need as the same softness met my dick, thrust after thrust.

"Ohh god, I felt loved when you were winking at me and flirting while you worked on assembling the props." She was ready with this one, avoiding any gap between the last thrust I gave her, so I rewarded her, squatting lower and pistoning in and out of her, her wetness reverberating in the room as I made love to her.

"Yes, oh, don't stop... When you told me you'd set up chairs and tables for the parents and kids to sit in the lobby without me having to ask."

"Fuck, Baby Doll, I'm going to need you to tell me quicker."

"Yes! When you pulled me aside to hydrate and take a minute because you noticed I was getting a bit tired."

She was barely pausing between statements anymore, both of us lost in the feel of each other. Aisha had started to meet my thrusts, her ass jiggling, our bodies slapping against each other. The scent of us together made my mouth water, and I gripped her hips to ground myself. My chest was tight, and my spine tingled with the myriad of emotions threatening to make me lose myself inside Aisha.

She deserved all of this and more. She deserved it all...

"Ahhh, when you told me 'I love you' and kissed my temple." I snaked my hand around her neck and pressed her fully against me. I tasted the spot I'd kissed earlier while I tightened my grip on her neck, her ass bouncing against me with each thrust.

"And right now, I feel all the love you're pouring into me with your groans and your moans and your kisses and bites and...oh, Sir, I'm coming!"

I ground my dick into Aisha, our hips mimicking the African dancing she taught as we let our bodies speak their own language. Making love. This was making love, music, laughter together. This was making memories, tenderness, and care together.

"I love you," I whispered in her ear, and I let her take me away as we both made love to each other, as we made each other become love.

Thirty-Five

Aisha

Showtime.

Every single time I've been part of a cast in a ballet or a musical, that first day has been riddled with nerves. I would second-guess myself all the way until my feet hit that stage, then it would all melt away. My confidence and adrenaline would bolster me through the entire performance and every night after that.

So, when I woke up full of nerves, I was expecting that. What I wasn't expecting was to find out that part of the setup we required in the dressing rooms to check in all the dancers hadn't happened as expected.

Nerves threatened to get the best of me, but with Mila's finessing and Sal's no-nonsense attitude, we managed to get the venue to do the setup as required. By ten in the morning, we were ready to go as the dancers started arriving with their costumes.

We had staggered arrival times to ensure we could manage the influx of dancers. The oldest ones arrived first in their jumpsuits and sweatpants with their costumes in dress bags, chatting in excitement, all the way to our three-year-olds already with their beautiful costumes on, tights and pretty little hair bows fixed, holding their parents' hands.

"You good?" Knox approached my registration table while I checked in the last dancers, bringing a bottle of ginger ale. He sat next to me and smiled.

"I'm alright. Did you check on Trin, is she all good?" I said, accepting the bottle and putting it on the side.

"Yeah, she's chillin' in her dressing room, and Chantal is gonna change her for jazz after she does her ballet choreo. Ok, I'm gonna need you to drink this ginger ale. I get you can't take any food in, but the drink will at least give you some calories and settle your stomach."

I paused, then stared at him. "That's the most dad thing you've ever done since I met you, and I've seen you do some dad shit."

"Oh, ho! You cursed!"

"Never mind." I dismissed him and opened the bottle, taking a refreshing sip, then, before I knew it, I was finishing it in a few gulps.

"Better?" he asked.

"Better. Thanks, love."

"Good, my work here is done. The props are all set for the first number, and we've put signs in all the dressing rooms with the order of the show, so the dancers are aware. We have two staging areas for the smaller kids' parents to come and get their children after. Sal and the chaperones are all in place. Mila is up doing sound check, and Devon is with the dads making sure everything else is good to go. So can you stay still for twenty minutes before we get ready for showtime?"

Beaming, I threw myself on his lap and feathered kisses all over his face. His laughter made us both shake as our lips met.

"Come on, you're gonna get all mushy, and you should be working right now," he said, and I laughed happily.

The hour progressed as every single dancer prepared themselves for their moment. The riot in my stomach calmed down to a dull protest, but it didn't let me go.

The theater filled up, the murmurs of the public rose, and then eventually, the lights dimmed as the voice of God announced that the show was about to commence.

The first dance was beautiful. Our ten three-year-olds showed up in their red and white outfits, doing their pliés and retirés, and at the end, skipping away in giggles.

I stood in the wings, directing our dancers. When it was Trin's ballet number, I gave her a big hug, and she squeezed me with her little arms.

"You're going to do great, Ms. Trin!" I whispered to her.

"Thanks... Can I call you Aisha when we're not at school? We already hang out outside of school, so..." she timidly asked.

"Oh, honey, it would make me so happy!" I said, my throat closing off with the threat of tears.

Not that I'm biased—ok, maybe I am—but in Trin's group, she was the one who truly shined. When her number finished, I could hear Knox's whoops on the other side of the wings where he was volunteering to line up the dancers, and I was pretty sure I heard Pops' loud "Yeah!" from the seats.

We progressed to the older dancers, and I stood there to give a last word of encouragement.

The dance crew excelled in their choreography, getting a standing ovation from the public, filling my heart with joy.

Then, right before it all ended, the dads came on stage. Knox walked out from the opposite wing, blowing me a kiss as he sauntered in his black sweatpants and the graffiti t-shirts they'd selected for their number.

The number started with "Step Into A World" as the men two-stepped energetically to the beat of the music, transitioning from '90s hit to '90s hit as they started getting into the groove, popping and locking, following the steps they'd tirelessly practiced during the evenings. The crowd was on their feet, clapping on the twos and fours as the guys really showed some of their moves.

"It Takes Two" by Rob Base blared on the speakers, and all the attendees whooped and clapped as the guys got into a circle and the freestyling started. I couldn't stop laughing at the goofiness that ensued; the boys showed up, from the Dougie to the Biz Markie. Mila, Sal, and I all beamed from the wings as they rocked the stage.

When it was Knox's turn to go, he pointed a finger straight at me, then pretended to look out on stage and blew a kiss somewhere to the audience, which I knew was probably to Trin. I screamed like a teenager at her first Usher concert. I didn't care; that was my man, and he was about to show them all his moves.

All smooth swag, he bounced his shoulders and showed his footwork, then spun and started doing the Humpty, and I lost it.

He hadn't wanted me to see what he was going to freestyle, and I knew it would be worth the suspense. When my cheeks couldn't spread any wider, the rest of the guys brought out these signs that I'd missed during all the hubbub.

"Ouch!" I complained as Mila squeezed my arm.

"Read it, Aisha!" Sal said with an urgency uncharacteristic of her.

Squinting, I finally read the letters, which said:

MOVE IN WITH US, MS. MAC, with a heart sign at the end.

He wants to what? My heart somersaulted in my chest as the stage went black.

Epilogue

Aisha

Two months later

"Aisha, if you don't stop rushing me!" Momma pushed my arm away from behind her as she navigated the path leading to the main door of their love bungalow.

The bungalow was a homey furnished efficiency in our backyard with all the trimmings. Momma took out her key and inserted it into the white-painted double door. Only Knox had a copy of their key, the treachery.

"Stop it, woman; she's just trying to help you. You slow, and she gotta go," said Pops, zooming past us in his new scooter as Momma opened the door.

"Go, baby girl, you got that class, and we're good here. Tell that boy to take it easy with you, alright?" she said, and I stood close to her, receiving her soft kiss on my forehead, inhaling her scent of cinnamon and Momma.

"It's ok, Devon is doing this class. I don't have to rush no more!"

"Good baby, girl, now go on. We'll have dinner in our suite tonight. I know Trin is at her mother's."

Trin had officially become Momma's and Pop's great grand and loved all the attention. She was gonna spend the week at Chantal's, a trial that had both Chantal and Knox a bit nervous, but I knew it would work out well. They'd agreed to do one week per month instead of alternating.

I jumped in my car and took the long way to the studio, basking in the sudden quiet, which was few and far between now.

After thinking Knox had lost his ever-loving mind by wanting to join our households together, I caved after Christmas Day when he showed me pictures of a house minutes from the studio and his parents. The house had had a large efficiency with its living area, kitchen, a large patio, a nice playground for Trin, and three bedrooms, three baths.

Something deep inside was illuminated by the gesture, and I spoke with Momma and Pops, then agreed to move in together.

Two months later and it was the best decision I'd made in a long time.

The parking lot was full of cars as I navigated a parking spot. The newly installed camera doorbell winked at me while I entered with my key.

"My love. The kids just went in for the advanced ballet class."

"Hi, Mr. Receptionist." I beamed when Knox stood up in his black suit and crisp white shirt.

"I figured I'd take a long lunch break and man the door while you took Momma to her appointment." He stalked toward me and embraced me in his strong arms. I sighed, letting all his love surround me.

"You didn't have to," I mumbled into his chest.

"Yeah, I did. Mila had class too, and Sal... Well, you know she's been acting a little dodgy lately."

"I know." I frowned but lost the tension as soon as his finger ran from the nape of my neck right below my hair and ghosted down till he met my hips. I shivered at the contact.

"No worrying today," he commanded in a whisper, then bit my ear.

"Yes, Sir."

"Good, Baby Doll. I have something special planned for tonight."

"Really? Is that why Momma is talking about not having dinner with us?"

"Actually, my plan starts after dinner—we are going to the Gold Room."

All the hairs on my arms stood in attention to the promise in his voice.

"Oh, so what are we gonna do in the Gold Room tonight?" I asked, burrowing into his delicious scent.

"Not for you to know yet, but know that you will feel all my love."

I gazed up at him, our eyes locking. So much had evolved since that first day that I overheard him talking ill of my business to now, him supporting me, walking side by side into our future.

"I love you, Knox Davenport, you know that?"

"I know it. You tell me every time you look at me like that, Aisha McKinney."

"Good, I just wanted to make sure."

And we stood there in our embrace, our lives enriched

by each other as we never imagined they could be, just because we decided to trust each other.

"So...have you been stretching and doing your pliés?" Knox whispered in my ear.

This man...

THE END

Acknowledgments

2022 was a hard year for my family and for me, but a bright light through the year has been this amazing community of readers, content creators, and authors in the Indie space, especially the Black indie, the Latine, and the LGBTQIA book community.

Thank you to the people that helped make this book what it is today, the ones that met Knox at his roughest :) Meka, Gaby, and Marty!

Kaitesi, thanks for your patience, notes, and encouragement; they mean the world to me!

To my family and their immense patience with me. For their love and their support. Thank you, my loves.

To everyone that fell in love with the Firecracker Cousins and is now joining this Wicked Moves journey, and for those new to the ride... This thank you is for you.

About the Author

A.H Cunningham is an introvert that weaves lovey-dovey contemporary romance and erotica. Her characters are Black and Multicultural adults, trying to navigate their grown folk lives while contending with all the horny feelings and falling hopelessly in love in their journey. In her writing, you will find a deep love for the entire Black Diaspora and all the ways we connect through our heritage. When she's not writing, you can find her reading, snacking at odd hours, dancing some Panamanian song, and playing the metaphorical Tamborine as her family navigates a new move.

Join A.H's newsletter to get all the latest updates!
http://www.ahcunninghamauthor.com

- facebook.com/ahcwrites
- twitter.com/ahcunningham1
- instagram.com/ahcwrites
- tiktok.com/@ahcwrites
- goodreads.com/ahcunningham

Also by A. H. Cunningham

The Firecracker Cousins Series

Alight

Ablaze

Embers

Toying with Temptation

Holiday Shorts

'Tis The Season to Release

Anthologies

Current: An Anthology for Jackson Mississippi - Vol 1

www.ingramcontent.com/pod-product-compliance
Lightning Source LLC
Chambersburg PA
CBHW060756240525
27179CB00034B/703